Praise for
New York Times bestsel

"Heather Graham delivers a harrowing journey as she always does: perfectly.... Intelligent, fast-paced and frightening at all times, and the team of characters still keep the reader's attention to the very end."
—*Suspense Magazine* on *The Final Deception*

"Immediately entertaining and engrossing... Graham provides plenty of face time and intimate connection, all lightened with humor, to reassure and satisfy romance readers. Though part of a series, this installment stands well alone."
—*Publishers Weekly* on *A Dangerous Game*

"Taut, complex, and leavened with humor, this riveting thriller has...a shade more suspense than romance, [and] it will appeal to fans of both genres."
—*Library Journal* on *A Dangerous Game*

"Intense... A wild, mindboggling thriller from start to finish."
—*The Reading Cafe* on *The Forbidden*

"An enthralling read with a totally unexpected twist at the end."
—*Fresh Fiction* on *Deadly Touch*

"Graham strikes a fine balance between romantic suspense and a gothic ghost story in her latest Krewe of Hunters tale."
—*Booklist* on *The Summoning*

HEATHER GRAHAM

MARKET FOR
MURDER

mira

ISBN-13: 978-0-7783-1050-1

Market for Murder

Mira
22 Adelaide St. West, 41st Floor
Toronto, Ontario M5H 4E3, Canada
www.Harlequin.com

Printed in U.S.A.

For Rich Devin with tons of love
and so many thanks for so many things!

CAST OF CHARACTERS

The Krewe of Hunters—
a specialized FBI unit that uses its members' "unique abilities"
to bring justice to strange or unorthodox cases

The Euro Special Assistance Team, or "Blackbird"—
a newly formed group created to extend the Krewe's reach
into Europe to assist with crimes abroad

Carly MacDonald—
amber eyes, dark hair, a Blackbird agent known for
her effortless ability to work undercover

Luke Kendrick—
six-four, green eyes, dark hair, a Blackbird agent
with a military and police background

Brendan Campbell—
clean-shaven head, a determined and intelligent leader,
with the National Crime Agency

Daniel Murray—
handsome and young, cut out for undercover work,
with the National Crime Agency

Mason Carter—
six-five, blue eyes, dark hair, head of the Blackbird division

Della Hamilton—
late twenties, five-eight, green eyes, light brown hair,
Mason's partner

Michael MacDuff—
gruff and serious, head of the local investigation
with Police Scotland

Jordan Dowell—
thirty, solid detective, working under MacDuff

Dr. Foster—
on-site medical examiner

William MacRay—
a bartender at Filigree

Marjory Alden—
another Filigree bartender who may have a secret

Kaitlin Bell—
a helpful ghost found haunting Filigree, died in 1838

Keith MacDonald—
a ghost in a jacket and kilt with a MacDonald tartan, died in 1838

Dr. Leith Forbes—
tall and trim, dark hair, head of the transplant unit at the hospital

Selina Caine—
nurse and assistant to Forbes

Dorothy Norman—
head nurse in the transplant ward

Milly Blair—
a friendly nurse in the transplant ward

Rusty Teller—
an orderly at the hospital

Winston Culpepper—
a member of hospital security

Prologue

She lay in beauty.

Almost like a fairy-tale princess. Her blond hair radiated out from beneath her head like golden rays of the sun. Her cheeks were fair and her lashes lay softly against her skin, for surely she had simply fallen asleep in such a peaceful and stunning position.

Eyes closed and her hands folded prayer-fashion over her chest.

She'd been out for a night on the town, or so it appeared. She wore a stunning sequined blouse or dress… It was difficult to tell.

Because it seemed she'd brought a blanket with her, almost as if she'd intended to fall asleep in the vennel, or alleyway, right behind the popular club with nightly entertainment that was just off the Royal Mile.

Aye, she lay in beauty.

But she had to wake up and move. Edinburgh was not only Scotland's capital city, but it was also a prime tourist location. And people sleeping in the streets— even if they were beautiful—was not something that encouraged tourism.

Doreen Gantry, just arriving for the breakfast shift at the nearby café, hunkered down and was determined to wake the young woman gently.

She touched the young woman's arm, and it was ice-cold.

Of course, it had been a cold night, but...

She moved the blanket. At first, she just stared in horror, frozen in place.

She tried to scream and couldn't. Then she found her voice.

And she screamed, and screamed, and screamed...

Doreen Gantry knelt there, frozen, simply frozen in form, until someone arrived at last and dialed the emergency phone number. She knelt until officers from Police Scotland arrived. She stood, finally, when one of them gently pulled her away from the sheer horror of the body.

One

Carly MacDonald studied the skeleton displayed before her at the special exhibit in Edinburgh. It was that of Mr. William Burke.

A monster? Certainly, to those whose lives he had ended and to their loved ones as well.

Now, he—or his skeleton—was on loan from the Anatomical Museum at the University of Edinburgh, and it seemed ironic to Carly that there was currently such an exhibit going on because a new form of similar crimes was on the rise. People were dying—so that others could live. But not on purpose, and there was nothing noble about what was going on.

Of course, it was ironic William Burke was here on display since his crimes had included selling his murderously obtained "fresh" corpses for dissection and display.

Medical science…few other areas of study had ever so advanced the quality of life for so many—and the length of life itself.

And in the early years of the nineteenth century, Edinburgh, Scotland, was at the forefront of medical science and anatomy.

However, at that time…

Corpses for study could only be obtained through those who had been hanged or died in prison, those who had died from suicide, and those who died as foundlings or orphans. Laws governing corpses were strange. The dead were always in demand, and thus there came into being a new breed of criminal known as "resurrectionists."

Body snatchers.

Of course, the bulk of society looked upon those crimes as totally heinous, against any form of religion, horrible! But resurrectionists at least stole the bodies of those who were already dead.

Burke, along with his partner, Hare—who managed to avoid the hangman's noose by giving state's evidence against his partner in a full confession and as witness—discovered the decent income to be made in selling corpses to Dr. Knox so that he could excel in his lectures at the university.

But digging up bodies was increasingly difficult as loved ones of the deceased began to demand more protection for cemeteries.

It was also a heck of a lot of hard work with the possibility of being caught hanging over one's head.

Of course, according to Hare, he was there when the murders were committed—but *he* wasn't the killer. He only watched as Burke killed his victims. Not with brutality or fury—simply for the business commodity of it all. Their first sale had been the body of a man who had died of natural causes, the complication being that he owed money to the rooming house owned by Hare's wife—common-law wife, most likely—Margaret. That's when they discovered the easy income and living to be enjoyed off the dead. But in different confessions, it came to light that both men were guilty. One man held a victim down while the other covered the victim's nose and mouth until they asphyxiated, which gave a new term to the English-speaking world, *burking.* They plied their victims with alcohol first, hopefully to make death easier for the victims? Or easier for Burke and Hare to accomplish their crimes. But this had been their method, except in the case of a poor boy some considered simple who'd had his back broken. By accident? As claimed by Hare. Or had a sense of cruelty come out in the killers at last? No matter the reason, their victims were usually drunk before being murdered, a little token of kindness one way or another. Then off the bodies had gone to the medical school for lectures on anatomy.

Dr. Knox had turned a blind—and approving— eye to the "freshness" of the corpses he received from Burke and Hare. Students even recognized the body of a beautiful young prostitute—a few of them had availed themselves of her services. They noted a few other characters who were often seen around the city as well. But the killers weren't caught until Burke convinced an older Irish woman, Margaret—or Madgy— Docherty, to come back to drink and stay at his lodging house. The two men had a small problem, but one that was easily solved.

Burke and Hare had met in 1827, and at first Burke had roomed with Hare and his wife at their lodging house. But then he and his "wife" Helen McDougal— records didn't show if they were legally married or something closer to common law—moved into their own lodging house by summer. A couple, James and Ann Gray, were already staying at Burke's lodging house—they had to be convinced to move to Hare's to allow for a room in which to commit the murder at Burke's. With the Grays gone, Madgy met her end and Burke and Hare hid her body under the bed. Alas for Burke and Hare, James and Ann Gray returned to their original room before they were expected and discovered an unwelcome surprise waiting for them.

And then in retrospect, it made perfect sense that Knox's students had recognized some of the previous "fresh" bodies in their anatomy classes.

It was the end of the game for Burke and Hare.

Only Burke, however, would go to the gallows.

"Carly!"

She turned. It was impossible to miss her partner, Special Agent Luke Kendrick, in almost any crowd. He was six-four and fit and walked with what was surely just about perfect posture.

And with purpose.

They'd first been paired together for the too-recent "H. H. Holmes Society" case. Carly had been impressed with Luke in many ways, she thought, smiling for a minute, just as she was impressed with their Supervising Field Director, Jackson Crow, a man who seemed to know instinctively who would work best together. Maybe because they were all so "unique in their talents," as she'd heard their team described, but also because he seemed to know human quirks and personalities.

She and Luke were a partnership, in every essence of the word. She was grateful they would be together while still in Scotland seeking new killers, along with

Police Scotland and the National Crime Agency. Brendan Campbell as the head of the Scottish component was always in close contact with Jackson, who was juggling all his agents in the States and abroad. She and Luke had started off together here, studying the displays, until she'd found herself all but hypnotized by the bones of the man who had once caused such pain and horror in this very city. Luke had gone on to observe other aspects and probably those milling around as well. He was a great people watcher. And it was true that those responsible for criminal acts were often curious to see the effects of their deeds.

"We've got to go," Luke said, and from the serious set of his face, she knew there had been another body found.

"Where's the car?"

"We're walking. She's in a vennel behind a popular club. But it's a narrow alleyway, and there's nowhere to put a car much closer than we are now. Come on."

Carly nodded and turned quickly to join him. "A young woman?"

Luke nodded. "This time."

The killer was—or killers were—all over the place when it came to victimology. She and Luke had been called back to Edinburgh from the Stirling area when the first bodies had been found, and the media began hyping the killers as "Burke and Hare Revisited."

She'd gone to see the display on Burke that morning specifically to try to understand more. There was no way a killer was going to sell cadavers to a medical college these days, but she had to agree with the media—the killings were for profit.

Victims were discovered minus vital organs. But

the care and transport of organs for transplant was tremendously precise and difficult! How was this killer—or these killers if there were indeed two or more—managing such a feat?

Or...

Are they just sadistic and brutal monsters, ripping people up for the emotional or sexual release it gave them?

All she knew right now was the murders were accelerating. There had been three bodies discovered before "Blackbird"—the European division of the Krewe, their unique unit within the FBI—had been called in by Brendan Campbell of the National Crime Agency.

"Don't you love the internet?" Luke murmured as they walked.

Carly frowned, wondering what had brought that on. "I love the pics I see of my family on social media," she said.

"Yeah. If it were friends and family pics and cool things, it would be great." He made a face and shook his head. "It also gives a platform to people who want to spew hatred, who want to form societies for people to mimic historical killers and—" he paused, glancing her way "—allows people to pick up on the media and give names to serial killers who love the attention!"

Carly shook her head in response. "Luke, I don't think whoever is doing this craves the media attention or ever wanted a special name. From what we've seen, they're stealing human organs—wanted by those who need transplants all over the world—for monetary gain!"

"That's true. But if that's all they were doing, why

display the bodies the way that they have?" he asked softly.

They'd walked quickly, and Luke had taken the turns that brought them off the Royal Mile and into the narrow vennel behind the popular nightspot.

He flashed his badge to the Police Scotland officers on duty, ensuring the curious didn't pass through the crime scene tape that cordoned off the area. The officers nodded grimly and they were allowed through.

"Campbell is waiting for you," one of the officers said.

"He's here? Already?" Luke asked.

"I think he *teleports*, like on *Star Trek*, when he feels he needs to be somewhere," the officer said dryly.

"Maybe," Luke agreed, almost giving the man a smile.

The discovery in the vennel had been just too grim for any real humor, even though those who dealt with death and crime sometimes had to find humor lest they lose themselves and their ability to function and reason. It was equally difficult not to take cases personally—the victims were human.

"Ahead," the officer instructed, although there was no other way to go.

They hurried along to where they saw a medical examiner bent low over a form stretched out near one of the large garbage receptacles just beyond the back door of the club. Brendan Campbell, two local officers and Daniel Murray, a young detective with the National Crime Agency, a man with whom they'd very recently worked, were standing nearby.

Daniel looked at Carly as they arrived, shaking his head and wincing. She arched a brow and nodded, looking down at the woman on the ground. The medical examiner was hunkered down at her side, and he looked up at them, scanning the faces of the law enforcement personnel surrounding him now. "Well, as ghastly as the scene appears, I don't believe she suffered much. I don't have test results yet, but close as I am, I do believe the young lady had a great deal to drink. I also believe you'll be relieved to hear she was suffocated—dead before the evisceration of her body began."

He spoke quietly, his gentle Scottish burr something that seemed to soften his words as well.

"Different, but the same," Carly murmured. "Not tortured, rather taken for the monetary value of her death to her killers."

"Aye, and *burked*," Daniel Murray said, his tone hard.

"I believe," Luke said, looking over at Brendan Campbell, "the killers—and there is more than one—are simple psychopaths with no thought whatsoever about the lives they are taking. However, they are not brutal or sadistic. The kill has to do with the fact it's a means to an end. Somehow, they have a market for human organs. While human life means little to them, they are aware there are those across the world who would give anything to survive—and that chance to survive depends on a viable heart, lung, kidney or liver."

"We've already heard my theory, but what do you think about the display?" Carly murmured.

Luke looked at her. "All right. They started out just being in it for the money. Maybe things changed. The media gave them so much attention that maybe they discovered they loved it. I don't believe they started out to be Burke and Hare. But because they are killing for the money a body can bring, and once they read that they were being compared to Burke and Hare, they decided they enjoyed the media sensation. They might even enjoy the fear it's creating in the city, or the historic significance of being compared to Edinburgh's most infamous killers. The first body, sir," he said, addressing Brendan Campbell, "it wasn't discovered in such a pristine and...peaceful state."

"Edge of the park," Campbell told him. "And, no. It was Mr. Walter Freeley, on vacation from Toronto. He was discovered off the road, covered with tree limbs."

"And the news media got wind of the body parts being removed," the medical examiner told them. "The next thing was that every news medium was comparing them to Burke and Hare. Of course, it helped that this is Edinburgh."

Carly spoke up quietly. "Sir," she said, addressing Campbell, "I suggest we study each case and each site bringing us up to date on exactly what happened where and when, who the victims were and how they were chosen, and the geography of the sites where they've been discovered. This woman wasn't killed here—there had to have been blood loss even if the heart was stopped when the removal of her organs began, and that isn't apparent here."

"Aye, you're right, of course," Campbell said. "Dr. Foster, your preliminary report—death by asphyxiation—the woman under the influence of alcohol at the time and..." His voice trailed and he shook his head.

"And as you can see," Dr. Foster continued, "the body was then dissected carefully from the throat to the groin, and the vital organs were removed with only the intestines left in a pile in the cavity that was created."

"Thank you," Campbell said, turning to the different law enforcement agents and officers surrounding him. "We have a headquarters set up in one of our holdings, just on the edge of Old Town, a place we've used before. Several bedrooms and a large dining room that suffices quite nicely as a meeting forum. We also have rooms for you there, for those of you who are not local. That would be you, Carly, Luke and, though he's local, we have a room for Daniel, too. And you need to know Inspectors MacDuff and Dowell, local detectives, are on the case," he finished, nodding toward the two officers they were just meeting.

MacDuff was about fifty, with steel-gray hair and deep brown eyes. Dowell was younger, maybe thirty, a tall, fit redhead who nodded grimly at the introduction, adding, "Carly MacDonald and Luke Kendrick. I see Campbell using your given names. Mine is Jordan and this old hand here is Michael."

Carly smiled and offered her hand as the others did.

"I have had everything sent to the headquarters— or house. You'll find you're set for whatever you need. And, of course, I'll be working on this as well," Campbell told them.

"And at this time," Michael MacDuff said, studying Carly and Luke, "you are the fresh eyes we need on this."

"Obviously, we all want this stopped as quickly as possible," Luke assured him.

"One more thing: your American coworkers are in France clearing up the recent Holmes Society creations there," Campbell said. "They'll be joining us as soon as they possibly can. Of course, one may not let one killer go to secure another."

"All right, then," Luke said, looking at Carly. "Let's

get moving. These killings are happening quickly. Four victims in so many days. Let's see if we can stop this before we have another on our hands."

Luke hated it when killers were given cinematic names by the media. With most criminals in his experience, it heightened the delight they took from their crimes.

Of course…

These killings were different.

He sat at the table in the dining-turned-conference room and studied files on his computer, looking at the large corkboard that showed pictures of the victims along with the crime scenes—taken at different times during the investigation.

The first victim. Walter Freeley, thirty-five years old, Canadian, fond of hiking, a man in excellent physical form—until his death. Left by the road at the edge of Holyrood Park, covered with tree branches.

Killed elsewhere.

Like their recent victim, his autopsy had shown a heavy alcohol consumption prior to asphyxiation, death before the removal of his organs.

Victim two, Brian Dresden, thirty-nine, a businessman from New York, had also been discovered semi-hidden, this time in an extremely small vennel between two larger homes in Old Town, several blocks off the Mile. Coworkers had informed the police via video interviews that he seldom drank—but the alcohol content discovered in his body at autopsy had also been high. Like Walter Freeley, he was in excellent physical shape—before death.

The third body discovered had been that of Lila

Strom, a budding actress from Hamburg, thirty-two
years old, a dancer and in excellent form. She had been
the first to be *displayed*, and like their victim this morning, she'd been discovered just off the Royal Mile.

Displayed beautifully. Her hair had created a magnificent golden halo around her head. An elegant silk
trench coat had covered her lower form, and the sanitation worker who had discovered her had thought at
first she'd had too much to drink and simply passed
out in the vennel.

Until, of course, he'd moved the trench coat.

Luke set aside his computer and looked over at Carly,
who was still studying her screen. Daniel Murray was
watching him—as were Michael MacDuff and Jordan
Dowell.

They were gathered at the house just on the edge of
Old Town that would be their headquarters; as Brendan
Campbell had promised, it was set up for them to work.
It was both comfortable—more so than a hotel room
since it offered a kitchen, space to be together and space
to be alone. Apparently, it was known by the powers that
be that he and Carly were a couple in every sense of the
word, so they'd been assigned a beautiful room with a
king-sized bed and a handsome refurbished bathroom,
which even offered a whirlpool tub.

Carly had smiled at that, impressed. And he almost
smiled in return, thinking what a lucky man he was.
Carly was striking with her slim and shapely physique,
dark hair and eyes. She would be notable almost anywhere on earth, he thought. Her name might be Mac-
Donald, brought to the US by Scottish ancestors, but she
had gained her stunning coloring from a grandparent
from the Middle East. Such was America, he thought

with a certain pride. Americans were everything—a people from just about every culture known to man.

And Carly…

She was amazing. A sharpshooter, able to be the most diplomatic person known to the universe and, in modern vernacular, kick ass with the best of them when a situation demanded such action.

He loved being with her in any situation—in the few moments when they'd been "off" and when they were working together as well. They both brought different thoughts or insights to a situation and respected those of the other.

"What are you seeing?" Michael MacDuff asked him.

"The killers aren't sadists. They aren't attempting to torture their victims in any way. In fact, they are purposely inebriating those they have targeted—"

"Wait," MacDuff said, frowning. "You are certain there are two—"

"Or more," Luke said. "Perhaps one plans the abduction without the victim having any idea whatsoever they're being abducted, leads them back to their killing grounds and then they work together to finish off the victim and—"

"But *two*?" MacDuff said, frowning. "If only one needs to find their chosen target and lure that target to a killing zone, why would they need—"

"I believe there can be only one reason for this—the sale of human organs. And if I'm right, the killers would need to see the organs are carefully preserved from the second they're obtained. Therefore, we don't need to just find these killers—we need to find their brokers."

"Brokers," MacDuff murmured.

"Whoever is paying them for the organs and seeing they are safely delivered—" Carly began.

"I know what a broker is!" MacDuff snapped.

"I apologize," Carly said.

"Don't mind him," Jordan told Carly. "He's an old fart!"

"Eh!" MacDuff protested.

Jordan shrugged and for a moment, they all smiled.

"My apologies, Special Agent MacDonald," MacDuff said, but he was smiling as well. "I am an old fart. I've seen my share through the years, but this case… In all this, forensics hasn't been able to find a print, a hair, the weest spec of a fiber! Four now dead—and we have nothing!"

"We will," Luke assured him. "They are a few assumptions we can make. They are still identifying our latest victim, but first, none of the others were local. They are targeting visitors to the area, those who might need guidance through the city. Most probably outgoing people who are happy to meet locals—"

"Y'think a Scot did this?" MacDuff demanded.

Luke smiled and shook his head.

"Sir—"

"Neither Burke nor Hare was born a Scot, y'know!" MacDuff told them indignantly. "Irishmen, they were!"

"I'm not blaming a Scot or an Irishman," Luke said.

"Good," MacDuff put in. "My wife is from Dublin."

"No one is blaming anyone—yet," Carly said. "Please, sir, every nation out there has produced horrendous individuals just as every nation has produced brilliant men and women."

"Eh! You know what a Scot invented—the flushing toilet!" Daniel pointed out. "Well, in 1775, Alexander

Cumming filed the first flush-toilet patent. To be fair, Englishman John Harington started the whole thing back in 1596, under the direction of Queen Elizabeth I, and then after Cumming in 1860, a bloke really named Thomas Crapper created all kinds of modern improvements." Daniel grimaced. "Guess that's why we still go to the *john* or the *crapper*!"

They all stared at him and even Michael MacDuff burst into laughter.

"We needed that," Carly told him.

He smoothed back his unruly hair and grinned. "Aye, now, I'm useful at times."

They all nodded and glanced at one another. Carly said softly, "Seriously. Every country in the world has produced monsters. I don't believe we know who we are looking for now. Not necessarily a Scot, but someone who has come to know Edinburgh, the streets, closes, vennels. It's an old city, an old city that's arisen through the centuries on an extinct volcano, which allows for all kinds of things happening underground—if you know where that underground is."

"You think they are killing people underground?" Jordan asked.

"Not necessarily," Carly assured him. "I just think there are partners, and one—or both—of them knows the city of Edinburgh. I also believe they're trolling the nightspots, looking for their victims. They don't break into any homes with alarms. They watch out for businesses where others might identify them as someone a victim has been with. Here are the things we need to do—divide and conquer, for one. We need to go to nightspots and watch what's going on. Play the game ourselves—obviously, Luke and I make the best tourists. We don't have your beautiful accents."

Jordan laughed at that.

Carly arched a brow.

"He just means an accent is only cool when it's not your own," Daniel supplied.

"See, your accents are *cool* to us," Jordan assured her.

Carly smiled and Luke was glad to see it. Being immersed in so much that was painful sometimes made it difficult to hang on to humanity.

"Well, thanks," Carly murmured.

"So," Luke continued for her, "tonight, we all hit the town. You two—" he motioned to Jordan and Michael "—will need to give us the names of places where people hang out the most. I think we're all up to speed on the victims. Now we'd like to see the dump—and/or display—sites. And of course, I assume there has been a tip line set up? Discussions with the families or friends of the victims? Have the pictures of the victims been run through the various places we'll try out tonight?"

"Tip line, aye, thousands of calls, most of them bogus. With the recent trouble regarding the Holmes Society, both Police Scotland and the National Crime Agency have been stretched thin. As far as the calls go—"

"I understand," Luke interrupted, "but we can help with that. Jackson can set up a relay so that they're getting everything at our headquarters in the US as well. That can help thread through those just calling in because they're paranoid or need the attention and those that may really give us something."

"Then," Carly said softly, "we need to find the brokers. Their method of selling the organs to the highest bidder."

"I'll pick up some info from our people at headquarters and be back in half an hour to tour the sites you wish to see. I'll do the driving," MacDuff informed them.

Carly arched a brow and noted, "There are five of us."

"He has an NCA Escalade—we'll be fine," Jordan assured them. "Thirty minutes!"

"I'll be ready," Daniel said, rising as they did. "Quickie shower—I feel…" He looked from Luke to Carly and she finished for him.

"Icky?" she suggested.

"Aye, that's the word!" Daniel said.

She grinned. "Me, too. I need fifteen minutes."

"And she means it," Luke assured Daniel. "She's faster than the speed of light."

"In all things?" Daniel queried, grinning. "Whoops, sorry! You know, I meant with work and all!"

"Go take your shower!" Carly moaned, and Daniel quickly disappeared. She slid behind Luke, looking over his shoulders, her hands upon them. "I get his feeling. But we'll never wash off this horror, will we?"

Luke turned to her. "Oddly, as bad as the bodies may be…death was quick. And if they were seriously inebriated…"

"Right. We've seen worse. Still, I am going to take a shower."

"Go ahead." He looked up at her. "I'm not as fast as the speed of light," he teased. "You know, temptation and all that…and I want to give Jackson a call. He'll need to set up our people listening to the tip calls. I know they're good here, amazing maybe, but they have been stretched thin. Jackson can get some profilers in and maybe give us some insights we're not seeing. There's one thing I find curious, but that might get back to our killers being ordinary Joes, capable of seducing people—and I don't mean so much sexually, but as friends. Helpful people, ready to give tourists information on the best places, or even give them rides. I'm curious because our one victim…" He hesitated, referring to his computer again. "Brian Dresden. Friends and coworkers said that he wasn't a drinker. How did they get a man who seldom drank inebriated?"

"Seldom isn't never," Carly said. "And that's back to the friendship thing. He was probably out, possibly for a meal. He wound up talking to someone who gave him advice on what to do with his free time. He was talked into sampling whiskey and did it so that he'd be sociable with someone who was welcoming him to the country."

"They might not have started out as Burke and Hare, but they might well have accidentally made use of some of the ruses that the pair had practiced in their lethal form of body snatching," Luke told her. "It's not such a bad idea that we do study the original duo—now the killers have embraced the monikers, or so it seems. Historic information may prove useful to us."

"And tonight?" Carly murmured. "I think we'll need to split up—"

"Not necessarily. These people aren't seeking sexual partners. They just want healthy individuals. And we both fit that bill."

"But they haven't taken two victims at once."

"True. If we think we've got something…"

He broke off, shaking his head. "I've been investigating the illegal organ trade. Think about it. Say you're a billionaire. You have a child who desperately needs a kidney. You're going to pay anything to get it."

Carly nodded. "I was just reading about a case in Pakistan. Police raided an apartment building where twenty-four people were being held—alive, but as part of a human-trafficking organization—there for when their organs were needed. It's not an American thing, a European thing, or a *thing* that belongs to any one nation. This is just people wanting…"

"To be alive. To live themselves or to see a loved one live, and I imagine those who go to the illegal trade are simply desperate," Luke said. "The original Burke and Hare specimens had to have piqued Dr. Knox's suspicions, but he felt his need for the bodies in his classes was greater than his need to check on the origins of the *product* Burke and Hare were offering. With buyers of human organs, I believe those receiving them or procuring them for a loved one don't allow themselves to think of how they might be obtained. I'm sure they don't ask. They're just grateful and maybe lie to themselves, thinking that a widow, widower, children or parents of someone who died naturally might need the money."

"Whatever causes it, these people have a worldwide market. We're going to need to stop them—and just as importantly, stop the buyers! Maybe I should say the brokers. I think it must be…well, you have the killers who procure the organs. But I believe there must be someone else who knows where they need to go to fetch the highest price."

Luke nodded, leaning back. "So…you going to dress up for the night out on the town?"

She laughed softly. "Later, Romeo. Right now, jeans and a denim jacket. We're going to go play in the dirt at the dump sites and maybe need another shower after. And you, please! Tell me you'll clean up, too." She wrinkled her nose teasingly.

He sighed. "So picky! Sure, I'll shower."

Grinning, she touched his shoulder and headed for their room.

"Oh, hey! E.T., don't forget. You're supposed to phone home."

"Will do!"

He smiled, watching her go, but it faded as he stared at the massive corkboard again. Four lives. Stolen.

They needed clues. They needed something to go on.

He pulled out his phone and hit the speed dial for their headquarters back in the States.

He spoke with Jackson, who brought Brendan Campbell in on their conversation. Between Police Scotland, the NCA and their unusual bureau team, they would get it done. They had the best tech support in the world and a vast number of soldiers on the ground.

Yes, they would get it done.

When he ended the conversation, he found himself still staring at the computer.

And looking up everything he could find on the original Burke and Hare.

Because they might not have started out that way, but...

But the killers were now copycats. And sometimes, just sometimes, because of the past, copycats might be easy to catch out in a "historic" mistake.

Two

It certainly wasn't a hardship being assigned to Scotland. And among the beautiful cities to be found in the world, Edinburgh might well find a place at the top of any list.

Carly didn't know it like the proverbial back of her hand, but she had been there often enough growing up since her father's parents had immigrated to the States from the country. But she did know and love the Royal Mile, Edinburgh Castle, Holyrood Park and so much more. Of course, nothing in the world really ever stood still. Things in existence when she'd been younger might not be there anymore, and other things might be in place. But in such a historic place, there were bound to be locations like the castle, Holyrood Palace, St. Giles' and more that had stood not just from decade to decade, but for hundreds—and hundreds—of years.

Walter Freeley had been discovered on a road accessible only on foot—but not far from the main road.

When they arrived after parking on an embankment and being led the rest of the way by MacDuff, the crime scene tape had been removed. And the site where Freeley had been discovered appeared to be nothing but peaceful and shaded by a beautiful elm; the remnants of the ancient volcano upon which the city of Edinburgh had grown all around them, majestic cliffs, soaring rocks and forests and manicured paths.

"This is not right at all," Daniel murmured. "Holyrood Park is just there, and it's been a refuge and a wonder for the people of the city—and tourists—since its inception. So beautiful, so many natural wonders. People hike, they love going up to Arthur's Seat and seeing the old volcanic vents and the city below and…"

"We understand completely," Carly assured him. "Central Park is a mecca for New Yorkers and visitors, but sometimes…it's misused."

"And there's nothing like a body dump in the Everglades," Luke murmured.

"He was right there, and of course, there's little to be seen now," MacDuff said. "We arrived on the scene after being called by a terrified hiker who met us on the road—she'll never come this way again. Anyway, she wanted to head up that hiking path and thought something that might trip someone was covered up by the tree branch. But when she went to move it out of the way… Well, she saw his face. Screamed, called us immediately… We arrived, medical examiner arrived…forensics…by that time, of course, the media had gathered."

"But," Jordan Dowell told them, "the circumstances of death weren't known immediately—apparently they leaked after the second body was found." He shrugged. "The city powers that be wanted it all back to a pristine condition as soon as possible, and of course…"

"He wasn't killed here—he was dumped here. So it

was easy enough for your forensic people to finish up as soon as possible. And they found...nothing?" Carly asked.

Luke was seriously studying the scene, shaking his head. "Whoever is doing this is good. They might not be in forensics, but they've studied forensics. They were wearing gloves, of course." Luke looked from MacDuff to Dowell. "But they didn't find a hair, a fiber..."

"Nothing," MacDuff said. "And they tried, and whatever you may be thinking—"

"I'm think your forensic people are good," Luke said, "which is why I believe whoever is doing this has some grounding in medical knowledge and forensic science."

"So, a forensic medical examiner?" Dowell asked dryly.

Carly smiled grimly. "The person isn't necessarily a professional. And I seriously believe there must be at least two people doing this. They're doing the killing elsewhere. And the display portion of what they're doing didn't come about until the press decided to label them Burke and Hare?"

"Exactly," Dowell told them. "So, again, I'm afraid the crime scenes can't—"

"Right. They don't exactly give us clues, but then again, they do," Luke said. "We know someone drove to a point, and then they had to carry Walter Freeley's body here."

"Onward, then?" Daniel asked.

"Onward. We may not get exact clues from the locations, but—"

"Sure, we understand," Dowell said. He grimaced at MacDuff and turned to Luke and Carly. "Told you. He's an old grouch!"

"Eh!" MacDuff said, frowning fiercely.

"But damned good at what he does!" Dowell said, grinning.

MacDuff just shook his head. "He's an uppity lad, but he's pretty good, too," he said. "And working on this case… Well, we do need to lighten the load now and then."

"Agreed," Carly said, smiling at Jordan Dowell, who grimaced. She liked the younger inspector. They all worked hard on some of the most horrendous things human beings could do to one another, but he also managed to keep a balance between what they did and saw, and the need to keep their own lives on keel so that they *could* help others.

She was equally glad Michael MacDuff—as grouchy as he might be according to Jordan Dowell—seemed to have absolutely no difficulty being the local lead on the team he and Dowell had been assigned to with two Americans and Daniel from the National Crime Agency.

While they didn't need to be best friends for life, it was important in this investigation that they respect and listen to one another and act as team players at all times.

MacDuff saw good things in his partner as well. He was teacher and student, Carly thought, because he respected Jordan Dowell in return. Each generation brought new knowledge, especially where tech was concerned, and MacDuff was truly a professional, a man who would respect the opinions, intelligence and knowledge of others.

They stood a moment in silence, studying the location and all that was around. And it was strange, but she understood Daniel's feelings of anger regarding their location.

The site was beautiful. And it was peaceful. Truly, the edge of the kind of refuge that took people away from the general cares of their day. The air was cool and just slightly moist. The breeze was gentle.

"Well," MacDuff said. "We need to move onward. It was after the discovery of Brian Dresden that the media gained the information the bodies were being gutted, and the headlines started to read *Burke and Hare, at it again.*"

"But his body wasn't on display—like the two women who were found next," Carly murmured.

"No, it was after the headline that the display part began. They may not have meant to be recreating anything, but…they are enjoying their moniker," Dowell said.

"We move on," MacDuff said.

As they drove to the eastern outskirts of Old Town, MacDuff told them, "The crime scene photographs have been sent to you. When we return to the house, there should be plenty of time for you to study them and place them in your minds along with the places we'll have been. Of course, you have already seen the last location."

"Of course. Thank you," Luke told him.

"This next location is not quite like the first one," Dowell murmured.

When they arrived, Carly thought it might not have been as majestically beautiful and natural as the area fronting Holyrood Park, but it was still oddly charming. Two old estates existed side by side with well-maintained foliage and old brick walls separating them—along with a small alleyway, the kind the Scots referred to as "vennels."

The vennel was only accessible by foot, and MacDuff parked by the road before leading them halfway down the alley beneath the shade of a giant oak.

"Again," MacDuff told them, "the body was covered in branches and discovered by the homeowner to our left at about eight in the morning—the owners are friends."

"Wealthy friends," Dowell said dryly, indicating the majesty of the old medieval homes behind the brick walls. "They often have morning tea together and Mr. Connoly—house to the left—was headed over to see his friend, Mr. Douglas."

"And good thing it was Mr. Connoly and not Mrs. Connoly. She was a complete wreck when we arrived at the scene, though we spoke with her in the house and she never saw the body," MacDuff told them. "I doubt if she's been in the vennel since."

"I guess it's not easy accepting the fact a mutilated body was found just outside your home," Carly murmured. "May we speak with the Connoly couple?" she asked MacDuff.

He arched a brow. "We interviewed them. They didn't see a thing. These body dumps are occurring in the middle of the night. And if Ewan Connoly hadn't gone to share morning tea with Ian Douglas, he might have been in a wretched state of decomposition by the time he was discovered."

"Still, if it's possible—" Luke began.

"Come, then—there's a call box back at the front of the vennel," MacDuff said.

A woman's soft voice came through the little metal call box near the gate to the house. MacDuff identified himself and she quickly said, "But, but… Oh, we've

spoken with y'sir! We… Oh, shall I never forget what…
I cannot live here anymore!" she moaned.

"Mrs. Connolly—" MacDuff began again.

A male voice then came over the box. "Sir, I'm opening the gate. Please, come in."

MacDuff glanced at them and nodded. They heard
a click and the gate opened. The five of them headed
up the long stone path that led to the medieval house.
Carly wasn't sure a property could be described as a
"Tudor" house in Edinburgh, but the home they approached reminded her of Harvington Hall, a massive
mansion built circa the same time period. She had visited it once in England with her parents.

A stone path led through an alley of manicured trees
to a stone building that offered a grand entrance and was
surrounded by three other smaller buildings.

The double doors opened as they approached the
house. A man of about forty-five stood there, dressed
casually in a T-shirt and jeans. His hair was dark, cut
short, and he had a defiant way of standing, legs slightly
apart, feet firmly on the ground, hands on his hips.

"MacDuff! What can we do for you now?" he asked.

Either the man was mocking them with an American accent, Carly thought, or more simply he was an
American.

"We believe we have yet another victim of the killer
who left the body in your vennel, sir," MacDuff said.
"We've added to our team, and we'd like to hear about
the morning you found Mr. Dresden again."

"As my wife said—"

"Ye've been over it, aye, sir, we know. But the situation is extremely grave."

"Fine, come in. We'll have tea," Connolly said.

"Sir, we do not mean to put you out," Luke said.

Connoly studied Carly, Luke and Daniel for a minute.

"You're American," he said.

"Not me!" Daniel protested.

"You're an American," Carly said.

"Yes, and no," Connoly told them. "My folks were working in Chicago when I was born, lived there for about fifteen years and returned here." He shrugged. "Hard to turn it down when you're left a place like this in your parents' will. It would be... Well, they'd be turning over in their graves if we hadn't made it back home."

"It's an amazing place," Luke said.

"So, please do come in," Connoly said. "And tea is no trouble at all—neither is coffee. Your choice of either. The wife makes the best scones on the planet, so please, it will calm her a bit to go about being a good hostess."

They entered the grand mansion. Mrs. Connoly was standing in the entry, her hands clenching and unclenching nervously.

She was an attractive woman with light brown hair that curled gently around her face. She was slender and tiny, a mere five-one or -two against what Carly figured to be her husband's six-foot frame.

"Lily, darling—" he began.

"I'm sorry, ever so sorry, but..." the woman began.

"She's still so upset," her husband explained.

"I didn't see, but I knew... I knew!" Lily said. "And it's ever so horrid! Why? I've been a wreck ever since. And when my husband is not here, I keep the dogs in the yard and I let no one in! Why, why did they choose our place to leave the poor lad?" she demanded.

"Mrs. Connoly," Carly said quietly, "we believe it

was simply a place where they might leave the man and not be seen."

"We have four massive Rottweilers—in their kennel at the moment—and the gate and even the walls are set with alarms, as is the front door of the house," Ewan Connoly said. "Ian Douglas has the same kind of security, I believe. 'Tis a pity the wretches didn't think to make use of our properties—they'd have had sirens blazing no matter the time."

"Do you think I'm safe?" Mrs. Connoly asked. "Ne'er mind! Fer now. Tea... I will let the lass know. Oh, tea or coffee? Please, sit. I will be right back and I'll bring the tea and coffee."

She disappeared before they could stop her. Ewan Connoly shrugged and lifted a hand, indicating they should follow him into the next room, a massive parlor or perhaps once upon a time a ballroom. It now offered a game table in one section, a connection to a dining room table that could seat at least twelve people, and a section with a massive television screen, stereo equipment, and a grouping of period chairs and sofas with a large old oak coffee table between them all.

"Please. Have a seat," Ewan offered.

He waited politely for them to arrange themselves. Carly, Luke and Daniel sat on a sofa facing the coffee table and screen. MacDuff and Dowell were on two side chairs that allowed Ewan Connoly to take a chair opposite the two men with the short end of the table before him.

"I do realize how serious this is," Connoly told them. "I just don't know what more I can say. I mean, I started a usual walk to my neighbors' house and ran into a body!"

"Did you hear anything at all the night before—or perhaps in the very early morning hours?" Luke asked him. "Are your dogs out at night? Did you hear them putting up a fuss about anything?"

Connoly frowned as he thought. Then he looked at Luke and twisted his head at a thoughtful angle.

"Come to think of it, yes. I almost got up to go and give a piece of my mind to the pups, but then they stopped barking."

"You didn't investigate?" Carly asked.

He smiled. "I've explained my property. No one who doesn't belong gets in here."

"Do you and your wife have children?" Carly asked.

"Indeed, a handsome son."

"Does he live here?" Carly asked.

"Aye!" Lily Connoly said, coming back into the room. "When the lad is home from university, aye, indeed. But my husband insisted he go to Harvard in America and…" She shook her head, letting out a sigh. "The lad is twenty, a good boy, I swear it. But alone in that country… I mean, not to offend yer beautiful country. It's not here. It's far, far away!"

"We understand perfectly," Daniel told her. "Me mum was a wreck just because I went as far away as London," he assured her.

"Who else lives here?" Luke asked.

"Flora, and ye'll meet her…now!" Lily said. "Now, most obviously, I believe, the urn has coffee and the pot offers tea. And the scones… I do make the best in the world. Simple plain and a few with blueberries and a few with strawberries. Please."

A young woman with long sandy hair, dressed in a black uniform and bearing a heavy silver tray, arrived from the kitchen region. The men stood again immediately since the tray appeared to be heavy, but the young woman quickly assured them, "Ah, gents! I carry the like all the time but thank you!"

She set the tray down and looked at Lily.

"Shall I pour, ma'am?"

"No, no, lass, we can manage, thank you, Flora," Lily said. "Oh, my pardon. This young lady is Flora MacDonald, aye just like the same Scottish heroine, Flora MacDonald, who helped save Charles Edward Stuart, our Bonnie Prince Charlie, from troops after the Battle of Culloden in April of 1746! And these people are—"

Carly stood quickly to offer her hand to Flora, grinning. "I'm Carly MacDonald, perhaps a distant cousin!" she told the girl.

"Another MacDonald, eh?" Flora said, grinning. "I do trace back to the MacDonald clan of Sleat, but I'd be happier if I were heiress to the McDonald clan of the Happy Meal!" she said lightly. "Perhaps we are long-lost cousins."

Carly laughed. "I'll have to get on an ancestry site and find out," she told Flora. "Flora, this is my American partner, Special Agent Luke Kendrick, and these are our members of Police Scotland, Michael MacDuff and Jordan Dowell, and the handsome young fellow there is Detective Daniel Murray with the National Crime Agency."

"Flora, a pleasure," Daniel said, smiling.

Flora was pretty—but then again, Carly thought, so was Daniel. Well, handsome, to be more linguistically correct. But she could have sworn she saw a few sparks fly as they met and shook hands, smiling at one another.

"Thank you, Flora," Lily Connoly said again. "I will pour, lass."

Flora nodded and turned, about to return to the kitchen.

"Flora, do you live here?" Luke asked her.

"Oh, no," Flora said. "I'm a student at Edinburgh University. I work four days a week and take classes on the other three."

"Busy girl!" Luke noted.

"But we do keep a room for the dear lass!" Ewan said. "That way, she can head in and study when she wishes and also get a good night's sleep."

"Wow, a property this big!" Carly said. "Does anyone else help maintain it?"

"We have the dogs, Flora stays now and then, and when Grayson—our lad—comes home from school, he sometimes brings a tribe!" Lily said.

"But we like our privacy. A cleaning crew comes every Monday. Lily and I are delighted to have the property, and we don't mind a wee bit of work ourselves, eh, Lily?" Ewan Connoly said, smiling at his wife.

"Not one wee bit!" Lily said. She seemed to have relaxed some since they'd come and since Flora had brought out the tea and coffee. "Now. Please. You must indulge. I shall pour and I shall start with you, dear," she told Carly. "Coffee or tea?"

"Coffee, please. I need to stay awake and alert!" Carly told her.

"Cream, sugar? Ah, nay, yer a cop. Well, an agent, same as a cop! Black, eh?"

"I do hate to ruin a good stereotype, but I'd love a drop of cream," Carly told her.

"As you wish!"

Lily saw to it that all her guests had something to drink, and she was insistent that they try the scones as well.

The scones were delicious—sweet but not too sweet.

And as they ate and sipped their drinks, Carly and Luke continued to ask questions.

Had they noticed anyone they didn't know looking at their property, studying the vennel, their habits, any such other occurrence?

No.

Did Ewan remember the time the dogs began barking?

Perhaps about four in the morning, give or take a few minutes.

And finally, they finished refreshments and questions.

Their host and hostess were thanked politely, and they all rose to leave at last. Luke produced one of the cards Campbell had ordered printed for them when they'd started on their last case revolving around the H. H. Holmes Society, asking them to call if they thought of anything, anything at all.

"We have Detective Inspector MacDuff's card as well," Ewan told them.

"And you're welcome to call any of us if you think of anything that may be helpful," Luke assured him.

And after that, they left.

"We'd like to speak with the Douglas family as well," Luke said, once they were in the alleyway again. "There must be a way into the vennel for them, too."

MacDuff nodded. "They, too, have a wee box to call from the vennel—and a gate that leads into the estate."

"These are really beautiful homes," Carly murmured.

"Off the beaten path, and yet not far at all away from the excitement of the Royal Mile, shops, restaurants…"

"Filled with tourists for the picking," Luke put in.

"Right. Come on, this way," Dowell told them.

They headed down the vennel again and found the call box and keyed in the code that allowed entry to the Douglas residence.

But there was no answer.

"We can call them and arrange for another interview," MacDuff said.

"I wonder if they're in there and just not answering," Daniel said.

"Well, if they are, there's nothing we can do," Jordan told them. He looked at Daniel and grinned. "Besides, their maid is about fifty, way too old for you and plump as a ripe cherry!"

"Ha, ha!" Daniel responded.

"Children!" MacDuff chastised, but he spoke lightly and said, "There's nothing we can do right now. We'll need to reach them to arrange for an interview. We have no right and no cause to scale their wall. If we could, I do believe we'd trigger an alarm and half the men and women on duty for Police Scotland would hurry on out to arrest us."

"We do want to see them," Luke murmured. "But you're right. Nothing else to do here now."

In the Escalade again, Carly said, "It ties in. I'm not in medicine, but if the corpses had no livers, it would be impossible to tell time of death through the temperature method. But it seems the amount of time needed to remove organs coincides. Say these people are found just being social and friendly, that their new *friends* buy them doubles when they think they're drinking singles, or whatever their method. During the week, most night-spots close around midnight, if I'm correct," she said, and waited for either MacDuff or Jordan Dowell to let her know if she was or wasn't.

"They can set their own hours but you're correct. It's usually eleven during the week, and then midnight or later on the weekends. It's a university city," Jordan Dowell reminded her. "People love to crawl in the older darker pubs in Old Town, or cross the bridge and enjoy the trendier places that are in New Town."

"And none of our victims disappeared on a weekend. Always a weekday—and they were found on a week-day," MacDuff added.

"All right. So, our victims meet their killer—or killers—sometime late at night, but before 1:00 a.m., most certainly. Then...they are somehow encouraged to imbibe copious amounts of alcohol. They are quickly dispatched. The simple removal of organs from a dead body by someone who had learned or been told what to do might well take a few hours. And then, at that time of morning, they've checked everything out and they know where to dump the bodies where they won't be found until they're long gone," Carly finished.

"Any exact time of death is hard to have 100 percent right no matter what, and certainly harder when there are no organs in the body," Luke agreed.

"And again," Jordan said, twisting to look at those in the back seat of the car, "I remain perplexed about victim number two. We spoke to his boss in the States and to his coworkers. The man simply didn't drink. His boss told me he'd walk around social events with a lime and soda so that people wouldn't want to buy him drinks. He told his boss once that he didn't like the taste of alcohol period, and he'd seen it do too many bad things to too many good people. So, how did they get him drunk?"

"What did the ME say?" Carly asked. "Was it forced down him—"

"Well, he was asphyxiated, so there were wounds around his mouth and nose. It would be difficult to know because of that if his mouth was pinched open. And we all know the rate of inebriation one acquires has to do with the alcohol content of the beverage," MacDuff said. "They might have acquired something super-charged." He shrugged. "We are famous for our whiskeys, and they do come with differing degrees of alcoholic content. Most are sold at about 40 percent strength. Some at 60 percent. But I imagine it's possible to go over that, and if you don't drink at all…"

"One drink might leave you in a position to do whatever you were directed to do," Luke said thoughtfully.

Daniel groaned softly. "So, we're looking for a whiskey distiller with a medical degree or an obsession with videos depicting autopsies and/or transplants. Charming and friendly, great at nightspots. But as we've discussed before, there are only hours until organs stop being viable. Where and how are they getting the organs to buyers?"

"Or," Jordan said dryly, "are we dealing with a group who aren't selling the organs, but simply making meals out of them?"

Carly groaned and hit him playfully on the shoulder. "This is bad enough."

"But he could be right," Luke said.

"Right. We can't forget that although he never quite confessed to it, prosecutors believed Andrei Chikatilo, the Butcher of Rostov, consumed parts of his victims. You had the relatively unknown German serial killer, Joachim Kroll, the Duisburg Man-Eater, who also dined on his kills. Then closer to home," Luke said, looking at Carly, "we have the very well-known Jeffrey Dahmer—and there was also Ottis Toole, the Jacksonville Cannibal."

"Of course, not to be outdone!" Jordan Dowell added. "We have our own infamous Scottish cannibals, Alexander 'Sawney' Bean and his forty-five-member clan known for getting away with murder for twenty-five years with, legend estimates, a thousand victims in that time, only stopped when King James sent out a search party. Kind of, to use a great Americanism, *icky, icky, yucky.* The clan were his children and their children who were their children's children, clan incest—"

"Okay, okay!" Carly protested. "Yes, cannibalism exists and we all know it, but…"

"But we also all believe this has to do with the illegal organ trade," MacDuff said.

"All right," Carly said, leaning forward. "Where are they going to harvest the organs?"

"Just about anywhere private," MacDuff said. "Our privacy laws are similar to yours. No illegal search and seizures. Unless they worried about being suspected or seen…they could go just about anywhere."

"Right," Carly agreed. "But then…oh, my God!"

"What?" Daniel asked.

"I read somewhere that there are about nine-hundred little islands off Scotland, some of them public, some of them privately owned," Carly said.

"That's true. There are little islands that look like they're no more than big rocks dropped into the ocean,

big enough for one house, accessible only by boat or...
maybe by a parachute," Jordan said. "Others are a little bigger, as you know, part of the Hebrides, the Shetlands, the Orkneys... You can buy an island here. We
sell to foreigners, too."

"That must be it!" Carly said.

"So, we should parachute to nine hundred islands?"
MacDuff asked.

Carly grinned. "No, and we don't know if I'm right.
But say the killers have the organs. They might be able
to take them out quickly, but surgery to replace a living
human being's organ is going to take longer, and you'd
need recovery time. Where could you go where you are
on private property that's only accessible by a boat—or
a parachute jump—and where you were fairly certain
of privacy and not being interrupted by anyone for all
the time that was needed?" she asked.

"It's quite possible. We'll get our techs working on
islands and sales, though of course, say that what you're
saying is right. This person—these persons—might
have owned their island for years," Daniel reminded
them.

"We're looking for properties that aren't large at all,
that may have just one home, like you were saying,"
Luke said. "Well, being that small does bring the number down, right?"

MacDuff laughed. "I've been here me entire life! I
can honestly say that while I've been to the Shetlands,
Hebrides and the Orkneys, no one has yet invited me
to a private island. Then again—"

"I'm sure our great computer people can narrow
numbers down for us," Luke said. "Off the subject a
bit. Lily said Flora MacDonald didn't live there, but

she did have a room and stayed sometimes. I could be wrong, but it seemed to me Lily wanted Flora back in the kitchen quickly."

"Lily wants to forget any of it ever happened," MacDuff said.

"Maybe," Luke mused.

"Seriously?" MacDuff said, frowning as he drove. "The woman is a shattering pile of tears."

"She is. But I would have liked to have talked to Flora a bit more, too," Carly said. "Flora is a student. We should be able to find her through the university and perhaps speak to her away from the Connoly property."

"Or, she may just call us," Daniel said.

MacDuff's frown deepened. He was driving and he didn't turn to look at Daniel. The others twisted to do so.

He smiled. "When we shook hands, I slipped her *my* card," he told them. He shrugged. "She might not have been there that night, maybe there's nowhere to go, but…"

"You slipped her your card because you think she's cute," Luke suggested.

"Well, there's that, too," Daniel said. "But convenient, right?"

They all smiled again, even MacDuff.

And it was good, because they were almost at their next destination.

"And this," MacDuff announced, "this…the murder of the young and lovely actress and dancer, Lila Strom…" He broke off as he shook his head.

He began to speak again, his voice dry.

"This is where legend takes over, where the media stepped in," he said. "Lila was the first to be *displayed*, left as if she slept in peace. Her disposal site allowed the killers their moment of amusement and irony. This was where the case became Burke and Hare—revisited."

Three

They were approximately two blocks off the Royal Mile. And as they had been that morning, they were in a narrow vennel.

Worn crime scene tape still blocked off an area, but it was fading. And as they walked down the alley, MacDuff shook his head and went to rip away the tape. "They're done here," he told them. "As we all know, killing and disemboweling takes place elsewhere. And as moving around today has shown us, they're scoping everything out and just delivering the bodies to these locations. But..."

He paused, pointing to a place between the rear of two businesses. "That's where she lay. Even when we arrived, she looked as if she were sleeping. She was discovered early, around six thirty in the morning by Quint Robertson, a sanitation worker. He tried to wake her. She was covered not with a blanket, but with her trench coat. He threw the coat back on top of her the minute he saw her torso and called us. We were here soon after. We've been careful. Absolutely no photos have gotten out in any way, shape or form."

"That's good to hear," Luke told him. He pointed to the wall and the doors on either side of the area where MacDuff had indicated the corpse had lain. "What are these two businesses?" he asked.

"McKinley Accounting Associates and a place called Lock-It," MacDuff said. "Lock-It is a company that designs individual high-tech security systems. Both places close at five in the afternoon. None of the employees—only six between the two, three accountants and three consultants—were out in the vennel the day she was discovered."

"No security cameras out here?" Carly asked. "And the one company designs high-tech security systems?"

"Ironic, huh?" Jordan said dryly. "No. According to Kent Logan, owner of Lock-It, no one is ever back here—no reason for anyone to ever be back here—and there is continual video being taken at the front of the business."

The alley was narrow and led to a wall. It was kept clean.

There was nothing in it except, as in other areas they had been, large dumpsters or trash receptacles.

"Quint Robertson was here for the trash—they come from the main road with receptacles to take them from here. With only two businesses here, it's usually an easy gig for the workers. The trash tends to be paper, so not too messy."

Luke nodded and walked over to the receptacle.

"I take it that—"

"Aye, forensics went through the trash," MacDuff assured him.

"All right, then," Carly said, standing by Luke's side. "Thank you, Michael—"

The man grinned. "You can call me MacDuff, I won't be offended. The kid goes by Jordan but somehow, my surname became the name everyone uses for me—including my wife."

"Well, that's because MacDuff is a cool name," Carly told him.

"Almost as cool as MacDonald," he teased in turn. "All right. Let's get back to headquarters. Our headquarters. I mean the house."

It took less than five minutes to return to their home base.

"Weeknight," Jordan said, as they keyed in the code to get through the gate. "Do you think they'll be out tonight? The speed seems to be picking up—nothing like a major moniker in the media to get a good serial killer going. But I believe they'll give it at least a day's cooling-off period."

"And you're probably right," Luke agreed. "But you have a list of places where the victims were seen before they were discovered, right?"

"We have a list. Obviously, we've been to all of them. But you need to remember, pubs are friendly places. Bartenders remember the victims, but they saw them talking to several people, none of them regulars. I believe the killers are purposely choosing people who are tourists or in the city for business. That way, they're not known by the regulars. But…"

"Yeah, we've been on this before. It will be good just to go out, speak to the bartenders or waitstaff again," Carly said. "We don't need to grill them—just chat and let them know we're working the case, and we're here if they see anything suspicious."

"Tonight, how about this. MacDuff, you and Jordan

know the terrain, the bartenders and the waitstaff, and probably some locals who are out. We can split into two groups to cover more ground. Jordan with a couple of us and you with…"

"If Jordan and I head out together," Daniel said lightly, "we might have to spend the evening fighting the lasses off!"

MacDuff groaned. "Jordan, you head out with Luke and Carly. Daniel, you'll come with me. That will keep you safe from those voracious lasses."

"Great, I get to go with McGruff!" Daniel said, grinning. "MacDuff! Sorry, sorry. No, not really, I was teasing, but the thing is, of course, it's a deadly—in every sense of the word—situation. But we're going to need to behave like people just out for a wee bit of night life ourselves."

"Exactly," MacDuff said. "And indeed, lad, I like that! MacGruff. Don't you forget it!"

"Okay, so we need to head out early. How early?" Carly asked.

"Let's say six. I'll go through some establishments and make suggestions. Of course, it won't be so bad since we've had Mrs. Connoly's scones and little else. Dinner will be fine."

"Agreed," Carly said. She headed toward the table and her computer. "Until then… I'm going to go through those crime scene photos," she announced.

Daniel joined her at the table and Luke did the same.

"See you in a bit," MacDuff said. "I've, uh, seen more than the photos."

He headed toward his room, and Jordan did the same.

Luke sat, turned on his computer and stared at the screen.

The photos weren't as grisly as they were tragic. The victims had been carefully slit open, their bodies cut in what was almost a heart shape from just below their collarbones to their groins.

There was very little blood to be seen.

But as he stared at the photos, Luke murmured, "Hmm."

"What?" Carly asked him, and he realized she and Daniel were staring at him.

"Sorry. I was wondering how this person could have delivered these bodies to these locations without…well. Even if they had bled out elsewhere, in order to lift them, carry them, lay them out…they had to be covered in bits of flesh. They had to have blood on them. And as we all know, everything leaves something behind. They're choosing their places where they don't believe anyone will possibly see them at a chosen time. But they must have a car nearby, and that car…if we can find it, I believe we'll be able to find hairs, skin, epithelial cells…something."

"True," Daniel agreed. "We just need to find whatever vehicle they're using. Which, of course, is easier said than done. But it's my understanding Police Scotland has increased patrols at all hours. It is going to get harder for these people to carry out their…their dumps, if nothing else."

MacDuff reappeared from his room.

"I've spoken with Campbell and your man in the States, Jackson Crow," MacDuff told them. "I've suggested they do computer searches of the small islands. His second-in-command, Angela Hawkins, is apparently brilliant when it comes to computer traces. She's also going through all the footage from the front of the shops. Checking traffic cameras, anything."

"That's great," Carly told him. "Angela *is* brilliant. They do have a great team, though of course, there are great teams here. These people will be found. It's a matter of…"

"Just how many may die until we do stop them," Luke finished, looking grimly at MacDuff.

MacDuff walked over to the table. "We are the lead team. We are the investigators, but I swear to you, lad, Police Scotland and the National Crime Agency are working twenty-four seven also. We're not alone."

"We do know that," Luke assured him. "You just know, of course, as we do that it's incredibly frustrating when we have so little." He frowned. "I still want to have a conversation with Flora." He glanced at Carly. "Well, we could even do it as a friendly thing. MacDonald! We could say—"

"I don't think we're going to need to do that," Daniel said.

They all looked at him, and he grinned as he showed them his phone.

"She texted me."

"She texted you—and what did she say?" Luke asked.

"That it was a pleasure meeting me. And I now have the lass's phone number!" Daniel said, grinning at them.

"All right, then, you need to arrange to meet her and ask her a few questions," Luke said.

MacDuff frowned. "Do you think the lass could be involved?"

"No," Luke told him.

"Then," MacDuff said, frowning, "you think the Connoly couple could be guilty in some way? I can't imagine why. They obviously don't need the money."

"Well, we can't be sure of that. Despite the property," Carly said, "they could be in hock. We'll have their financials checked as a safeguard. And we will check on Ian Douglas, the neighbor, and his situation also. We just need to eliminate all those we can."

MacDuff nodded slowly. "Because we never do know. As we've all seen, the most charming and upright individual on the outside can be the most warped on the inside."

"Sometimes we can only go by what we see on paper," Daniel said. "But I do think I might get to know the lovely young Flora MacDonald. I mean, after all, she's a descendant of a historical heroine! She comes from a very helpful line!"

"Maybe we should just start calling him Casanova," Jordan suggested.

MacDuff groaned and they all laughed.

"Getting close to time to see about some dinner," Jordan reminded them. "I'm going to spruce up a bit!"

He grinned and left them.

Carly stood. "Think I'll change for our night on the town," she said. "We were both here for a bit before, you know," she told MacDuff. "And I came many times while I was growing up and even in recent years. I know a few places, but of course not where our victims were last seen."

"Aye, and that is even my problem. Naturally, we toured the area with pictures of our victims—in life— and queried everyone everywhere. But restaurants and pubs can be busy. They may have been in one place and gone on to another, but not have noted where they went next. But…"

"Don't worry," Carly assured him, smiling. "We are very good at pretending to be eager American tourists!"

She disappeared down the hall to head to her room and change for the evening.

Luke realized he was watching Carly and that in turn, MacDuff was watching him.

"Most unusual," MacDuff told him.

"Carly?"

MacDuff laughed. "You and Special Agent Mac-Donald. It's rare that such a partnership and relationship can work. But you two are it. Most unusual. Quite the team. Very rare, indeed."

Luke lowered his head for a minute.

He doesn't know just how rare we really are, and that in working the last case, we discovered Daniel Murray, too, is among the "rare."

He looked up, shrugging. "We somehow do make it all work."

MacDuff nodded. "My wife," he told Luke, "was a barrister. Now, that didn't work out well, since it would most obviously be a conflict of interest were she called upon to represent someone I had brought in. But she found she loved and preferred teaching. Though, I swear, while we were in a bit of a quandary, I did offer to find different employment. She was adamant that I stay on the force. She'd been called upon to defend a few people she found to be indefensible morally if not professionally. So here, I believe you are perhaps on the right track—both on the same side of that track."

"You're right. At least it's easier for us. We are on the

same side," Luke said. "That must have been something. I'm happy for you and that you two worked it out."

MacDuff grinned. "We have three fine children and our first little grandchild on the way. May your life be so blessed, and I think that it will be. Well, hmm. I shall get myself into something more presentable to wear."

"I'll do the same," Luke said.

MacDuff disappeared into his room but before Luke could reach his own, Daniel appeared in the hallway.

"Luke," he said, almost whispering, trying to make sure neither Jordan nor MacDuff were anywhere near them. "There was something…"

"Something, Daniel, what do you mean, something?" he asked.

"I know that… I'm new to discovering our, uh, talent, or whatever one calls this strange ability—"

He was referring to the ability of Krewe members to see and speak with the dead who remained behind, and who realized that they might be seen and heard, and wanted to help. Apparently, Daniel had always sensed them, but during their last case, his own ability had flourished. He had been incredibly relieved to realize he wasn't losing his mind—and not alone in the ability.

Luke grinned at him. "Some would call it a curse."

Daniel grimaced at him. "When we were near the park, the first crime scene… I didn't see anyone but… I sensed we were being watched. I think if we can get back there, just you, Carly and me…maybe we can find someone who did see something." He cast his head to the side. "Because unless these people doing the killing somehow happen to be blessed with this ability along with their penchant for cutting up the living, the dead would be those who might have been there when something was happening."

"You realize, Daniel, that even if we do find something out, we'll need evidence," Luke reminded him.

"In the greater area here, there are at least five-hundred thousand residents," Daniel reminded him, his Scot's burr growing deeper as he hurriedly spoke. "If we know where to look for evidence—"

"Daniel, you're right. Tomorrow we'll find a way to get back there."

"You believe me? You trust me?" Daniel asked him anxiously.

"Very much so," Luke assured him. "We must use anything that we can." He smiled. "That's why we're a special part of the Krewe of Hunters, Daniel. We're the team who goes in when unusual crimes demand unusual law enforcement."

"Aye, right, of course," Daniel murmured. "So, I'll be off with MacDuff. I'll take care—"

"Of course you will. I know you will. But seriously, Daniel, I don't know why—I think it's going to be important to keep that relationship you have going with Flora. I can't explain why. The Connoly couple appear to be solid, and I'm not saying they might be guilty of being involved in any way. But I simply have a gut feeling that we've missed something. And we still want to speak with the neighbors—the Douglas family. But there is only so much that can be done in a day. Tomorrow, however, we will get back to that area near the park, and we'll go by to see the Douglas couple and whoever else lives at their estate, and—"

"And we'll meet with Flora. I'll see that it happens," Daniel vowed.

"Perfect. Well then, Casanova, go get dressed and I'll do the same!"

Luke left Daniel and went on into the bedroom.

Carly had dressed for the evening in a soft knit maxi-dress in a deep navy color, one that seemed to enhance the dark swirl of her hair and eyes. It was conservative, but the knit also clung to her in the right places.

"This okay?" she asked him.

"You look stunning," he told her.

She laughed. "Ah, but does it make me look as if I'm perfectly healthy and fit?"

"Oh, so far beyond!" he told her, taking a minute to pull her into his arms. "Hmm, what can I wear that will come close?"

"You can wear anything," she assured him. "You know, we've tried this before, searching for the Holmes associates."

"And it's still a good plan," he told her. "Especially when I believe there is little else we can do until morning. I'm no slouch at a computer, but we have people way more talented than you or I when it comes to gleaning information from the internet. I want to get back to the Douglas house, and we need to see what Daniel can glean from Flora... Anyway, we do need to eat."

She smiled at him, reaching up to move a lock of hair from his forehead.

"True."

"And..." He hesitated.

"What?"

"Daniel thinks he sensed...someone at the first location near Holyrood."

"Sensed? You mean—"

"Exactly. There might have been a dead man or

woman watching. We were listening to MacDuff, and…
okay, This is Edinburgh. The scene of some tremendously violent history."

She nodded. "And many of the dead we've met through
the years don't particularly like to hang around in cemeteries. They love to go out and see the action, and while
a living person might not be able to point out someone a
victim was with…maybe a dead person can?"

He nodded. "That's our talent," he reminded her
lightly. "Finding information when others can't, because
they're not able to talk to the witnesses we may find."

"Yes, of course." She smiled. "Daniel is so new at
this, and yet—"

"Good. And besides that he's rakish and charming,
and I can't help but think there's something we can learn
from Flora MacDonald."

"I just can't believe that girl is a killer or the accomplice of a killer," Carly said.

"That's because her name is MacDonald."

Carly laughed and protested. "No! She just seems
so…open."

"I didn't say I thought she was guilty of something,
but I believe she may know something, or she might
have seen something. Maybe she doesn't even know
what she's seen or knows, but one way or the other,
the dump sites are being scoped out. The killers now
want their victims discovered in their beautiful displays, but they don't want to be caught while they are
setting them up."

"That is true. So, tomorrow, we're set. And for tonight,
we get to eat dinner."

"And conversation. With others—besides ourselves."

"So, get dressed for a night out!"

He groaned softly but went ahead and dug in his luggage. He chose a newer pair of black jeans, tailored shirt and a long suede jacket. He shook his head as Carly watched him.

"Is this okay?"

"Very okay. You'll be giving the handsome young Daniel Murray a run for his money!" Carly teased.

"Hmm. I think tonight is going to be a learning experience. These killers—and there is no way that there is just one killer—are growing bold. They are amused and pleased by the press they're getting, but I think they will take a little care. They're not going to strike immediately."

"Ah, maybe not. But I also believe they work on supply and demand."

"Angela is checking out the islands along with others who know the country far better than any of us. No matter how many times we've been here, we need their help. Angela and the team here—and I never lie to those guys—I know they're good."

"Okay, so tonight, dinner and lots of charming conversation with bartenders and waitstaff at the restaurants and pubs. But, Luke, don't you think people are going to be more careful now, and they're going to be wary of strangers?"

"Yes," he said. He sat on the foot of the bed for a minute. "So, who do people not see as strangers?"

"Policemen and women?"

"Gotta trust a cop," he murmured.

"You think maybe someone in Police Scotland is guilty of this?" she asked.

Luke shook his head. "I think it's possible that at this point, someone has or will steal a uniform and start using it. Dinner! Let's go. Let's try to stop innocent-looking people if they look like they're going to go with a stranger, a pickup in a bar, whatever. You're looking especially lovely this evening, *lass*, and I'm also growing hungry."

"You know, we are familiar with so much on the Royal Mile, Luke. We've been here before, searching in the same way. I just wish—"

"That we could stop it tonight? Carly—"

"I know, I know. Fine. Dinner!"

She drew away, beckoning to him as she walked to the door.

Jordan Dowell was waiting for them.

"Daniel and MacDuff just left. MacDuff and I studied the places where the initial investigation showed us the victims had been during the night. They're heading to a new Italian place on the edge of New Town. The bartender there *thought* he recognized Brian Dresden. I thought we'd start out off the Royal Mile near Grey-friars Kirkyard where there's another up and coming restaurant, Filigree." He shrugged. "Great fish, shepherd's pie—"

"And haggis, of course," Luke said.

"Only on the weekends, so you're safe," Jordan said. "Ready? We all figured it was a walking night—more to see with people milling on the streets."

"All right then, lead the way," Carly told him.

"Aye. And by the way, you're exceptionally lovely this evening, Special Agent MacDonald."

"Thank you," Carly told him.

"Oh, sorry. You, too, Special Agent Kendrick. It's just she's my preference, I mean nothing wrong with it if she weren't, but—"

Luke laughed. "That's fine. I feel the same. Nothing wrong with it. But as you have all figured out, she is my preference."

Grinning, Jordan headed out of the house. Luke, taking up the rear, keyed in the house alarm and the alarm at the gate as they departed.

The streets were full at this time of night. Some tourists—maybe a bit nervous—were going to the hotels on and off the Royal Mile.

Luke assumed some people were part of the local population and were heading home from work, stopping to shop or perhaps to grab something to eat. And likewise, he assumed many were tourists busy trying to get in what they could before darkness fell.

He didn't think the killers were necessarily taking their victims at night. Darkness was simply a time of day that was instinctively feared more by most people. But it was also the time when far more people were prone to drink. For those who didn't indulge often, a few drinks often led to sleep. For those who enjoyed a little indulgence, it was the time when they could spend a few hours perhaps savoring a couple drinks slowly while spending time with friends and shaking off the day.

"Just people, pretty people, thinking people, heavy people...a few kids," Jordan murmured. "All moving about because we all need to move about. This is really..."

"We need more to go on. But we will get it," Carly assured him.

Jordan took a turn, leading them off the Royal Mile. As they walked along Greyfriars Kirkyard, Luke found himself pausing.

"Resurrectionists?" Jordan asked him. "Before Burke

and Hare, people became paranoid about their dead, their loved ones. There were patrols, of course, and there were those who were caught trying to dig up *fresh* corpses, and they were prosecuted. Many people opted to buy what they called *mortsafes* for their loved ones, which were basically metal bars that made it extremely difficult and time-consuming to even attempt to get into a grave. From all I've heard, though, Burke and Hare didn't dig up bodies because they feared being caught. And most of all, they didn't want to be bothered by the work. When they had their first corpse fall into their hands through natural causes, they realized the value. And, of course, I never knew, either, but from what history tells us, they simply found murder a much easier means to an end."

"Right," Luke said. "There is sad history here, and touching history, too. This is where the little terrier, Bobby, sat at his master's grave."

"And Bobby is here, now, too, near his master but outside consecrated ground. The kirkyard is fascinating," Jordan said. "Oh, that sounds terrible—"

"Not at all," Carly assured him. "Graveyards are filled with history."

Jordan laughed. "Edinburgh is filled with history." He winced. "Odd as it may seem, Burke and Hare cost many people their lives, but into the following years, maybe they saved a few from like ends. The Anatomy Act of 1832 changed the regulations regarding the legal supply of corpses for medical purposes."

"Trust me, I understand laws, and they must protect the innocent as much as they must give us recourse against those who break them. But that Hare got off scot-free—oh, sorry, is that where that saying came from?" Carly asked.

Jordan laughed. "Maybe. It's disputed, from what I've read. A *scot* or a *scat* might have been part of a tax payment at one time, but some say it comes from America, from a man who escaped his slavery, Dred Scott—except the American Supreme Court at the time decided that as a slave, the man wasn't a citizen. To this day, many people consider it the worst decision the Supreme Court ever made!"

"Horrible, and in retrospect today, we all wonder how any human society could consider slavery right, except that—"

"In places and through crime, it goes on to this day," Jordan said. "I'm not picking on Americans!"

Carly laughed. "I didn't think you were doing so. History is history. We can't change it. We can only go by the philosopher George Santayana, 'those who cannot remember the past are condemned to repeat it.'"

"True. So, we remember," Jordan said. "Why can't we remember that murder is wrong?" he asked. He shook his head. "I worked robbery for a while. Stolen goods were evidence, but then returned to their owners. With this…these people are stealing organs! The organs can't be returned to their owners."

"No, because this stealing is murder," Luke said. "I've been reading. There have been cases across the world where people manage a medical facade and take one kidney from a person to sell to the highest bidder. There have been cases in which people didn't even know one of their kidneys had been taken out. But they were left alive, and a human being can survive with one kidney. This is far worse."

"But these people are being stupid. They embraced the Burke and Hare attention. That's going to make them easier for us to get," Carly said determinedly. "Oh, I see the restaurant ahead. That's it, right, Jordan? Filigree?"

"That's it." He gave himself a shake. "I'm really looking forward to good food. So let's, um, shake this grave dust!"

He hurried on. Carly grimaced at Luke and they followed.

Four

The restaurant might be new, but it was already gaining a nice reputation and following. They just made it in before those who came in after had to wait for a table.

Carly checked out the restaurant. It had a large semi-circular bar toward the rear and offered about forty tables. The bar seated twenty or so, she thought, and there were two bartenders busily serving those who were seated before them and those who stood next to those who were seated. They did have help. She saw that someone came in with a bucket of ice and a case of liquor and then refilled the well with fresh bottles as the other two scurried about.

A fellow wearing a name tag that identified him as Gregory arrived at their table soon after they were seated and offered drinks after introducing himself. He was a young man, sandy-haired, with a quick smile and pleasant attitude. It was a perfect combination for being part of a restaurant staff, Carly thought. He suggested the salmon—not a surprise—or their roasted chicken, which was served with the finest neeps and tatties to be had. "Oh, that's turnips and potatoes," he added, having ascertained through their greetings that Carly and Luke were American.

Carly opted not to tell him they did know. So she smiled and thanked him.

"Fish and chips are wonderful here, too," Gregory told them. "My favorite, in truth! The breading is so light, the haddock always fresh…excellent."

"You sold me on it!" Carly assured him.

"I'll have the salmon, and we can have a taste of both," Luke said.

"Scotch pie, please," Jordan said. "With whatever!"

"Your food will be out soon, and we'll be dropping off our complimentary shortbread as well! It is also the very best," Gregory promised them. He hurried away to see to their order.

Jordan sipped his water and spoke behind his glass. "One of our inspectors spoke with the young bartender there, the man with the reddish hair, William MacRay. And he believed he recognized a picture of our German tourist. But he also said she was here early, at about this time, and she ate at the bar. But he didn't see her speaking with anyone. He was horrified, of course, to hear she had been murdered. He didn't want to believe that anyone who could do such a thing might have met her here."

"Maybe I'll have a chat with him," Carly murmured. "Except…"

Just as she spoke, a woman rose to leave her chair and was followed by the man who had been standing at her side.

"Never mind!"

Carly leaped up and made her way quickly to the bar, managing to do so with a finesse that kept her from "stealing" the seat from anyone who might have been heading toward it at the same time.

There was a second bartender, an attractive young woman, but she seemed to be working to the left of where Carly had grabbed a seat.

The seats weren't just stools, they were tall chairs with wooden backs and soft cushions. It made it a very comfortable place to drink, something surely suggested by an investor in the new restaurant.

She was there about a minute before the man Jordan had identified as William MacRay came before her and smiled. "Evenin', lass. What can I get for you?" he asked her politely.

"A nonalcoholic beer, anything," she said pleasantly.

"Ye've come to a pub in Scotland for a nonalcoholic beer?" he inquired with a friendly grin. "Now I can tell you—"

"No, thank you, sir. I really need just a moment of your time. I'm with a team investigating the crimes that have recently taken place—"

Panic seemed to seize him. He frowned and shook his head. "Ever so sorry, lass, I'm swamped at the moment. Did you really want a drink?"

"Not really. When are you not—"

He set his hands on the bar, sliding them toward her, as he leaned in to speak. He smiled and nodded toward her table, saying politely, "We're a wee bit slammed here tonight, lass, so I will just get you that beer and see it's added to your tab. Here, as in America, lass, your server might have done that for you!"

"I'm sorry, I just wanted to see the bar," she said, realizing he had slid a piece of paper toward her.

She took care to slide it unobtrusively into her own

hand before rising with a smile as he handed her the beer, and she turned toward her table.

"That was not a long conversation," Jordan said dryly.

"He seemed to be afraid of something or someone here," Carly said. "I think he gave me a phone number, or…"

She reached into her purse and pulled out her wallet so she could pretend to anyone watching that she had taken the slip of paper from it rather than having received it from anyone here.

She slid it carefully on the table and told them, "He gave me his phone number. That's all that it is. Obviously, he doesn't want to talk to me in front of someone here."

"Great. There are between staff, people eating, people waiting and people milling around the bar…at least a couple of hundred people in here," Jordan pointed out.

"And while only a few people might have heard you at the bar, someone could be watching from anywhere," Luke added. "Let's just keep our eyes open. And what did you get there?" Luke asked Carly, amused with a brow lifted at the can and glass she was carrying.

"Um, I don't know… Tennent's Zero!" she said looking at the can.

"One of our best nonalcoholic brews," Jordan said gravely.

Carly took a sip. "And not bad at all. A choice drink for staring at people and trying to be a mind reader."

She broke off and frowned. There was someone in the crowd who didn't seem to belong. She was wearing a dress that looked like it had come from the Georgian era, and she was watching their table with a frown, studying them curiously, oblivious to the people around her.

As they were of her.

Dead. She's a spirit. And one who just might know something.

Carly looked at Luke. He had seen the woman, too. He gave her a slight nod.

"Ah, well, I need to go to the ladies' room. One never knows what one might discover there."

"Ah, dear lass, you should see the men's room upon occasion," Jordan said dryly.

"I'll leave that to the two of you," Carly said, rising, nodding toward the spirit. She didn't know how the woman might have recognized her as someone who might be able to hear her, but apparently she had.

When Carly walked toward the restroom, the woman followed. It was always intriguing to watch a spirit walk through a crowd. While an incredibly small percentage of the world's population could actually communicate with the dead, there was another percentage who seemed to be able to feel them. One woman standing with friends at the bar seemed to shiver as the spirit walked by her, frowning slightly as she tried to ascertain what had touched her, if anything.

Then again, it was a restaurant and pub.

All manner of "spirits" could be found there.

Carly moved on ahead. Maybe the restroom hadn't been such a great choice. There was a line for the stalls, and several young women were at the sinks and mirrors, laughing and chatting with one another. But even as Carly started to turn to leave, thinking she'd need to slip out of the pub for a minute, one of the young women reminded the others, "We go nowhere alone!

Linda, tone down on the whiskey! We are a group. We stay together so we don't wind up dead!"

"Right, right, right!" another woman said.

Lowering her head and smiling, Carly turned to leave, almost walking through the spirit as she did so. She nodded to her, indicating the fullness of the restroom. The place was loud, of course. Rock music was playing, but the music was low in comparison to the conversations going around the large room.

She pulled her phone out and indicated she was heading to the door, trying to make a call that she needed to be able to hear.

Once again, the spirit nodded and turned to join her.

Outside, there were still people walking about. Night was coming on in full, but Edinburgh's lights were up and bright. There wasn't as much of a crowd as there had been, but people still wandered up and down the street, some probably returning home, some out for a meal or errands, or just for the fun of being out. She reminded herself the capital city was a popular destination.

Even with killers on the loose. Then again, there was always something going on in the world, and one thing about life was that people needed to live it.

Just live it carefully. But the conversation she'd overheard in the bathroom had been a good one. A person had to go on living.

Just very carefully.

Carly put her phone to her ear as if she were listening to and speaking with someone on the other end of a call.

"Thank you," she said quickly to the spirit. "My name is Carly MacDonald. I'm with an American law enforcement team, but we work internationally. I believe you have something you wish to convey to us. You know something about what's happening here. Thank you. We're grateful for anything you can tell us!"

The woman studied her a moment and smiled at last. "Aye, lass. I didn't know…until I saw you look back at me, and then I realized you saw me. It's been years since I have spoken with the living! I'm Kaitlin Bell, and when I heard about the first murder, I was horrified. Not sure at all, of course, if there might be anything at all that I might do, but…" She paused, taking a deep breath. "I was not a victim but I lived in Edinburgh at the time of the Burke and Hare killings. Daft Jamie… I'm terribly sorry, that's what we called James Wilson, a poor boy who was slow, and he was just eighteen when he was killed. The sweet lad wandered the streets here most days but so many of us cared for him…and it came out at the trial that they didn't even suffocate the poor lad, he had his back broken after his granny had been killed. And even Burke admitted he was haunted by that killing! And that Dr. Knox—Jamie had deformed feet and limped, and he was recognized and Knox knew, surely, he knew, and he removed the lad's head and feet and… I am sorry, I go on and on about the past and it has come and gone. And now there is a new horror happening today, a new way to make murder a business!"

"I'm so sorry for the losses you knew," Carly said gently. "And again, I am grateful for anything you can tell me."

"Not much, I fear, but that is why I returned here. I saw the lass, the lovely young actress or dancer… She might have been both. She came in alone—she sat at the bar. She joked with the two working at the bar here and stayed a bit. Had a wee meal, but right at the bar."

"We know she was here," Carly said.

"But so was the bloody rat who did the lass in, or someone in contact with that person!"

The spirit of Kaitlin Bell appeared extremely agitated.

"You see, I heard someone telling her she must be careful when she left, to walk the main streets, but she should stop in at another new place, called Kevin's on the other side of the cemetery, before going in for the night. But there's no way to reach Kevin's on the main streets without going back to the Royal Mile and along the other side of the kirkyard. I was intrigued by her, a lovely lass, a German girl with lovely English, and I meant to follow her immediately, but the news came on the telly above the bar and I paused, listening…and when I went to find her, I could not."

Carly frowned. "If she left here and didn't take the main streets—"

"She was a strong lass and I doubt she would have taken a much longer path to reach her goal when she knew she could cut through the backstreets. And that's when she was taken, I'm quite certain of it!"

"When she was found and her autopsy was done, the ME determined she had a very high blood alcohol level in her system. Was she…"

"Nay, she wasn't drunk!"

"Then somewhere, between here and her death, she either willingly—or unwillingly—consumed a great deal more alcohol."

"She did not appear to be drunk," Kaitlin said. She hesitated. "I do not know, but I believe that she was sent out to be taken. The lass was in wonderful good health and she was alone here. She was so pleased, she'd been selected for a special performance here of dancers from around the world. She was chosen, I'm telling you, please believe me!"

"Thank you, yes, of course I believe you! I will tell my colleagues—"

"You'll tell those who don't believe?" the spirit asked skeptically. "They'll think you quite mad, you know, taking advice from a woman who died in 1838."

Carly smiled. "We've been doing this for some time. Two of my colleagues are like me—"

"Two!" Kaitlin interrupted, stunned.

Carly's smile deepened. "Yes. I come from a special team of people in the United States who are those with this ability. And another of our colleagues here, a Scotsman, is equally able. I can speak freely with them. I believe we might take that walk through the backstreets to Kevin's—"

"You must not! It is too dangerous!"

"We're armed," Carly assured her. "We're among the few with the right to carry our arms in the United Kingdom."

"Still, one must take the greatest care—"

"Tonight, there are three of us. These killers attack those who are alone," Carly reminded her. "But we will take grave care. And again, I will tell the truth to my friends who can see and speak with you."

"I must meet them! One can go decade upon decade without speaking with the living, and now you tell me that there are three of you here?" Kaitlin asked.

"Five, if a few of my coagents return from France," Carly said. "And yes, I promise, I will see to it you meet them. The one gentleman with me tonight is one of them—"

"Ah, and that's why he seemed to watch me, too."

"Exactly," Carly told her. "Kaitlin—may I call you Kaitlin?"

"Indeed, please."

"Keep watch here when you can. And we will start investigating everything you said and try to find out who here might have been communicating with the killers," Carly promised.

"Thank you!" Kaitlin whispered.

"No. Thank you!" Carly told her.

Kaitlin turned and simply drifted through the door. Carly had to open it.

She did so and returned to their table. Of course, the food was there. Her fish and chips remained untouched.

Jordan and Luke had eaten half their meals.

"We tried to politely wait for you," Jordan told her, "but…"

"No, no, no, that's fine!" Carly assured them. "I'm sorry. I talked to a few people outside, just warning them to be careful. I was trying to watch a few of those leaving the bar area."

Luke, naturally, knew she was lying.

"The food is delicious," he said.

"I think yours might be a wee bit cold," Jordan warned her.

"That's fine, I'm quite accustomed to cold food," she told him, and she leaned low with her fork in her hand, speaking softly when she added, "I heard talk from a few people about another newer place called Kevin's. They were saying they should walk back to the Mile and go from there, that it might be dangerous to take the streets back here, around the kirkyard. I think we might want to pay a visit in that direction."

"And you need to call the lad at the bar," Jordan reminded her.

"I don't want to put him in a bad position while he's working in case he's being watched," Carly said. "But..."

"But you could write him a come-hither text, and he'll have your number," Luke reminded her.

Carly smiled and pulled out her phone again.

I would simply love to see you again! she texted.

"Done."

"All right. Let's finish and check out Kevin's. Unless you think there's something else we can do here," Luke said.

"No, it sounds like a decent plan," Carly said.

She glanced at the bar. But if the young man had something to tell her, she couldn't endanger him by doing anything more.

They finished their food. Even cold, Carly's fish and chips were excellent.

They paid their check and left. Once outside, Carly noted there were now just a few people walking on the backstreet, a young couple and a trio of college-aged men passed them, politely nodding, and that was it.

"Lead the way," Luke told Jordan.

They passed by ancient walls, old homes, businesses, all wearing the look of the Old Town, charming with the richness of history and the lights that always illuminated the city by night, but far dimmer here than on the Royal Mile.

"You know," Jordan murmured as they moved along, "there isn't actually a street named *Royal Mile* on or near the Royal Mile. It just refers to the approximate distance between Edinburgh Castle and Holyrood Palace."

"Well, I guess it is a *royal* mile, then," Carly murmured.

"We do have a wee bit of the odd history, too," Jordan murmured. "Just odd—nothing quite so bizarre and horrid as Burke and Hare and their…well, their copiers now. But," he added with a grimace, pointing to the churchyard they passed, "in 2003, the very distinctive tomb of one George Mackenzie was broken into by a pair of teens. They slipped through a ventilation slit, made it down to the lower vault, reached the coffins and…"

"And?" Carly asked.

Jordan grimaced. "Well, the lads were caught because they were playing kickball with a skull!"

"Well, at least they only kicked someone already dead!" Carly told him.

"Hey!" Luke said suddenly.

He walked away from them to a spot where a patch of grass grew richly between two old stone buildings.

"Luke?"

"What is this?" he murmured, pulling a glove from his pocket and picking up something he found there. He lifted it for her and Jordan to see.

"Glass?" Jordan murmured.

"A broken glass. Someone brought a drink out here," he said. "You have another evidence bag, either of you?"

"A broken glass?" Jordan murmured.

"Well, I'm thinking it may mean someone had alcohol out here, and they managed to get it into our dancer before she ever reached Kevin's," Luke said.

"And you think we'll find DNA or prints," Jordan said.

"Not just that. I think we can find out if someone has an especially potent whiskey or other alcohol that they're using. How else do you get a nondrinker blitzed?" Luke asked.

"Good call," Jordan murmured. He frowned as he looked toward the churchyard.

"The church is open all night. Therefore," Jordan said, "the kirkyard is open all night. And it's huge, with clan plots, gated and fenced or not. Time takes its toll. The art, of course, is phenomenal. It's said it's the most haunted burial ground of any kind in the world. There are all manner of tombs, single graves, vaults, pathways. Do you think that maybe they dragged her into the kirkyard? And remember, the city is built upon an extinct volcano. You've been to Arthur's Seat at Holyrood Park, I imagine…and this area…so many little nooks in the ups and down. Of course, the wall surrounds many areas and there is a fence, but…"

"Maybe," Carly murmured.

"Otherwise," Jordan asked, "how could the killers be sure they were not seen or heard? It's night, businesses are closed, but still…people who work or have small children are usually in, but…"

"Possibly, they made use of the kirkyard. Possibly not," Carly began.

It was night, yes. And someone might have heard something, but…

"They might be sweeping their victims up in some kind of a vehicle, too," she finished.

"Anything is possible. And some idiot might have just dropped a glass on the way to wherever they were going," Luke said. "But let's get it tested."

"Let's do it. You two go on and see what you can learn at Kevin's," Jordan told them. He pointed. "You can't get lost—it's right there. I'm going to take this in. We have a night crew who can get right on it."

He reached for the evidence bag that now contained the broken shards of glass.

"Don't forget! It's a hilly place!" Jordan reminded them.

"That's okay! We're both pretty decent at walking!" Carly said.

Luke handed the bag to him. They started off walking together, but Jordan took a turn when they needed to keep going straight.

When Jordan had left them, Luke looked at her curiously. "Well?"

She shrugged. "You have the gist of it. The woman I met is Kaitlin Bell, she was here during the Burke and Hare murders. And she likes the *telly*, so she knows what is going on. She saw Lila Strom at the bar in the restaurant. She believed that someone there was setting Lila up to be met or detained by someone outside of the bar."

"And they told her to try Kevin's, I take it," Luke said.

"Exactly. Of course, whoever it was warned her to return to the Royal Mile and not go through too many side streets, but Kaitlin took a look at Lila and knew she was a strong and determined young woman and not afraid of the dark. And at that time, the two people who had been murdered were men, though…"

"We always think things can happen to others but not to us," Luke said. "So, you think she came this way?"

"I do."

"Then maybe someone met up with her with that glass, and it was filled with a super-potent whiskey," Luke said.

"Let's see if Lila Strom ever made it to Kevin's," Carly said.

"And I am willing to bet that she did not," Luke replied.

They walked on. Carly glanced back at the kirkyard.

"It is supposed to be the most haunted graveyard in the country. Plague victims, prisoners, religious war… Bloody Mackenzie, he of the broken-in tomb, apparently ordered all manner of executions and starved prisoners to death as well," she murmured as she realized Luke was watching her. "They even called his era *the killing time*." She shrugged. "The cute little dog, Bobby, seems to guard the place in the front, but they say visitors have come out scratched, bitten…and terrified."

"Right. They scare themselves to death and then trip and wound themselves. I haven't met a spirit who ran around punching people yet," Luke said. "But if you think—"

"No. I think we're going to need to find the spirits who aren't haunting a graveyard," Carly said. "Like Kaitlin Bell."

He smiled at her. "I agree. Still, maybe, when this is all over—"

"There's so much I want to do before we go home—"

"Or move on to the next case," Luke pointed out.

"Hopefully, when we finish this case—and we will catch these monsters—we'll have a bit of time? There are so many museums here we haven't gotten back to. So much to do and see. I especially want to go back to—"

"The Anatomical Museum?" Luke asked.

"No!" Carly said emphatically. "But the Museum of Edinburgh, the National Portrait Gallery. Oh! And the

Museum of Childhood, Harry Potter sights! You know. Surely, you remember? Fun and enjoyable things to do in an exceptionally beautiful and historic city!"

Luke, she saw, was smiling. "Sure. Here's hoping. And there is Kevin's right before us. Handsome architecture. Love the brick and the columns. So, what was that beer?"

"Tennent's Zero," Carly told him.

"Well, let's go have a few. Though…"

"Though?"

"Someone is spiking drinks with something even worse than a date rape drug," Luke said. "We need to watch everything going on."

She nodded. "But I was given a can, remember?"

"Right. And if they're spiking something, I think it would be the whiskey," Luke said. "Take a country's pride and twist it. Anyway…straight for the bar? This place wasn't on the lists that MacDuff had where inspectors had gone out with images of the victims and found out they had been seen there."

"I don't think anyone is going to have seen Lila at Kevin's. I don't think she ever made it that far," Carly said.

"We'll find out. Straight to the bar," Luke said.

Again, the place was busy. But they were lucky. Even as they stepped in and looked around, a young couple left the bar.

They quickly gained their seats.

Kevin's might have been in Old Town, but it had a New Town vibe. The rock music was louder here, the furniture was modern, and the lighting was dim and twisted with many colors. The clientele was mainly young; most everyone looked to be in their twenties or early thirties at the oldest. But as they took their seats, a smiling bartender came toward them, a man who appeared to be older than the rest of the customers and waitstaff, maybe even fifty.

"Welcome! What may I do fer ye?" he inquired, his brogue thick.

"Two Tennent's Zeros," Luke said. "Please."

"Not drinking?" the man asked.

"We just love pubs," Carly said sweetly.

"A true modern pub!" the man said. "But—"

"Sir," Carly said. "We're working with the National Crime Agency. We need to know if you remember ever seeing this woman in here." She produced her phone with a picture of Lila Strom.

The man, slightly gray with a clipped but graying beard and mustache, frowned with serious dark eyes. "I saw that picture. I saw her on the news. I heard what happened."

"People say she was on her way here. Did you see her? Did she make it here?" Luke asked.

"Sorry, I'm the Kevin of Kevin's, Kevin Burns," the man told them. "And I've been here every night since we opened the pub. I've been very grateful to be a success so far, but business is starting to go down. People are too frightened to go out. I did not see the lass, but I'll be glad to speak with all me staff and find out if anyone did see her."

"That would be very kind of you," Carly said.

"Oh! May I see your credentials?" he asked. "Forgive me, but these days—"

"Of course!" Luke assured him. "And you're right. You can't be too careful."

They showed him their badges and he nodded grimly.

He walked around to the back of the bar, speaking to a young woman who was also working the bar area. She frowned, shook her head and pointed to one of their customers.

Kevin frowned and hurried back to them.

"Catherine, my bartender, says that she was speaking yesterday to the young woman in the booth back there. The young woman is waiting for her father and her brother—she got out of work late and is afraid to walk home alone. She told Catherine yesterday she had seen the young woman who was killed back at another restaurant, and they'd talked about coming here. The lass's name is Jane Durfey, and Catherine says she knows she'll be happy to speak with you."

"Thank you!" Luke said, producing a credit card next. "We'll take those Tennent's Zeros, sir, and do our best not to scare anyone out of your pub."

"Thank you. On the house, please!"

He dug into a cooler and produced the beers. Carly said not to worry—they didn't need glasses. Then she looked at Luke.

Kevin of Kevin's seemed truly ready to help them. His bartender, Catherine, moved over to the table first, flashing a smile but explaining to the young woman who they were.

Carly looked at Luke.

No, they were both sure Lila Strom had never made it to this pub.

But they just might learn a little bit more about her final night.

Five

Apparently, those they were encountering seemed well aware there might be ears listening in on conversations throughout the public areas of Edinburgh, Luke determined.

Because Kevin and Catherine were careful to make it look like business as usual.

People at a pub, being friendly.

Jane Durfey was a young woman, a local, Luke assumed, if she was waiting for her father and brother. She had long soft brown hair and big amber eyes, and when they approached her table, she stood, greeting them warmly as if they were long-lost friends.

They quickly slid into the booth where she'd been seated, both smiling as if yes, they were good friends and it was great to see one another.

"I am so frightened! My father and brother will come so I'm not alone. I must work, as they must work, or we won't survive. But…" she began, leaning close over the table, her face scrunching in worry even as she tried to appear like she was laughing with friends. "I saw Lila, I talked to Lila. We talked about coming here. I had just met her, and I was with other friends. She was going to come and join us when she finished her drink at Filigree. I didn't realize until I saw the papers that something had happened. I have been so afraid, so afraid that anyone might be listening. I was terrified even to go to the police because they don't know... They can't protect each person, and whoever was there said something to her... That's how we heard about coming here, to Kevin's, and..."

"Jane, it's all right," Carly said gently.

"How can we go about, knowing..." Jane murmured.

"First," Luke told her, "you're being smart. Don't go anywhere alone. Whoever is doing this is looking for people who are alone, who appear to be vulnerable. We believe if they haven't gotten their victims to a state of inebriation so they do anything they're told, they're managing to get them onto a road off the beaten track. Somewhere they can slide by with a vehicle and force the person into it."

"They may also be slipping an especially potent whiskey into other drinks, something way over any legal alcohol limit," Carly told her. "So never—"

"Don't drink anything that isn't in an unopened can or a bottle," Jane said.

"Exactly," Carly said.

"When...how does this stop?" the girl whispered.

"I wish I could give you a promise," Luke told her. "But know this, every available means of law enforcement is working on the case. And with people like you, brave and *smart* about the way they're doing it and talking to us, we are getting closer. They are growing careless. They like being compared to Burke and Hare, and the comparison does exist because it's murder for money. From you, we know she did walk alone from Filigree to Kevin's, and she was stopped along the way. We will eventually have evidence we can trace to one of the people involved. Despite being told to walk back to the Royal Mile, she wasn't the type to be afraid of ghosts, so she probably took the side streets around the kirkyard. Jane, don't do anything alone or go anywhere alone. There is strength in numbers. You're smart, you're waiting for your dad and brother."

"Whoever took Lila saw me!" she whispered.

"But you won't be alone," Carly told her. "What Luke just said is the key for now. Don't be alone."

Jane nodded, looking toward the door. "My father and brother are here!" she said.

Luke looked toward the door of the establishment. A tall man of fifty or so was entering with a man who appeared to be his younger clone. Both men wore beards and mustaches in a sandy red color, with the father's showing signs of gray.

Luke stood politely, and Carly also slid out of the booth, allowing for the newcomers to sit. But Jane stood as well, hurrying over to them and hugging them, whispering to them as she did so.

Then her father and brother moved across the room to greet Luke and Carly, also behaving as if they were greeting old friends.

"We'll leave you," Luke said quietly. "You have a very smart daughter, sir," he added.

As they spoke, Jordan Dowell reached the pub, and Luke gave Jane a little nod to let her know Jordan was with them.

Again, greetings went around like old friends who made a chance meeting at a pub.

"Perhaps you should join us," Jane's father said.

"No, we never meant to intrude—" Carly began.

"And we should get back and get to sleep," Luke said. "We have work in the morning."

Jane looked bereft. They had made her feel more secure, Luke thought.

But Jordan solved the problem. He smiled at the group and glanced at Luke for approval. "I can stay a bit, if you'll have me."

"Please!" Jane said.

"And the two of us do need a bite to eat!" her father told them.

"Jordan, that's great. Oh, you delivered that bit of mail, did you?" he asked.

"Aye, that I did!" Jordan assured them. "See you at work, bright and early," he promised cheerfully.

"We'll just go tell Kevin how much we like his place!" Carly said, nodding at Luke. And he knew, of course, she wanted to thank Kevin and Catherine. It was gratifying that while Kevin and Catherine needed to stay in business, they were also concerned for their patrons' safety and tried to do what they could.

Kevin nodded gravely to them, and Catherine took a moment to speak with them to thank them in return.

"Hey, don't you leave here alone. I know they're putting out extra patrols on the streets, but still—" Luke warned her.

Catherine laughed. "I'm okay. Kevin knows I work with the energy of a busy bee—we both live near here, so I walk in with him, and I walk out with him. He sees me to my door!" she assured them.

They managed to leave at last, glancing back at the

table where Jordan had now joined Jane Durfey and her family.

"Strange," he murmured to Carly.

"What's that?"

"Both our handsome young lads seem to be finding romance as we investigate," he said.

"You think?"

"I think—and I think it works. Well, I mean, who knows? They might have a single date and move on, but Daniel and Flora seem to have a bit of a thing, and now…ah, Romeo Jordan Dowell, smiling with the lovely young Jane!"

Carly shrugged. "Not a bad thing. We met working together."

"True. Of course, the road to true love is never easy. They could date a night and discover that they don't get on at all, or go for weeks and one of them meets someone else, or—"

"Bah humbug!" Carly said. "Wow! What a pessimistic way to look at things. Should I be—"

"No!" Luke paused, turning to grin at her. "Never," he assured her. "You are the other half of me."

"Well, that's what partners are," she assured him.

"In every way, right?" he asked. "I was just…"

Carly laughed. "Being a total pessimist for our young friends. Hey, those two just met. And Daniel hasn't met up with Flora yet. That comes tomorrow." She paused, frowning, questioning his route with, "Shouldn't we be headed back toward the Royal Mile—"

"We're both armed. I thought we should take the route of darkness where bad things might happen."

"Ah, good thinking."

But that night, they traveled the back roads seeing no

one. It seemed the citizens of the city were taking care, a very good thing.

At one of the graying ancient brick walls that bordered the Greyfriars Kirkyard, they came upon a patrol officer who frowned and started to warn them to be careful on the streets, but Luke produced his badge and the man nodded.

"Thank you," Carly told him. "Great to see you out here. And…"

"Not a thing tonight, thank the good Lord above us! We are vigilant—we will be vigilant, but we are grateful for all help."

"As are we, always," Luke assured him before wishing him a good night.

When they reached the house, they discovered MacDuff and Daniel had just come in.

"Ah, and so, the troops return. Anything?" he asked, taking a seat at the table.

MacDuff and Carly joined him, and Daniel shook his head but did the same. "Nothing," Daniel said bleakly. "Well, not nothing. We did have a good dinner. We walked the area by Holyrood Park, and we cruised a few of the beaten paths…"

"And you?" MacDuff asked.

"A little better," Luke said, telling him first about their arrival at Filigree, the few things they'd "overheard" and Carly's communication with the bartender. She expected to hear from him again.

Carly had just begun to explain about going to Kevin's when MacDuff suddenly frowned and interrupted them.

"Jordan! Where is Jordan?" he asked.

"Still on the job. Speaking with a young woman I

was about to tell you about," Carly said, explaining how at Kevin's they met Jane Durfey.

"He's alone out there?"

"But by UK law, he has a special permit to carry a firearm. I sincerely doubt anyone is going to surprise Jordan. He knows not to drink. In fact—"

"Aye, we need a news conference. The National Crime Agency needs to handle that—Brendan Campbell will take the lead," MacDuff said.

"I'm off to bed. Tomorrow will be long," Daniel said.

"Good plan," Luke said. "Carly and I are going to get some sleep, too."

He stood. MacDuff didn't. He was seated at the table, frowning.

"Sir?" Daniel said, looking at him.

MacDuff managed to give himself a shake, look at them and grimace ruefully. "Feeling like an old da, here, worried about the lad."

"That's easy to solve," Luke assured him, pulling out his phone and hitting the speed dial that now went straight to Jordan Dowell.

Jordan answered immediately.

"What's happened?" he asked anxiously.

"Nothing. I think tonight was a quiet night, just as we all thought it might be. But, of course, under the circumstances in which we are living and working, we're just checking on you."

"About to key in our code and enter the yard, in the house in less than two minutes, I do believe!"

"Great. And how—"

"Lovely people. I've made sure they have all our information. And we can end this call now. I'm coming in the front door!"

Jordan entered, closing the door, keying the alarm and then looking at their group who were gathered and staring at him.

He started to laugh. "Wait, I shouldn't be laughing. Glad you all were worried for me!"

"We will all worry for each other until this is done," Luke said, and glanced at Carly. "Strength in numbers. That's probably the most intelligent thing I've said all night."

She grinned. "Probably. All right, good night, all."

"Good night all, indeed," Daniel said as he started for the hallway, but he paused and turned back.

"Hmm, two mantras, a bit at odds! Strength in numbers, and divide and conquer!"

"But I don't think we should be dividing into less than twos," MacDuff said. "So, divide and conquer but strength in the numbers two and three!"

"Agreed, all," Jordan said.

"That from the lad who stayed on his own."

Jordan grinned. "I wasn't alone. First, I was with the lovely Durfey family. Secondly, I was with Christie."

"Christie?" Carly asked.

"His gun," MacDuff said dryly, rolling his eyes. "Fine! To bed!"

He passed by Jordan in the hall, shaking his head. His door closed with a bit of a slam.

Jordan laughed, turning to the others. "An old grouch as I said, but one of the best men I've come across, ever."

With a wave, he headed into his room.

His door closed quietly.

With a grin, Daniel headed in and closed his door.

Carly looked at Luke with amusement and they headed into their assigned room together.

After they put their guns away and shed their clothing, Carly headed for the shower.

"Hey! What is your obsession with showers?" he called after her, thinking they'd curl in and see if the comfort of the bed sent them immediately into sleep— or something different.

She turned back to him.

"My obsession?" she queried, leaning against the doorframe. "Hmm...heat, steam, the deliciously sensual slickness of soap, heat, steam, bubbles...heat..."

"Gotcha!"

He leaped up in seconds flat to join her.

The comfort of sleep would come soon enough.

It couldn't have been more than six in the morning when Carly's phone started ringing.

They knew they'd be starting early, but she'd hoped for at least another thirty minutes of sleep! Of course, she answered it immediately and realized it was a call she had been anxious to receive, a call from the red-haired bartender at Filigree, William MacRay.

He started speaking in a rush as soon as Carly answered and identified herself. Luke rolled around on his pillow to look at her.

She hit the speaker button.

"I don't know what's going on. I mean, I wish I did, but someone at Filigree is involved. I don't know how. I don't see how they could be working and killing people at the same time, but..."

"Thank you and slow down, please!" Carly said. "Again, thank you. Are you in a safe place to speak?"

"Aye, I'm at home, wanted to call when I came in, but the hour was wee, nearly two in the morning, but I reckoned that you rose early and I've not been able to sleep."

"I'm so sorry and thank you for calling. But what have you seen? What do you know?"

"I know that the young German lass, Lila Strom, was taken soon after she left the restaurant."

He suddenly stopped speaking.

"William, please, what is it?" Carly pressed.

"I know what I was serving her. I know that she was not drunk. But I couldn't just stand in front of her. She was sweet, she was friendly. She talked to those around her. But…"

"William, please," she pressed gently.

"Marjory served her, too. And when she left, I saw Marjory make a phone call. I think that Marjory may have a special bottle somewhere that is spiked in some way and that… I think that she is working with the killers."

"All right. William, what is Marjory's last name?"

"Alden. Marjory Alden. We've worked together since Filigree opened. We're the two main bartenders. But when we started…she was easy, open. She's divorced, has a nanny who watches her children by night. I've met her wee ones, Reggie, six, and Alana, four. She was such a good friend, not in a dating way, just a friend and then suddenly, she clammed up. She'd answer questions, never ask any, avoid me… Something changed, something happened to her, and then I started to see she was topping off me drinks, giving free drinks…listening to people and making calls," he said.

"But…you didn't call the police or speak with the

inspectors who went in there, asking about those who were discovered dead?" Carly asked.

"Speak about this—in front of her? And I can prove nothing! I dared not speak in front of her. These people are killing men. I leave there alone at the wee hours. I..."

"I understand—"

"And it was just this vague idea until...until I saw the pictures of Lila Strom. Until I remembered her smile and her laughter. And how she had chatted with Marjory when Marjory topped off her drink and then made the phone call. And I didn't know if I was being a tad on the side of paranoia, of suspicion because we're all wired with a bit of fear now. Perhaps I was just seeing things that weren't there. And I thought she had a bottle somewhere else with whiskey, but I could never figure out where, and so... I don't know. But last night I felt I had to talk to you, no matter how silly or panicky I might sound, and..."

"What you've done is right, William, and we truly thank you." She glanced at Luke and he nodded. "We'll be there tonight, William, with some research done ahead of time. Seriously, thank you for calling me, thank you. You are helping us hopefully save lives."

"Tell him to act as if everything is normal," Luke reminded her. "And, let's help him out. I believe he's really onto something—"

"Who is that?" William asked, fright in his voice.

"My partner. William, it's all right."

"Special Agent Luke Kendrick," Luke assured him. "As grateful for your help as Carly, William. And I don't want you to worry today. We're going to talk to our teammates with Police Scotland and see you're given protection during the day."

"Thank you!" William said.

"We'll see you tonight at the pub," Carly said. "And please, go to work, behave as if everything is as always."

"I hope I'm a decent enough actor," William said.

"I know you can be. And you have my phone number. If anything happens that frightens you in any way, please call me immediately."

"I'll be in my house until this evening. You can trust in that!" William said.

"And patrol will see you get to work safely," Luke assured him.

"If I'm seen with police—"

"You won't. They know how to keep a safe distance," Luke assured him.

"I will try for sleep, then!" William told them.

"Tonight," Carly said, and ended the call. She looked at Luke. "I saw Marjory, of course. But I didn't see her doing anything that appeared suspicious," she told him.

"Maybe she has a sixth sense—not the ghostly kind—just the self-preservation kind," Luke told her. "Or, you were talking to William and then you left the bar quickly. Maybe there was no one who appeared to be a good candidate at the bar. Maybe William has imagined his fears and suspicions. But I am going to speak with MacDuff right away and see MacRay is protected."

"Good plan," Carly agreed.

Luke swung out of bed, dressing quickly. She did the same.

"Not quite seven and we're moving forward," he murmured to her. "That's not too shabby."

"Right. Let's see if our teammates are moving. And—"

"And I didn't lie—we'll report on William's call and get him protected," Luke said.

He collected his Glock, concealing it in the holster at his side under his jacket, and opened the door for Carly. She had chosen stretch pants and a knit shirt—and a long suede coat that covered the Glock she, too, was carrying. Thank God they had the special permits.

They were the first in the dining room/conference area, and the first to the kitchen, where Luke let out a sound of delight.

"What?" Carly asked, looking at him.

"Sorry," he said with a laugh. "The little pleasures in life. Someone set the coffee to brew this morning for seven. Just perked, fresh and strong. And who ever said Scots only drink tea?"

Carly smiled in response. "I don't think anyone ever said that they only drink tea—just that they drink more tea than we do in America. But I'm with you on the gratitude thing for whoever remembered to set the pot to brew!"

"That would be me," MacDuff announced, joining them.

"Then thank you!" Luke said. "And I'm glad you're up—"

"Of course I'm up!" MacDuff said gruffly.

Luke smiled at Carly and continued with, "We have a lead."

He went on to explain Carly's—and then his—conversation with William MacRay.

"And you think this Marjory, the other bartender, could really be guilty in this?" MacDuff asked.

"I don't think she's killing anyone. But I do think

she's calling them when there's a possible victim about to appear out on the streets. And that maybe, just maybe, she does have something with which she's spiking drinks. Bartenders do buy drinks for clients, or top off what they've already purchased. It would be easy enough for her to get away with it," Carly told him.

"All right, we'll look into the lass. And I'll see to it Mr. MacRay is guarded in his living quarters and on his way to work," MacDuff said. "And I've spoken with Campbell—he's giving a press conference at nine this morning to warn people to travel in groups and take grave care with what they're drinking."

"Important advice," Luke said. As he spoke, Daniel entered the kitchen. Luke didn't need to speak with him.

Daniel just lifted a hand and said, "Aye, I will be talking to Miss Flora MacDonald quite soon. She has an eight o'clock class, and I'm to meet her for coffee right after."

"Not alone," Carly murmured.

"What?" Daniel asked her.

"Men have a natural instinct to worry about women, which is human and caring," Carly said. "But these people just want human organs. And we seriously don't know who is involved."

"I believe she's trying to help us and may have important information," Daniel said, not being argumentative, still just confused.

"I believe that, too," Luke told him. "I think we all do. But since we don't know anything for sure yet—"

"I'll be his wingman," MacDuff said.

Jordan walked into the kitchen, grinning. "What a wingman!" he said.

"Unobtrusive and sitting at a table nearby," MacDuff said, ignoring Jordan.

"This is serious," Luke said, "and Carly is right. We don't want to become victims ourselves while we're investigating."

"Easy enough, you two are a duo," Jordan said, helping himself to coffee.

"And we can become different duos when needed," Luke said. "We need to bring everyone up to speed on everything."

They sat at the table. Luke and Carly told Jordan and Daniel about William MacRay and their plan to be at Filigree again that night. They talked about Jane Durfey and her family, and how Jane's information had gelled with something going on with someone at Filigree.

Their phones all chimed at once, and they looked at one another and then at their phones, dreading the possibility of another victim.

"Report on the glass shards!" Jordan said. "Our forensic crew worked fast for us!"

They all looked at their phones and read.

There were no fingerprints on the glass, other than those belonging to Lila Strom; saliva found also matched her DNA. If the killers had touched the glass, they'd worn gloves.

But what was interesting was the residue of the contents of the glass. It was well over the highest proof of alcohol that was legally sold in the United Kingdom.

"Okay, so, we're taking steps forward," Luke said, still looking down at the text they were all reading. "These people are being given spiked or enhanced drinks. They are watched by accomplices who let the killers know when a possible victim is on the move.

We've suspected as much. So, these are the variables we're working with—finding out who has the resources to create such a potent brew, who has the facilities for murder and organ removal, and just how they are getting them to the buyers. We're also looking for someone with medical knowledge. A person can murder someone and disembowel them easily enough, but doing it in a manner that will allow for a transplant is another story."

"We have a doctor involved. Or at the very least, someone who knows about anatomy and how to make sure an organ can survive. But even then, given the time frame on transplants…" Carly said, and lifted her hands.

"Do you think the transplants are being done somewhere here?" MacDuff asked.

"Not necessarily. By plane, you can reach many other countries within an hour or two," Luke said. "But there is always going to be a time element involved."

"Unless someone is just chopping up people for the fun of it, for special or ritualistic meals—" Jordan began.

"They left some of my favorite bakery's scones in plastic wrap somewhere in here," MacDuff said, striding along the counter. "Ah, here! A plate of them."

"Nice. Cannibalism makes him think of scones!" Jordan said.

MacDuff just shook his head.

"Um, not the most appetizing conversation," Carly said, "but I'll take a scone!"

Despite the topic, they all wound up grabbing scones. Every one of them was convinced the killing going on was murder for profit. While the last two bodies had been displayed, there was nothing to indicate a cult being busy at work.

Unless, Carly thought, *a business enterprise that involved murder could be considered a cult.*

A call came in, which they picked up. It was Jackson, and it was a video call to all of them, and it also included Brendan Campbell.

"We've been investigating on several ends," Jackson told them. "And almost always, there's a small private island for sale off the Scottish coast. As I'm assuming you already know, some are big enough for cottages, some are buildable...all different. We're researching twenty-two that have been purchased in the last few years and three that have been owned by the same families for decades but haven't been inhabited by those families for years and have been let as rental properties. We're still working and will keep working along with the tech team there."

"Closer to home," Brendan Campbell told them. "Thanks to your tip we have everything available on Marjory Alden. I believe your source told you she was divorced. Her ex-husband in now living and working in Ireland. She has full custody of her children, but apparently the children's schools were told they're spending time with their father in Cork, so they're out of school for a bit. The nanny is still being paid so Marjory doesn't lose her services, but the nanny has her own apartment with a number of friends. Marjory is basically living alone at this time. She has no record—so far, the woman appears to be an upstanding citizen. We've also researched the Douglas family, and right now there are no red flags. But! No offense, MacDuff. Today, Jordan will need to be Daniel's wingman. The coffee shop that Flora suggested is near campus. Jordan can keep his distance. If he's seen, he'll just greet

Daniel and act as if he's enjoying a little time away from the grind."

And so it was decided.

Daniel—with Jordan as his "wingman"—would be heading out to meet Flora MacDonald.

MacDuff had arranged for Carly, Luke and himself to visit the Douglas family. Carly thought it would be interesting to see if the Douglas couple watched the news—and if Brendan Campbell's news conference for the National Crime Agency would play while they were there.

MacDuff drove, knowing the ins and outs of the streets of Edinburgh better than either Carly or Luke—what was pedestrian-only, what was one-way, and what led to a tiny vennel or a dead end. It was a great city for walking, and Carly loved just looking at the weathered buildings, thinking of all the things that had gone on in the past, and how it had developed into such a vibrant city known for its citizens' contributions to the arts and sciences.

They didn't arrive the way they had before—they came to the front of the grand properties. But just as in the back, there was a call box that allowed entry to the Douglas house. A man answered and welcomed MacDuff. They were expected.

Ian Douglas clicked the lock to the gate open and they entered. Again, Carly found herself marveling at the historic grandeur that could be found in so many places. Not that there weren't stunning and expansive estates in the United States, but like his neighbors' house, Ian Douglas's home was truly unique.

"There should have been a pack of spirits running around these halls," Luke whispered to Carly.

She smiled. Thinking of the history that occurred in or near them, yes. But if ghosts were haunting the historic manors, they weren't making any efforts at communication.

"Come in, come in, please," Ian said, welcoming them at the open door to his house. "We would do anything to help you in any way! You must be the Americans," he said. "Pleased to have you here. Mellyora has a snack ready, I wasn't sure if you'd had time for a meal."

"We had a few scones," Carly said, shaking his hand and introducing herself and Luke. "But it's lovely you're so willing to help us."

Ian Douglas was a man of about fifty, tall and dignified with silver hair. He swept out a hand, indicating that they come through what must have been a great hall at one time and now, as in his neighbor's house, had been brought up to the present with a TV screen that might have done a small theater proud, a stereo system and comfortable seating to go with it all.

They were led into a dining room. One thing was certain, whether anyone here was guilty of collusion in any way, they were not just polite—they were warm and welcoming.

"My wife, Cassandra," Ian said, introducing the woman who waited for them in the dining room. She was about five-six with dark hair neatly trimmed to frame her face, bright blue eyes and a friendly countenance.

She greeted them warmly, sweeping her hand out to indicate the table. "Shortbread, of course, oatcakes, and the little pies are smoked salmon. I tried to keep it to little bits of food that might be held in one hand. Please, I do hope you will enjoy. I didn't do the cooking myself. I wouldn't do that to you. All is from our favorite grocer."

"This is incredibly nice of you," Carly said, smiling.

They were all seated. They passed around the delicacies. Carly glanced at Luke. If nothing else was gained, they were able to sample some fine food on their expeditions.

Cassandra glanced at her husband. She sighed and looked back at Carly, and then at MacDuff, back to Carly and then downward.

"To be quite honest, I feel terribly guilty," she said, as if she were speaking to her lap. "There is something that I didn't say...and I don't know if it's important or not."

"What is it?" Luke asked her.

She glanced nervously at her husband again.

"Cassandra, please, just speak to them. They won't think you're horrible, and I know they'll be very careful and discreet."

"Please, what is it? We're eager for any help in any way. And as your husband said, we investigate everything very carefully and don't need to tell anyone where we learned anything," Luke said.

Again, Cassandra glanced at her husband.

"Where else could they have learned this?" she whispered, but Carly reached across the table and gently set a hand on Cassandra's.

"Please," she said softly.

Cassandra winced.

"All right, I thought at first, I mean it may mean nothing, but..."

"But?" Luke prompted softly.

"I saw our neighbor in the alley that night. I—I saw Ewan Connoly in the alley just before dawn, and I thought after we'd learned what had happened that the poor soul who was murdered must have been back there then…but I might have been wrong! It was dark. It might have been someone else, I just thought it was Ewan, and if I'm wrong… What am I doing?"

Six

"Don't upset yourself," Luke said quietly to the woman, "but let me make sure I understand what you're telling me. You were awake—and you came out back?" he asked.

"No, I woke up and I don't know what it was, but I thought I heard something from out in the back. I looked out the window from our bedroom. And then I just thought, how odd! Ewan must have been back there and it seemed strange, but then I was awake, so maybe he was awake... I mean, sometimes people have trouble sleeping and when they do, I know I'll come down sometimes and pick up a book, put the telly back on... anything to try to get tired enough to go back to sleep."

"But you're not sure it was Ewan?" Luke asked her.

She shook her head. "I thought it was him. The height and size seemed right. But then, of course, I was looking down from the window. Our bedroom is on the second floor."

"Does anyone else live here?" Carly asked her. "I'm sorry, I mean because someone else might have seen something, too?"

"No, um, our children aren't far, but they have their own apartments. Brianna teaches at the university and Westin is a doctor. He works at the hospital," Cassandra said proudly.

Luke knew Carly was looking at him.

Their son is a doctor. There are many doctors in Edinburgh, of course. The medical school remains one of the top institutions for learning.

But a body had been found here...

"Sounds as if you did a fine job raising them," Luke said, glancing at Carly. But she was watching Cassandra, too, giving nothing away in the manner she looked at her.

"Thank you."

"And neither of your children came home that night for any reason?" Carly asked. "We're just hoping someone else might have seen something."

But Cassandra shook her head. "I'm so sorry. It's all so distressing. Those poor people! They came to our beautiful city and..."

"Of course, you're distressed," Carly said gently. "And please don't worry—"

"Ye'll never tell Ewan that Cassandra worried he might have been in the vennel, eh?" Ian Douglas asked them.

"Not a word," MacDuff promised. He gave them both an assuring smile. "We have our ways of investigating that give nothing away at all."

"Thank you. I just..." Cassandra paused, looking at her husband. "I can't seem to help myself. I'm nervous when he comes now and—"

She broke off again. There was a tap at the door.

Curious, since you need a code to get through the gate.

Luke frowned and asked quickly, "Ewan doesn't need you to let him in? Or is that—"

"We have each other's codes," Ian Douglas told him. "And that must be Ewan coming for tea as he so often does! He always knocks at this point or opens the door and calls for us before entering. I'll uh…go get him?"

"Of course. And don't worry. We'll just say we hadn't been able to talk to you on the day we spoke with him— that's the truth," Luke said.

Ian Douglas stood and left the dining room to hurry to the front.

"It's all right!" Carly assured Cassandra.

Ian returned to the dining room with Ewan, and Luke quickly stood to greet him along with Carly and MacDuff.

"Good to see you again, I think!" Ewan told them. "Ian says he and Cassandra were out the other day, and so they asked you over this morning."

"They did, but…I'm afraid we still have nothing," Luke said, shaking his head. "But thanks to the two of you and your wives, we're eating well!"

"It's the least we can do," Cassandra said.

"Well, I believe we've eaten your lovely pastries and enjoyed the tea tremendously," Carly said. "But…well, we'd best move on and see what we can accomplish elsewhere."

"You've gotten nowhere?" Ewan asked them. "My wife is still in such a tizzy—so frightened that such a killer was here just outside our doors."

"Oh, we will find out what's going on," MacDuff assured him. "This is my city, and a treasure to the world. We'll not let it go on."

"No, we won't," Carly said sweetly. "Mr. and Mrs.

Douglas, thank you so very much for your hospitality. And please, Mr. Connoly," she told Ewan, "tell your wife not to worry. Police Scotland is vigilant and watching over this area, especially your beautiful homes. Oh! May we turn on the news for a minute, please? Brendan Campbell is giving a press conference right now!"

Luke lowered his head. Carly was right on. They could observe Ian Douglas and his wife watch the news conference, along with Ewan Connoly.

"Oh, I don't know! Should we see more—" Cassandra began.

"It happened," Ian Douglas said flatly. "It's important we know what continues to happen step by step."

"I believe he's mainly giving people a warning of what to watch out for," Luke said.

"Aye, that's his plan," MacDuff agreed.

"Shall we?" Ian Douglas led the way out toward the entry and the large parlor or ballroom where his entertainment system was to be found.

None of them sat. He found his remote control and keyed in to the news. Brendan Campbell was already on, stating that numerous law enforcement agencies were working day and night to bring an end to the nightmare. He went on to warn people not to be out alone, to be vigilant, to report anything they see as slightly suspicious.

Campbell was good; he didn't create panic, but he gave a clear warning.

The talk ended as they watched.

Ian Douglas hit the off button on his remote and turned to them.

"Numerous agencies! Someone must end this."

"Not to worry, sir. There are officers and agents

working around the clock, as Campbell said," Carly told him.

"Right, of course," Ewan said. "And thank you. There's always someone…"

"Watching, yes," MacDuff said.

"Good to know," Ewan told them.

They managed to leave, and when they reached the car, MacDuff leaned back in the driver's seat, shaking his head.

"So, she may or may not have seen Ewan Connoly in the vennel," he said.

"We have people researching both families," Luke reminded him.

"And Ewan now knows his home is being watched. If he or anyone there is guilty of anything, he's prepared. And now we know Ian and Cassandra's son is a doctor," Carly murmured. "I think I'm going to pay a visit to the hospital."

"And ask to meet him? Won't that be obvious?" MacDuff muttered. He frowned. "Daniel is meeting with Flora now. Maybe—"

"And maybe Flora may or may not know anything. Maybe she just likes Daniel—that's not a shock," Carly murmured. "But what I was thinking…"

"You're going to go to the hospital and ask to speak with an expert in transplants, just to find out more about what really happens when organs are taken and transplanted. Also, I believe transplant patients must remain on certain medications. Perhaps find out more from the pharmacy," Luke said.

"All right—" MacDuff said.

"No, not all three of us. Just me," Carly told him.

"We can't act as if someone there is being staked out," she explained.

"Aye, there's a point," MacDuff said. "But—"

"I'm fine alone. You'll drop me off right in front of the hospital and pick me up there. The two of you can meet with Daniel and Jordan and find out if they learned anything," Carly said.

MacDuff looked at her worriedly.

"I'm armed," she reminded him quietly.

MacDuff looked at Luke then, and Luke smiled and told him, "I wouldn't want any of us walking around alone at night now. Thankfully, Jordan got in okay last night, but none of us go off alone anymore. But we'll drop her right in front of the hospital and pick her up right in front of the hospital. Whoever is doing this— and yes, there are at least two people involved and probably more—wouldn't risk doing anything to anyone at the hospital."

"Right," MacDuff murmured.

Carly looked at Luke and whispered, "You know I'll be careful."

"Yes." Luke reminded them all, "The victims have been taken at night, to the best of what we've discovered. During prime time at pubs."

"And tonight, we go back to Filigree," MacDuff muttered.

"And we have people trying to find out more about Marjory Alden," Luke told him.

"So, right, hospital, here I come," MacDuff said. But he smiled to himself. "We do have more than one hospital."

"Whichever does transplants," Carly said.

"Aye, of course!"

MacDuff drove and they soon dropped Carly off.

They watched her go in, present her ID at the stand near the door and turn to wave to them.

"I'll call Jordan, see what's going on with Daniel and Flora," Luke told MacDuff.

Before he could make the call, he received one.

It was Jackson from the States.

"We have discovered something interesting," Jackson told him. "I've already let Campbell know. We reached Marjory Alden's ex-husband. The children are not with him. To the best of his knowledge, they were with their mother."

"Oh, God, you don't think—" Luke began. No, no mother would let her children have their organs taken from their bodies.

But…

"Someone is holding them," Luke said. "Someone took her children—and that's what they have over her. She is working for the killers—"

"So, we don't even need to play a game tonight," MacDuff said. "We go in and arrest her."

"We can't do that," Luke said. "We must find a way to find out what happened, and when and where those kids might be, or the next victims—well, I'm very afraid the next victims just might be little ones."

"Oh, Lord!" MacDuff exclaimed, shaking his head. He looked over at Luke quickly. "To punish her—and as a warning to anyone else they have something over! How in God's name do we deal with this situation?"

"Extremely carefully," Luke said. He leaned his head back for a moment. Catch-22. They would have to find the killers to find the children. But to find the children…

Somehow, they were going to have to find the killers.

* * *

"Miss MacDonald!"

When Carly reached the fourth floor, she was met by an attractive nurse with her dark brown hair pulled back in braids—best for work in a hospital and certainly when sterile conditions were so very important.

"Yes, thank you, I'm Carly MacDonald and Dr. Forbes has said he can afford me a few minutes of his time," she said.

"Aye, and forgive me. I understand you're with the team investigating the murders here, but…you're an American." She grinned at Carly. "An American—with a Scottish name!"

"Scottish grandparents on my father's side," Carly told her.

"But you're working with law enforcement—here?"

"Part of an international team," Carly explained. "And you're—"

"Selina Caine, one of the nurses in this department, and very happy to help you. And my apologies. Are you Officer MacDonald—"

"Special Agent is my work title, but Carly is just fine. I'm hoping to gain some knowledge from Dr. Forbes, I'm not really on the clock."

"Of course! Let me bring you to his office."

"Thank you!"

As Carly followed Selina through the hallway toward the offices, she noticed two other doctors and several nurses.

A few noticed her and looked at her curiously. A few did not.

"Dr. Forbes is our lead in this department," Selina explained, "but our doctors have different specialties.

We just passed Dr. Chou. If you ever have a kidney problem, he is the man you want to see."

"I imagine he's saved many lives."

"Oh, aye! And here we are."

They stopped in front of a door, and Selina tapped on it, heard a "Come in," and opened the door.

"Special Agent Carly MacDonald, sir."

"Thank you, Selina," Forbes said, rising from the swivel chair at his desk and addressing Carly. "Please, come in."

Dr. Leith Forbes was an impressive-looking man: tall, dark-haired and trim, a man who wore his white coat with great dignity. He appeared to be about forty-five, polite and ready to speak with her, because she knew she'd had no choice but to explain what she needed when she arrived at the hospital, wanting to speak with him.

He seemed perplexed as he offered her the second chair in the room and drew it up so they could look at one another.

"I'm sorry to take your time," she told him.

"If I can help, not at all. Still…since you're seeing me and you're law enforcement, I assume you believe the killers currently plaguing Scotland are disemboweling their victims for a reason?"

"Money," she said simply.

He shook his head. "There are incredible difficulties involved with transplants," he told her. "Of course, I've heard about the murders. No one in the city could possibly be oblivious to them. But I have believed—as most of the populace, I think—that the killing was done to appease a killer's horrendous mental sickness. Looking back at Jack the Ripper, the man tore women apart but did nothing with the organs unless, as one of his letters—real or bogus—explained: *I ate the other part.*"

"We don't believe we're looking for a cannibal, Doctor."

"Burke and Hare as the papers say?" he asked.

"Well, Burke and Hare sold the entire bodies of their victims," Carly explained. "They made money. The way that these corpses are cut…it does appear they're trying to preserve the saleable organs: heart, kidneys, lungs, livers… There is a worldwide black market."

"Aye, there is, but all kinds of difficulties are incorporated in that. First, the organs must be removed precisely by someone who knows what they're doing. They must then be implanted in the recipient with that same expertise. And there's a time limit involved with every organ—"

"Yes, Doctor, I looked that up."

"That's why it is so important that those who are on donor lists remain where they can be reached, where they can quickly and easily get to their transplant hospital in good time," he said. "And, of course, you must have sterile equipment and the right conditions. An illegal transplant could easily be signing one's own death certificate."

"What if a person was desperate?" Carly asked.

He shrugged. "I suppose, but…many transplants have now been done successfully for years, however, if an organ isn't taken and stored properly—"

"What if it is? Then this is all possible."

"Almost anything is possible," he agreed. "Still, so risky, and yet—"

He broke off suddenly and she frowned. He saw her look and said, "All right, I was thinking if something went wrong with an organ stolen from a murder victim… Well, those who do such a thing would just discard it. But! It's not speed dating, you know! Everything must be right for a person in need of an organ. I have seen families desperately search through every member of their clan when a child is going to need bone marrow…"

"But I believe these people have their own lists," Carly said quietly. "They know who needs what and if someone is on the bottom of a legitimate list, they might well be hoping for any small chance."

"Aye…" he murmured thoughtfully. "Still, it's a long shot."

"But a valuable long shot. And if you have several organs from one body, perhaps you only need to see to it that one person receives what they need; the cost would be so high."

"And a viable life would be lost so that…" Forbes paused, shaking his head. "Being a donor is a great and kind thing. But when a death is natural. To kill one person for another…"

"Doctor, we believe those who receive the organs— or have what is needed to pay for a loved one to receive an organ—are able to fool themselves. Perhaps they're being told the truth, that others are dying for them, but creating reasons they should die. Perhaps people don't even ask questions. Say you have a teenager who has advanced kidney disease, and dialysis isn't working. Your child. I think many people who see themselves as decent human beings might decide not to ask any questions when there's a chance they might save a loved one."

Forbes nodded slowly.

"I am aware that in poor countries people are willing to sell one kidney. I know that there have been scams around the world. But I know those working in this hospital—"

"Oh, Doctor!" Carly protested quickly. "I'm not suggesting at all that anyone with the hospital here might be involved. But there are doctors around the world who do perform this kind of operation, isn't that true?"

He nodded slowly. "Aye, that there are. And in many countries...well, the rich are very rich and well-educated, and the poor are very poor. Aye, there are doctors, nurses...across the world. Still, as a specialty..."

He frowned.

"They've been very careful. But...from what I've seen and read in the news, the organs are...just completely gone. Is that correct?"

"Yes, that is correct. And there is little if any blood found at the site where the victims are discovered. All different sites in different areas. We believe they are receiving an extremely potent whiskey before they are led out... We even believe that they're *burked*," she added dryly, "suffocated with one killer pressing the chest while the other—"

"Covers the nose and mouth," Forbes finished. "Aye, we've heard that the method has been asphyxiation," he told her. "I just never..." He stopped suddenly, staring at her in horror. "Oh, dear God on high! You don't believe that I—"

"No, no, no!" Carly assured him. "I thought I did the right reading and I had a decent understanding of all that was involved, but I wanted to make sure with you, with an expert."

He nodded, exhaling. "Such a thing...so very, very horrid!"

"But possible," Carly said. She stood and he politely did the same.

"Aye, possible," he told her. "And you must take my card. It has my direct number. If there is anything else I can do in any way, please don't hesitate to call me. These killers…what they're doing is more than sacrilege. There are so many people in the world who need help but seek it in the right way. This is so terrible that I wish…"

"Sir?"

He grimaced. "I almost wish we still hanged people here—and took their organs after, of course. Now, organs must be donated, but back then, the hanged were a free product to be picked apart. Burke was hanged—and his body was given over to anatomy lecturers!"

"Well, I don't believe that will happen now. We're just seeking to stop what's happening and let the courts deal with the killers. Again, thank you. And here's my card. If you see or hear anything…"

"My staff are golden!" he said quietly.

"But a patient may say something to you, Doctor Forbes. You never know. Here is my card, and again, thank you, thank you."

"Of course. Take care yourself, Officer MacDonald."

She grinned. "Special Agent. But my friends call me Carly. And you have truly been a friend," she told him.

"And you," he assured her. "Do you need—"

"I know the way out," she assured him.

She smiled and stepped out of the office.

His staff was golden. He truly believed it. And she didn't believe a man in his position would be someone behind all this, participating in this. But that wasn't it, she knew. Her gut feeling propelled that belief, along with his manner.

But she observed his "golden" staff as she left the hospital. Other doctors and several nurses. An orderly nodded to her as she made her way out, a man in his late twenties or early thirties. Other nurses appeared to be about the same age. She saw two who might have been older, one with slightly graying hair and an appearance that put her at about the age of fifty.

She reached the elevator and headed downstairs. In the entry, she called Luke and told him she'd spoken with the doctor.

After she called and discovered they were ready to pick her up, it would just be a few minutes, she walked over to the desk again, thinking that doing so was something she should have done first. If Westin Douglas was working, she wanted to meet him.

"Is Dr. Douglas working today?" she asked. "Dr. Westin Douglas?"

The woman behind the desk looked at her computer. "I'm afraid not. He has office hours two days a week and this isn't one of them," the woman told her. "You can call for an appointment with him, though. He'll be in tomorrow."

"Thank you very much," Carly told her, stepping away.

As she did so, two of the nurses that had been on the transplant floor came out of the elevator.

They both smiled at her and one asked politely, "Are you looking for help? If so, there is no one better or kinder or, most importantly, good at getting things done than Dr. Forbes!" she told her.

"He was very helpful," Carly said simply. "And thank you."

The woman speaking seemed to be in her late thirties; she was petite with blond hair. Her friend or co-worker was taller, dark-haired and maybe a few years younger.

"Aye, he's the best," she told Carly, but she seemed a little impatient as she said more quietly to the blonde nurse, "I've got to get out of here! Nurse Ratched was—"

She broke off, looking at Carly, realizing she'd been heard.

"Nurse Ratched, as in the movie *One Flew Over the Cuckoo's Nest*?" she asked.

The poor woman looked horrified. "Um…movie, umm…"

"It's okay!" Carly assured her. "I don't know anyone here, and I'm sure there are a few people who are total monsters when one is working hard enough as it is." She dropped her voice to a whisper. "I won't say a word, I promise!"

"That's an old movie! You saw it?" she asked Carly.

Carly laughed. "I did. Hey, you can stream just about anything these days. Which nurse? I'll make sure I never see her!"

"Oh, I've got to get going! My husband is waiting! Goodbye, um, nice to chat! We're really great here, I was just whining a bit!"

With that, she hurried out the front door. Her blonde companion laughed, looking at Carly. "She was referring to our head nurse, Dorothy Norman. And she can be very, very hard on us! But good—she's excellent at nursing, and she expects no less from those of us who work under her. Makes for a good department.

Well, we are the best!" She paused and offered her hand. "I'm Milly Blair, and if you're looking for yourself or a friend, we may whine a little, but seriously, you couldn't find a harder working and caring department anywhere."

"Carly. Carly MacDonald," Carly told her. She wasn't sure that it mattered if she gave her title or not. Dr. Forbes and others in the hospital already knew just why she'd been there. "Thank you. I was actually asking Dr. Forbes for help on understanding what exactly is needed in transplant situations, but I do appreciate knowing just how good the department is!"

"Right, well, we didn't mean to unload on you. Nice to meet you!"

"You, too!"

Milly Blair smiled, gave Carly a wave and headed on out, too.

Just as she did, Carly saw Luke and MacDuff had returned for her.

But they weren't alone.

Daniel and Jordan were also in the car.

Along with Flora MacDonald.

Carly was glad MacDuff drove a big Escalade, and Daniel and Flora MacDonald were in the far back, leaving her a seat next to Jordan in the middle seat.

Luke was next to MacDuff.

"Hi!" she said, getting into the vehicle.

This was something Luke might have mentioned to me when I called!

"We're taking Flora back with us," Jordan told her.

"Oh?" Carly said, twisting to look to the far back seat. "Are you okay, Flora?"

"I'm okay now!" Flora breathed. "Except…"

"Except she's frightened. She was accosted by a man when she was walking across the coffee shop after we met," Daniel said.

"Accosted?" Carly said.

"He had her by the arm," Jordan told Carly. "I saw it. When he saw Daniel and me, he took off. I pursued, but he hopped on a bike and I was on foot and…"

"Forgive me, I'm still confused!" Carly said. "He walked up to you and grabbed your arm, Flora?" she asked.

"No, not at first. He walked right up to me, and told me I was beautiful. He said he would love to just buy me some breakfast. I told him I had a meeting and I needed to hurry. He told me he would be way better than any meeting. I saw Daniel had stopped and was watching…and so I told him I just saw someone who was going with me. Then he grabbed my arm and told me he would be far more entertaining than any schoolboy and no meeting would be as important as what he could do for me. He—he scared me. Then he said, *just coffee.* I was afraid he would put something in the coffee, not that I would have had coffee with him, but…"

"But?" Carly persisted.

Luke turned around to look at Carly, telling her, "Flora thinks he might be the same man she saw in the vennel the night before the body was found there."

"But—I thought you weren't there!" Carly said.

"I wasn't. I was on my way home. The man passed me in a hoodie as he was heading toward a car. I didn't pay any attention to him then, and he seemed to want to just get past me…but now I know! He had something to do with it and…"

"And?" Carly asked, looking from Flora to Luke and back again.

Luke was trying to let Flora speak, she realized.

At last, she did, her voice tremulous.

"And I think I've seen him before at the Connoly house!"

Seven

With Flora in the car, Luke waited until they had a chance to be alone in the house before telling Carly what they had learned regarding the bartender, Marjory Alden.

"That's a critical situation! We must do something immediately, Luke. There are children involved and God only knows—"

"Carly, I know! But we need to move slowly and carefully. She wouldn't continue doing what she's doing if she didn't believe her children were still alive. So, we need to go about this as slowly and as carefully as possible."

"But we're nowhere near answers to any of this, even with Flora being certain that the Connoly couple are involved," Carly said. "And…so, at the hospital, pretty much everything that we thought is right. There is a strict timetable—and we need to be looking at a few medical experts, maybe a disgraced doctor or someone who didn't make it through medical school."

"Maybe even someone who needed a transplant him- or herself and figured out a way to get one, and then figured out it could be a very profitable enterprise," Luke murmured.

Carly let out a sigh and shook her head. "Finding those children must be our main priority now."

"Agreed."

"And the information Flora gave Daniel and Jordan? Anything real?"

"I don't doubt in the least that Flora MacDonald is frightened, nor do I doubt anything I was told by Jordan and Daniel that occurred right before MacDuff and I got there," he told her. "The problem is so far—other than knowing that Marjory Alden's children are not with their father in Ireland—we don't have anything that's concrete. Yes, Flora *thought* she'd seen the man who accosted her today before when she was leaving work at the Connolly house. She *thinks* he's been at the house. And I'm sure while you gained vital information regarding the medical portion of this situation, I sincerely doubt you discovered a doctor there who ran up to you and said he was transplanting stolen organs."

Carly shook her head. "The hospital is legitimate. As far as the doctors go—I sincerely believe that. However, I wasn't able to meet Dr. Douglas—he didn't have office hours today."

"Just because the man is a doctor—"

"Right. And he's not part of the transplant team," Carly said.

"So," Luke told Carly, "Flora is going to work with a sketch artist—we'll get out a bulletin and at the least speak to the man. It could prove that he's simply a jerk. He was obnoxious to Flora, hitting on her. And he ran when he saw Daniel and Jordan. He might have just looked at the two men and decided that Flora MacDonald wasn't worth the fight he might get into with the two of them. Between them…"

"Yeah. And we know there is a doctor in the Douglas family."

"But there are dozens, if not hundreds, of doctors in Edinburgh and the surrounding vicinity." Luke frowned thoughtfully. "And medical examiners."

"A medical examiner is a doctor—a coroner isn't always a doctor, but—"

"Right. My point is that an ME isn't usually trying to save a life—but he or she would sure know a lot about human anatomy."

"True!" Carly agreed.

"We need to get back out there and get a plan going. Here's my fear as far as jumping the gun with Marjory Alden. If these people believe that she's been compromised and might give them away, they might kill those kids immediately."

"So what's our plan?" Carly murmured.

"Pretty much what we thought before. Tonight, we head to Filigree. Somehow, one of us needs to talk to Marjory Alden without letting it be seen we're talking to her about anything that has to do with what's going on if that makes sense."

"I've already been up there and then I went back to the table, but tonight… I'll go in early. I can say that I just want to sit at the bar and have a few drinks alone," Carly said. "I can closely watch whatever is going on, maybe order a drink from her to subtly spill…switch to that Tennent's Zero in a can, and watch whoever might be followed—"

"And we can be ready to follow anyone she notes leaving," Luke said.

Carly nodded.

"All right. We need to gather as a team and go over it all," Luke told her.

She smiled and walked over to him, coming up on her toes to gently and swiftly kiss his lips. He caught her shoulders, holding her to him for a minute.

"What was that for?" he asked.

"Ye auld reminder that the world can be good!" she said lightly, but then she frowned and said, "Luke, we must find those children."

"And we will," he assured her. He kept his voice strong; he didn't want her to know that even he was afraid they might not find them, and if they did find the children, whether or not they'd be alive.

"Team time," he said.

She nodded and headed out the door, knowing he was following her.

Brendan Campbell had come while they were talking; he was at the table with MacDuff, Jordan and Daniel.

"Where's Flora?" Carly asked, frowning.

"Poor lass is really, truly terrified. She has said she'll never go back to work for the Connoly family. She doesn't even want to go to school until something has changed—until whatever is going on has been stopped," Daniel explained.

"I don't know if everything she has told us is right or true, but I do know it's what she believes with all her heart," Jordan said. "She told us that the night before the gutted man was found in the vennel, when she'd left the Connoly house, she'd known that either Mr. or Mrs. Connoly had been up, doing something—which hadn't really surprised her, except for what came after.

She thinks they had met with the man she believes she saw by the vennel that night, and perhaps either Mr. or Mrs. Connoly was standing guard while the body was dumped back there."

Brendan Campbell waved a hand in the air. "I have solved that situation. It was evident that Flora was trying to help us and in trying to help us, she may well have put herself in danger. I made arrangements for Flora to be taken to a safe house for the time being."

"That's great," Carly said. She let out a sigh. "Do we speak with them again, or—"

"As you know, I believe, she'll be working with a sketch artist," Campbell told them. "We'll then have Daniel and Jordan view the sketch, see if they think it's a true likeness, and we'll get our hands on him—even if just for questioning. We'll find out if he's just a jerk of a bloke, or if he's involved. As it is, I understand that your next moves are going to be this evening."

"We'll head out early again, for six, in just a few hours," MacDuff said.

"We first heard about Marjory Alder through her fellow bartender at Filigree, William MacRay, who contacted Carly. She believes she can get to the bar and get a rapport going with Marjory, let her know that we're aware of her situation, and find out if she can give us any help at all so we might possibly find them," Luke said.

"I'm good at listening, too, sir," Carly told him. "If someone looks like they're becoming a bit too inebriated, I'll alert the team immediately—"

"A few of us will be inside, and a few will be outside," Luke explained.

"And I have undercover officers pulled in from across the UK on patrol," Campbell said.

"Sir," Carly asked. "Does Marjory's ex-husband know—"

"That his children might be in danger? Aye," Campbell said. "He's returning this evening, but he knows he mustn't give anything away. Naturally, he's beyond upset she's been lying to him, telling him the kids are just fine, sleeping every time he tries to talk to them—but we've made him understand that him throwing caution to the wind could be the end for them."

"Then…"

"Our next moves are in just a few hours," MacDuff said. "Until then…"

"I think I'm going to church," Carly said.

"Not a bad idea," Campbell said. "We could use some help from on high!"

She smiled. "Indeed, something for which we're always grateful. But we also believe that people might be lying in wait at Greyfriars Kirkyard. I love Greyfriars itself, sir, and since the kirkyard is enormous, there might be something that…"

"Jumps out at you?"

"No one with a knife, let's hope," MacDuff muttered.

"That I see something—"

Brendan Campbell smiled and groaned at the same time. "So many so-called ghost-hunters call it the most haunted burial ground anywhere in the world. That brings out every fanatic known to man, even when there's a truly heinous serial killer—or killers—running around. They claim people have been bitten, pinched and scratched by the spirits."

"Great. Get beat up so go back," Jordan murmured.

Campbell shrugged. "My point is that the place does not help us much now. There is even a tour that operates at night, goes to the Black Mausoleum, even to the area known as the Covenanters' Prison, due to the many hundreds who were held there after the Battle of Bothwell Bridge, June 1679. Sad, to this day, men and women are still fighting horrendous wars over religion, but...the point is there may be a great deal of movement, noise and action within the kirkyard. Then you don't just have the crazies, you have those who love the dog, little Greyfriars Bobby! Ah, well, that's Scotland. Stories of love and loyalty—and stories about bloody battles."

"Not to mention Burke and Hare!" Jordan said dryly. "But back to the little terrier—such a charming story, which did allow for a darling statue and a great pub, Greyfriars Bobby's Bar!"

"I do like the pub. And as for blood and guts and love and charm... Hey, that's the story of the world," Luke reminded them. "Which might," he noted, "make it an even better place for someone to lie in wait. And if people are being pinched and scratched and letting out screams, other calls of distress might not be noted."

"True," Campbell agreed. "And...ah, well. I shouldn't be complaining. The Real Mary King's Close, the kirkyards, the castle, all haunted—makes good money for our tourist industry. But you're right, finding the children is a priority—along with stopping the murders, period. I believe, considering the circumstances, your plans are solid."

Carly stood. "I won't waste time—we'll meet here, be ready for the evening by five thirty?"

Luke rose. "I'll accompany you. No one goes out alone. And, of course, I'm going," Luke said.

"But of course!" Daniel agreed.

"One more thing. We do still have people research-ing the small islands," Campbell told them. "Here—and across the pond. You do believe someone is making use of the privacy such a place affords?" he asked Luke.

"I do. We're not ruling out any possibilities," he said. "But timing is everything in such a situation. One would need the right conditions and someone with enough medical expertise to see that the stolen organs are viable for those who have purchased them. It would be very easy to reach many of these islands quietly by boat. It would be possible for someone to have accrued a com-plete medical setup there, along with someone able to perform the necessary surgeries."

"I have alerted our people on the water. Just as in the United States, we now have laws against just breaking in on people and demanding to see what they've got. But if we find cause, we can get a warrant."

"Of course. We are law enforcement. That means we are beholden to follow the law," Luke told Camp-bell, smiling.

He headed to the door and waited for Daniel and Carly to go on out, and he started to follow them.

"Jordan? MacDuff?"

"We're going to go over and over everything we know for the coming evening," MacDuff said. His com-puter sat before him; he looked up from the screen. He had already started on his study.

"Aye, I'll stay with the old grouch," Jordan told them. He looked over at Campbell, wincing. "Sir, I didnae mean any disrespect—"

"It's fine, lad." Campbell grinned. "He is an old grouch!"

MacDuff groaned and then ignored them. Luke smiled and closed the door, keyed in the code on the entry pad, and followed Carly and Daniel out.

"I didn't mean to intrude if you were trying to be alone," Daniel said.

"No, you're not intruding, and we really want to get a sense of the kirkyard," Luke assured him.

"And I was hoping…"

"That we might find a helpful spirit?" Carly asked him.

Daniel nodded. "Supposedly, it's one of the most haunted cities in the world. One would think there might be many ghosts willing to give us a hand!"

Carly talked to him about Kaitlin Bell as they walked.

"Spirits can slip around, unseen—uncaring if they are seen—and even they haven't been able to fathom what's going on here," Daniel said.

"I'm hoping we'll see her again tonight," Carly said.

Daniel looked worried. He glanced at Luke and Carly and said, "Tonight, I believe that we will learn something. But I also believe this might have been on hold for a wee bit. Whoever is doing this knows the patrols are sweeping the city—they must be aware of the warning that Campbell gave with his press conference. I was thinking they might move on. Try their act in another city or town."

"That's possible," Carly said. "But you still have the problem of maintaining viable organs and a place where the transplant patients can have surgery. If their base is here, they'll need to target locations that are close by."

"Ice chest. Every law enforcement individual in the

city and beyond is on the lookout for ice chests!" Daniel noted. "Except—"

"Except if they have a killing place, an actual surgery they use before dumping the body, they wouldn't need ice chests," Luke said.

"Okay, that's true," Daniel agreed. "Have we heard anything on a distillery yet where a super-octane whiskey is being served?" he asked but answered himself. "No, because if anyone had any information, we'd all have it."

Luke nodded. "Right." He inhaled, looking over at the wall and facade of the church coming into view. "If they are making use of a private island, it might be just as easy getting there with a victim from cities or towns just to the north, south or west," he mused.

"Water and a boat," Daniel agreed.

"And here we are," Luke said, stopping and pointing out the statue of the loyal little terrier, Bobby.

Carly laughed softly. "He's wearing a sign! It reads, Please Don't Rub My Nose!"

Daniel groaned. "He needs the sign. There's a rumor that it's good luck to rub his nose. Problem is, too many nose rubs and it will wear down the statue." He shrugged. "You know, some believe that there's a curse on the castle, too. If students visit before a test, they may well fail it. Superstition!" He paused, studying the pub behind the statue. "Too bad we're not heading into Greyfriars Bobby's Bar! I could go for a pint—or a whiskey. No, a pint. I think it's the whiskey that's being tainted. These people want to strike Scotland where it hurts!"

"I think it's all for money," Carly said. "And these killers have been amused by the comparison to Burke and Hare. And that, yes, striking at one of a country's major exports, sure, why not? Except one is a secret pleasure, though Campbell did warn that people needed to take great care with their drinks."

They headed through the main entrance, with the great church or kirk standing before them.

Graves surrounded it, but the graveyard itself seemed to stretch forever. Paths led in several different directions.

And naturally, many people were walking through the grounds to admire the monuments, the aging walls and the history to be discovered.

"We're walking over the remains of over a hundred thousand people," Daniel murmured. "At one time, this was outside the main area of the city and St. Giles' was the center. Development meant they dug up the kirk-yard and many, many bones were reinterred here." He grinned. "Even for John Knox, the great reformer! His grave is a car park now, they think—then again, with all that went on during the centuries, he may be there or he may not!" He shrugged. "St. Giles' dates to the twelfth century, with the main buildings now having been constructed between the fourteenth and sixteenth centuries. Greyfriars—named for the clothing worn by the friars who at one time had a parish—is newer." He grinned. "Dates to about 1620. But then again, as I've noted... bones could be from about any of those centuries."

"Let's see the church itself," Carly said.

"I personally think it's quite magnificent. Oh, there are, I don't know, prettier kirks or churches about the world, but Greyfriars... Well, so much happened through the years, building on and off, a true place of community and...lots of the architecture, the nave, aisles, memorials, tombs... A lot is incredibly—cool," Daniel finished.

"Hey, you don't have to convince me," Carly told him. "Remember, I spent all kinds of time here throughout the years. And yes, it's wonderful, beautiful and unique. And that's why I feel like I'd love to go in." She pinched his arm. "I used to come to services here when I visited with my grandparents."

"Ah! A true parishioner!" Daniel said.

Carly liked the Greyfriars, Luke knew that to be true. But he also knew she, too, was hoping to find someone. A different kind of witness. One who couldn't appear in court but might still help them find the guilty.

And it was fine. Greyfriars was an amazing kirk, restored in the 1800s after a great fire. The stained-glass windows were magnificent, the organ was impressive and the pulpit, bearing the arms of Scotland, was fine as well.

But even as he took in the architecture and memorials in the kirk, he saw Carly had gone to take a seat in one of the pews.

And then almost as if he'd followed them in—as perhaps he had—a man in a kilt and jacket appeared. He headed toward the pew where Carly had taken a seat, and he smiled inwardly. The man, he thought, had been deceased for quite some time.

Perhaps he was buried just beyond the doors of the church.

Carly kept her head down as the man joined her, and he thought she was whispering something.

She was. The two rose and headed out of the church, wandering toward a path that would take them around to the largest section of the kirkyard.

Daniel walked up to him. "She's found someone!" he said.

"Leave it to Carly. She seemed to know that maybe someone had seen us before and would come to us," Luke said.

"But how do they know...?"

"They don't," he told Daniel. "They hope, just as we do. Shall we give them just a moment and join them? I believe the gentleman has something to say."

The gentleman who had come to her had passed away many years before, Carly was certain. He was kilted, and she smiled, wondering if he knew her name.

He was clad in the MacDonald tartan, a tall man with fine broad shoulders, a handsome head of dark but graying hair and a rich beard to match. He appeared to have passed away at the age of sixty or so.

"Keith MacDonald," he told her. "Among those in the yard since the year of our Lord 1844. I saw you at the new pub, that place with the neon sign saying Filigree, and you were with a dear friend of mine," he told her.

"MacDonald? Really?" she queried. She smiled at him. "Maybe an ancestor of mine?"

"Ah, lassie, there are many MacDonalds, but aye, perhaps at some point. Now, I be the one who should be asking *really*?"

"Really. My dad's parents are from here."

"And you walk about like a tourist," he said, nodding. "But you are no tourist."

"You saw me with a friend of yours—who?" Carly asked.

"Why, Kaitlin, of course," he told her. "Friends in

life, friends in death. Human flesh will always wear away, but the love in the human soul stays forever."

"And what about the sickness in a human being?" she asked him, wincing.

But he seemed to know she was here because of what was happening.

He shook his head. "There are people about. Come. Let's walk across the yard a bit, we're too close to the Black Mausoleum, the resting place of Bloody Mackenzie, and far too many come to see it."

She followed him, aware that Daniel and Luke were near, but trying to give her time to achieve a rapport with the spirit before they joined them.

"So, as I said, lass, Kaitlin was a dear friend then, and now. And we lived through that dreadful time when resurrectionists were tearing up graves, and Burke and Hare were creating their own corpses."

"She knew the boy, Jamie—"

"As did I. Poor lad. His feet were so severely deformed, but he had a heart of gold. Nothing to his name but the true care he gave to all." He paused, shaking his head. "Now, I also knew the two blokes, Burke and Hare—both men named William, therefore I will make it easy and make use of their surnames. The oddity of it all. Burke could be quite the gentleman. He worked real jobs at times, a cobbler, sometimes. He would entertain his customers and those around them, singing and dancing…he could be fine and polite. Now, Hare— the wretched bloke who turned state's witness and went free despite the horror of his crimes—was a wretch of a man. Rude, abrasive…not a fine fellow to be about in any way. Strange law, not guilty nor innocent but *not proven* let both the wives go free as well, though if they participated or not, I cannot say. But did they suspect or know? Most certainly."

"I'm so sorry," Carly murmured.

"We've witnessed much here, a country within a nation, so much bloodshed, but…now, as then, there is little quite so horrid as the thieving of one man's— or woman's—life, for the profit that's to be made from such a murder." He paused, still shaking his head at the events, as long ago as they had now been. "And Knox! Sorry, *Doctor Knox*, Robert Knox, not the reformer John Knox, but the anatomist! As if he—when his students recognized a few of the lasses plying the streets—turned a blind eye, a truly blind eye. Yet, at the trial, Knox said he had no knowledge of how the pair had acquired their corpses. The horse's arse! Begging your pardon, young lass—"

"It's quite all right," Carly said.

"Hare, of course, and his wife ran from Edinburgh, good thing. I'd have given the fellow a good auld *burking* if I'd had the chance, and like as not, I suppose, I'd have faced the hangman's noose. Knox, I do believe, lost his glittering reputation and left town as well, and…"

He let his words whisper away, but he looked at her, frowning a bit worriedly, and told her, "We're being followed."

She smiled again. "Those are my friends, sir. And they're…they see you as well, and, yes, they can hear you and speak with you."

"How very, very strange!" he said. He looked at her. "Time goes by, so much time…"

She decided she'd try to explain quickly. "There's a gentleman in the United States who founded a special unit of our FBI, I'm sorry, one of the American—"

"I know FBI," he assured her. "I loved—and still love—the theater. But I was quite entertained when I first saw the television come into being. Quite fascinating, what one can learn from it." He wrinkled his nose. "Then there are shows... Forgive me, lass, I digress! But the FBI—"

"Works mainly in the States. This gentleman, alive and well himself, knew about people who could communicate with those who had shed their earthly flesh but remained. And he had also spent his life helping others and was well-known by the right people, so he formed a special unit composed of people—like me. And we've recently formed an international unit, helping when called or when there might be an American suspect or..."

"Strange killing, eh?"

She nodded. "And those gentlemen—Daniel is with the National Crime Agency here, and Luke, the very tall gentleman, and I are part of the same team."

"Ah, so..."

"Speak freely. We've been hoping so desperately for help, though, of course, lest they lock us up, we don't explain to others how we received that help."

"Aye, and they'd be throwing you all out of court were you to try!" he said grimly.

"Most likely. And seriously, for a good reason. There was a time when they burned or hanged innocent midwives and others for being witches and—"

"Lass, I am aware of history. And aye, I understand. But these gentlemen—"

"Are truly my friends, and as determined as I am to end this horror that is occurring in this beautiful, beautiful city!"

He nodded. Carly beckoned Luke and Daniel, and they joined her and her ghost. The men and Carly ambled slowly as if they were about to discuss more of the sights.

Carly introduced them to Keith, and Luke and Daniel grinned. "MacDonald? A relative?"

"Perhaps," Keith said. "And proud I'd be if it were a fact," the ghost assured him.

"I've been so hoping," Daniel said.

"Sir," Luke told him, "we are truly proud to have made your acquaintance. We do believe we're moving forward. We are discovering certain clues, but we're hopeful—"

"Aye, hopeful that I may give you a name!" the ghost said. "What I know is this. I saw it but once, on a lovely lass, and she walked from the pub just fine, having imbibed a bit, but not…it was not until the gentleman stopped her, told her she must try one last drink. He followed her from the pub with that glass in his hand. She was still so sweet, saying she didnae need more to drink, and he kept begging her, please, just to taste, it was his family's special brew. And so she agreed, ever determined to just be polite and cordial. But then, even as she drank, the small van came by, and she was whisked into the vehicle, and it was the next morning that she was discovered."

Carly felt her phone vibrating and realized that Luke's and Daniel's phones had gone off as well. She excused herself and pulled her phone from her pocket and keyed in.

The message was from Brendan Campbell. It was short and sweet. Artist finished the rendering.

He was sending out the artist's image of the man Flora MacDonald had seen at the Connoly house.

The man who had grabbed Flora's arm at the café that morning. Carly looked at Daniel and Luke.

The sketch quickly appeared on her screen. She knew they had all received it, and she glanced at Daniel first, wanting to see his reaction since he'd been closest and had seen more of the exchange between Flora and the man.

Then she looked at Luke again.

Luke nodded to her.

She turned to her newfound ghost friend and asked him, "Keith, was this the man you saw with the young woman, running after her with a drink?"

She turned her phone so that the ghost could see it. Luke and Daniel looked at him anxiously, waiting for his reply.

"Mind ye, it was dark, and death, I fear, like age, does not improve one's vision."

"Aye, sir," Daniel said, "but—"

"I would say aye, indeed. That was the man," Keith said, his tone strong with conviction.

Eight

Carly was extremely glad they'd decided to visit the church.

Keith MacDonald might truly prove to be an asset to them. She smiled, thinking she liked him—she wondered what he had been like in life.

They left him soon after, promising him they were actively seeking the man he had seen and others, considering the scope of the situation, and they would all be working continually until the matter was brought to an end.

In turn, Keith promised them he and Kaitlin—and others they had yet to meet—would also be watching and doing anything they could.

Right before they left, Keith made one last comment. "I'm in a better position now to slip around and watch what is happening without causing alarm," he told them dryly.

And Carly told him their plans for the evening to head to Filigree and to find out what they could. "There's something about that place, indeed!" he had said.

"We do believe someone there is involved, and we'll

be working on that this evening. It's complicated. We're afraid children are entangled in this, so we need to be extremely careful with what we're doing," Luke had informed him.

"Trust me. I am capable of extreme care," Keith told them.

As they left the graveyard, Daniel looked at Carly with amusement.

"Could he really be an ancestor, do you think?"

She grinned. "Who knows? My grandparents came to the States right after World War II. But then again, even in the US, I can't tell you just how many Mac-Donalds there are!"

"It might be interesting to go on an ancestry site and find out," Luke told her.

She laughed softly. "Hmm. An idea, but I'm not always sure it's good to know about everything that might have happened with our ancestors. But…maybe!"

Daniel nodded. "True, but… Keith… He seemed like a fine fellow." He glanced at Carly and Luke. "I realize we're in the middle of something quite horrendous, but I'm grateful to you both. I knew I always *felt* things deeply, but until I worked with the two of you, whatever this sense is that we have, it wasn't developed in me. I supposed I might have been too afraid others might think me unwell."

"I wish I could say we'd had something to do with it," Carly told him. "But with our coworkers in the States, well there are many stories, people developing the sense at different times in their lives for different reasons."

"As far as the unwell part, we understand fully," Luke assured him. "I think we all go through that fear, and it's why the Krewe of Hunters is so important to us. We're able to share what we learn from the dead without fear of being locked up. But it's also extremely important you always remember this—we are part of the living, breathing world. Our dead friends can be extreme assets, but the evidence that we learn through law enforcement procedures remains paramount. Our investigation will be carried out to the best of our abilities resulting in the discovery of the culprits involved."

"Right," Daniel said. He grinned at them. "So, you don't think we need to stop, steal the sign and rub Greyfriars Bobby's nose?" he asked.

"I don't really feel like the populace hitting us—or winding up under arrest myself—would help our investigation!" Carly told him.

Daniel laughed and then grew serious.

"How do we find these children?" he asked.

Luke glanced at Carly and told Daniel, "If anyone can chat with Marjory, create a rapport and find out what the woman knows herself, it's Carly."

"Well, thank you," Carly murmured.

"If these people took her children, would they tell her where they were being kept?" Daniel asked.

"I don't know," Carly told him. "But they might have slipped and said something to give her an idea. And they might not even care if she knows, if they have her convinced that if she ever gives anything away, her children's lives will be the price she pays."

"And I think," Luke added, "the woman is probably in agony being so worried about her children. I don't think she'd ever kill anyone herself."

"Except maybe she is supplying the super-charged whiskey," Daniel noted.

"Again, maybe because she has no other choice?" Carly suggested.

They'd reached the turnoff to the house again. Luke keyed in their entry when they reached the gate and then again at the door.

"Campbell has gone on—he received a report from our techs. They've found five islands they're now doing their best to research, and we're sending *fishing* boats out around the waters to try to see if they can find anything that would allow us to get warrants," MacDuff told them. He shrugged. "Then again, maybe they're not out on an island. Maybe there's a house, a room... something right here beneath our noses that we're not seeing."

Jordan looked up from his computer and shook his head. *"Auld Reekie!"* he said.

Luke glanced at him and arched a brow.

Carly laughed. "That's what they called Edinburgh once upon a time. The city started with Old Town, of course. And there was a time where all the walls built throughout history closed it in. The population in such a small area was fierce with rich people getting their way. The rich lived on the second floors of buildings so that they didn't need to climb too many stairs, but they were above the filth of the streets, and poor people were relegated to the basements or attics, all together! Because of the walls and the fires for heat, there would appear to be a massive— stinky—gray cloud of stagnant air all the time. So..."

"Auld Reekie, got it," Luke assured her. He looked around at the others. "Well, so it appears as if we're about ready for a great rollicking night out on the town, all set in what one might describe as *business casual*. Should we make a solid plan and start out?"

"Solid plan," MacDuff said. "Carly befriends Marjory Alden at the bar. Senior man here, so I'll take a seat at a table. Let's see, Jordan—"

"Happy to sit with you, sir."

"Someone watches the entry and exit, I guess. And that will be me. Luke?"

"The bar always winds up being about two or three people deep with friends—or just those who don't really want a table—hanging around the stools. I'll be in the few-feet deep on the other side of the bar," Luke said.

"Won't you be recognized as having been together the other night?" Jordan asked.

"We can greet one another, we can be friends," Luke said. "But we need a close eye on what is going on there." He hesitated.

"If I'm trying to reach a point with Marjory where she might tell me things, I could also be in a position where she may try to ply me with enhanced whiskey. And if she does produce a bottle that's not obviously right there in the wall or on the bar shelves—" Carly began.

"I'll be in a position to interrupt and give Carly the opportunity to rid herself of that particular drink," Luke said.

"We're also on the lookout for our fellow in the sketch," MacDuff said. "But we don't know if he was in Filigree, or if he was alerted to watch out for Lila leaving the bar."

Daniel glanced at Luke and Carly. "Since we found the broken glass that was able to tell us about someone distilling super-charged whiskey, I believe he was indeed in Filigree, perhaps right at the bar, maybe blended in with a group that was pressed tightly—three deep as happens in such places. There's a good chance he'll be in there."

"And if he starts something up with Carly," MacDuff began, "we—"

"We let him follow me. If we see him, we will let him follow me," Carly said. "But remember, we need to discover what is going on with Marjory's children. It is becoming more and more obvious that several people are involved in this in one way or another."

"Earbuds, everyone on earbuds," MacDuff said.

"Works for me!" Carly told him.

"And no drunken shouting!" MacDuff told Jordan.

Jordan laughed. "Ah, sir, if only!" he said lightly. "So, we're on! I'll get the equipment," he said, referring to the earbuds and mics, their way of all knowing what was going on every minute on their determined course of action.

They tested the equipment and started out, staggering the way they walked so that they didn't appear to be a group.

They reached Filigree.

Carly saw William MacRay and Marjory Alden were the two bartenders just as they'd been before.

William MacRay greeted her. "Ah, lovely new American friend. Welcome. I'm delighted that you're enjoying our wee pub here so much!"

"It's a great place. And tonight I think I'll just have a seat at the bar."

He came close to her and pretended to flirt. "Tennent's Zero?" he asked her. "But I'll get it in a glass."

"Thank you," she said.

Luke was around the other side of the bar, standing

back, ostensibly in a conversation with two business-
men who were standing just behind the stools.

She knew Luke would be watching to make sure
nothing other than the beer wound up in her glass.

"And then I'll leave you alone," MacRay said, leaning close and smiling as if they shared an intimate secret.

Carly sipped the beer and remembered it was nonalcoholic and thought she should drink more so Marjory might check to see if she needed anything else.

She saw the woman was standing by the cash reg-
ister and leaning against the cabinets there, and for a
moment, her face bore a look of such hopelessness that
Carly felt her heart tear. The woman had to be stopped,
but she was certain they were right—her children were
at stake.

"Marjory, eh, lass! What's happening here?" the
older woman at her side asked as she lifted her glass.

"Coming, coming, Mrs. Dougherty!" Marjory said,
shaking off whatever worry had become so intense
that, for just a moment, she hadn't managed to hide
her agony. She hurried over to help the old woman. As
she did so, she glanced at Carly.

"Another whiskey, aye, luv!" Marjory said to the
woman. "Right on it!"

Carly could clearly see her pour the drink from a
bottle in the well.

But Mrs. Dougherty would not be a suitable victim.
She was far too elderly and while she might have decent health, she could also have a weaker heart than a
younger person or suffer from any of the other ailments
that attacked the human body as people aged.

No.

The chosen victims would be in their twenties to thirties…

Or perhaps even younger.

And as Carly had hoped, Marjory's attention switched to her.

"Hello and welcome! I saw you came to meet my mate here, Willy, the other night. Dining with friends, but…?"

"I love to sit at a bar and I'm obviously American, so… I'd love to get to know what it's like to sit at a bar in Edinburgh," Carly told her.

"Ah. And you saw Willy again, I see. But now, I do love the boy, but he's neglecting you! That ale is about gone. May I get you another?"

"I'm trying to keep it low-key. Kids, you know?" Carly said.

The woman's expression changed. The color seemed to seep from her face, leaving it white.

"Little ones, yes, of course. You have kids at home?" she asked.

"Well, not mine. But I'm with a friend, been with a friend… We're not a real thing, yet. He was divorced, and you know how that goes…takes a while. But if we do keep this thing going, I want to be a good step-mom. I would not take over or anything—their parents should always be their parents. But I want to be a good stepmom, and that means learning how to enjoy a bar without getting two sheets to the wind!" Carly said, improvising.

Carly observed the woman's reactions to her fabrication. Marjory appeared conflicted.

I'm a mother, I'm not a mother, I'm the person I'd want my ex to be with when she started a new relation-

*ship, someone who would care about and take care of
another woman's children but always remember their
real mother was their real mother.*

Carly heard Luke's voice through her earbuds.

"You're coming off a bit too decent and charming,"
he warned. "And don't tell me you can't help it, you're
just that charming."

She glanced across the bar. He was pretending to be
on his phone. He was watching her in return with a fair
amount of amusement.

But he was right.

"Then again, who knows?" she asked Marjory. "Maybe
nothing will ever come of the two of us. I don't have a
ring…"

"And yer out without him," Marjory noted. "And
you were out the other night, right? Didn't I see you at
a table as well as the bar?"

"I have relatives here," she said. "Oh, what the heck.
Maybe it's a night to indulge. Oh, how rude of me. Marjory, do you have children?"

Again, the woman couldn't quite control the pale-
ness that rose to her face.

"I do. Son and daughter. They're beautiful. Worth anything in the world," she whispered. "I'll get you a whiskey. Take a night to enjoy yourself!" she told Carly.

She hurried away, but she didn't grab the whiskey
in the well as she had done for the older woman sitting
next to Carly.

She walked around to the back of the bar.

"All right, she has decided you're not so nice," Luke
said. "But, still…the kids."

"I know, I know," Carly murmured.

"That's the stuff," she heard Luke say through the earbuds.

Marjory returned with her drink and apologized for the wait. "We're always busy in here. I am sorry to take so long," she said.

"Not at all!" Carly told her. "Marjory, what do you do with the kids at night? I'm always trying to figure that out. I mean, you're working with kids! It can't be so different here than it is in America. I'm in the travel business, and I work a lot of nights. Does your husband look out for them when you're here at night?" she asked.

"I'm divorced," Marjory said. "I have a good nanny. Except…my wee ones are on vacation with friends."

"Oh! Where did they go?" Carly asked.

"Um, I think they're traveling near, just south," Marjory said.

"Ah, maybe they're off to see Rosslyn Chapel. I want to see it myself! I loved the few minutes in getting to see it—the movie made from that book, *The Da Vinci Code*," Carly said. "The Knights Templar were persecuted, burned, hanged, tortured, all that, in the 1300s, and Rosslyn was built in the mid-1500s, right? So, I'm not sure the Templars could have hidden anything there—but then again, it was really all about the bloodline, right?"

"What? Um," Marjory murmured, looking as if she might have said too much and was stumbling to remain the friendly bartender full of information for tourists. "Aye, right, they find out, if I remember right, that the heroine was of the bloodline of Christ and Mary Magdalene."

"And a shadowy society guarded the secret! Something like that. But the chapel and the area are so pretty!"

"Roslin, Midlothian, Scotland," Marjory murmured.

"Only about twenty minutes from here, right?"

"Depends on where your car is and what traffic is like," Marjory said.

"I hear there are those who want all the vaults open, but then there's been so much fill, it would be just about impossible without the whole place collapsing. Still, I don't care about the vaults. I understand it's just beautiful, and that even the Arthurian legends seep into the building with all manner of carvings and—"

"It's quite beautiful. Drink up! That's a very special whiskey. Try it—let me know if you like it!"

Marjory, looking worried, turned to the older woman next to Carly and spoke briefly, seeing if she was doing all right, and then moved on.

"Dump the alcohol. MacDuff has called Brendan Campbell. They're getting people out to Rosslyn as we speak. May be made up, but we must follow every lead. Give it time. Let her bring you another, try to see if you can glean anything else," she heard through her earbuds.

Dump the alcohol. Of course, that had been her intent all along, but now it was easier said than done. She turned to Mrs. Dougherty, who was nursing her second whiskey.

"This really does seem to be a great little place! I love it when the staff is so nice," Carly said to her.

"Oh, aye, but we have many fine establishments!" the older woman said, looking at Carly. Her eyes were a bright blue and her hair was a beautiful, snowy white, puffing around her face like cloudy halos. "American, eh? Keep coming here. It's lovely. But you should also try a ghostly good pub, Banshee Labyrinth! Oh, and so many more, of course! Greyfriars Bobby's Bar is lovely. Oh, luv, if you want to sample some truly delicious Scottish fare, I say Howie's, right here in Old Town. Now, New Town has many of the more gourmet places, though some may be found near here. Still…"

She paused, frowning. Her napkin had slipped from her glass.

Carly used the opportunity to bend down to retrieve it, allowing the liquor in her glass to seep into the dark paneling of the floor beneath her.

"I'm so sorry, luv!" the woman said.

"No problem at all," Carly assured her. As she had bent down, she had seen that Kaitlin Bell was in the room and seemed anxious to speak with her.

"Dear me! I don't drink often, and it seems I don't do it well! I must take a trip to the ladies' room, but I don't want to leave my seat especially now that my glass is empty," Carly said.

"I shall guard it!" Mrs. Dougherty promised her.

"Thank you, thank you," Carly said. She left the bar area and she headed for the ladies' room. She hoped Kaitlin would understand she should talk, and Carly would just listen.

Thankfully, Kaitlin was shrewd and realized the situation. As Carly stood in line, Kaitlin spoke to her quickly.

"I think I know where they might be. A *foreign interest* recently bought land near Rosslyn Chapel. There were those who were upset, who wanted the ground purchased by a college or archeological institution. They believe there are tunnels beneath the two old cottages on the property that at one time connected to the chapel. It's all conjecture, of course, like almost everything about Rosslyn is conjecture or theory. But I believe the underground areas there really exist, which is why many people don't believe they should have been sold to any private enterprise, much less a foreigner. There were many news reports on it a month or so ago," Kaitlin told her. "Hardly world news when some are upset that a few cottages are sold, but children could be kept in the underground, a basement or even a tunnel."

Carly pulled out her phone and said, "Yes?" Then she looked at Kaitlin and said, "Thank you so much!"

"Take care, take care!" Kaitlin warned her.

And Carly nodded and said softly, "Thank you, again."

She pretended the line was too long and turned to leave, speaking quietly as if into her phone as she returned to the bar.

"Campbell should know of them. There are two possibilities, cottages built near the same time as Rosslyn Chapel, bought by a *foreign* interest. Some people are in an uproar. Could be nothing, but—"

"We heard Marjory. Daniel is on his way there already. He insisted Luke be the one to come with him," MacDuff said through her earbuds. "I'm still at a table and ready to follow. But buy more time. They need at least half an hour or more."

"Copy that," Carly murmured as she went back to the bar.

Mrs. Dougherty had kept her stool for her. Now, however, a new—full—drink had been put there for her to enjoy.

"Marjory said that one is on her. If you don't imbibe often, you should have some fun!"

"Well, that was quite kind," Carly said.

"And," Mrs. Dougherty said, leaning toward her, "a

very nice thing. She gave you a drink and felt that she was then obliged to buy one fer me, too!"

Carly laughed. "Well and good!" she said. "By the way, I'm Carly. Carly MacDonald."

"MacDonald?"

"I know. I don't look Scottish."

"Well, lass, yer quite beautiful. Those eyes! Dark and mysterious and lovely!"

"Thank you. We tend to be a mix of cultures and countries in the States."

"I'm Emily. Emily Dougherty. And I am a wee bit of a mix meself! Me da is half Irish and half French, and me mum is half Welsh and half Scottish!"

"We're like mutt puppies and they are strong. Stronger for the mix," Carly said. She smiled at the woman, looking across the bar where Luke had stood before.

MacDuff had left his table and taken up the position. He was chatting and blending in. She caught bits and pieces of his conversation.

"Carly?" Luke's voice. "Don't leave—we'll report back. Daniel wanted me to be with him because we ran into the gentleman we met in the street the other day. He had information on the cottages because a relative of his lived there or worked there or something years ago. Jordan is just outside where the drinking smokers gather. Try to buy more time."

"Right," she murmured.

And she did. It was easy enough. William MacRay came by to chat with her, and she smiled at him. He was better at acting completely normal than he had given himself credit for.

Emily Dougherty was happy to fill her in on all aspects of Edinburgh.

She managed to ditch the second drink. Of course, Marjory came by to serve her another one.

Half an hour passed easily and then a few minutes more.

She was about to figure out a way to speak to Luke and ask him his position.

She laughed at one of Emily Dougherty's descriptions of a young man at the bar and managed to spill another drink.

And seeing her glass empty on one of her rounds, Marjory Alden refilled it again.

"Private stash," she heard MacDuff whisper in her ear.

"Aye," she heard herself murmur, picking up the Scottish affirmative. And as she did so, she noticed something else.

A man who was the very image of the sketch created through the description given to them by Flora Mac-Donald was at the bar.

He managed to situate himself between those sitting and those standing behind them. He was almost lost in the crowded area.

He was keeping an eye on Marjory.

And, Carly thought, he was keeping an eye on her.

She had done it, she realized.

She had managed to make herself the night's chosen victim.

But…

She still had to wait. To play the game. And pray it had been easier than they had ever dared hope to find Marjory's children.

Daniel was doing the driving; he was familiar with the route. Luke sat beside him in the front passenger's seat.

And Keith MacDonald sat in the back, leaning forward so he could speak with them.

"Luke, thank you," Keith said. "We all know that… well, that you'd rather be one of the teammates watching over Carly. But Daniel needed backup, and he needed backup who could see and hear me."

"Carly is bright and knows what she's doing," Luke assured him. And that was true. But they all counted on their backup. And while he knew he was doing the right thing, the necessary thing under the circumstances, it was true; he wasn't happy about leaving the bar.

"Right," Daniel murmured, grinning slightly as he drove. "But when we get there—"

"Here's the thing, of course," Keith interrupted. "I can *will* myself through walls and enter through closed doors. But I can't just wish myself elsewhere. That's why so many ghosts are in their old homes or even haunting their burial sites. When we wish to go distances, well, as in life, we need trains, planes and automobiles. Well, it used to be horseback or buggy, but we've come a long way since I discovered that…I remained, but I was no longer alive."

"I'm not sure if I envy you or not," Daniel told him. "I mean through time, we see so much that is heartbreaking with our families, our friends…"

"That's true. We see so much that is beautiful and brilliant, too," Keith said. "Most souls just go on. I think we only stay if we have a purpose, and I've wondered through the years what mine might be. And now…now I believe I'm here because I could not help when Jamie died, but maybe I can help now!"

"We thank you," Luke assured him quietly.

"And here's hoping!" Daniel added.

Daniel was an extremely competent driver and managed to do the short distance to Roslin in just about twenty minutes.

The magnificent visage of Rosslyn Chapel came into view. Great pillars rose to pointed arches, and the chapel seemed to dominate the horizon.

"It's an amazing place, the stuff of legend, fantasy, theory and so much more. The columns and statuary are fascinating. Stories persist of King Arthur—from a way earlier time—but most have to do with the quest for the Holy Grail. Be it as some literature suggests, a bloodline or in truth a chalice or something of the like," Daniel murmured. "The cottages that were sold to the dismay of many were built before the chapel. They remain, though they were built for some of the workmen who came to do the building. And there...the first one lies just ahead."

"It was founded by William Sinclair, first Earl of Caithness—the actual construction began in 1456. But the charter received from Rome dates back to 1446, dates that confuse some people," Keith explained. "But they needed a place for workers. It's the third house of worship here, the first is in Roslin Castle, and the buttresses of a second can still be seen in the graveyard," Keith offered. "And there ahead is our destination."

Compared to the grandeur of the church, the cottages were small and simple. They were built as places for workmen to live and nothing more.

"Anglican now and, like us, went through changes!" Keith told them. "The chapel suffered a terrorist bombing in 1914, but visitors are welcomed and encouraged. The cottages we're heading for are not on chapel property, which is why they could be sold and are privately owned."

"One day, I'll get back here and really see the chapel," Luke said. "For now—"

"You have a plan?" Daniel asked.

"I do. If there's real trouble, Campbell has police who can be here in less than a minute—they've been waiting for us to act." They were out of range for use of the earbuds now; Luke had gotten a text from the man. "Keith, here's what I'd like to do. Daniel and I are both armed, but we don't want to go in as if we know something wrong is going on. I'll let Daniel do the talking. He's going to say we're with a division of child welfare, and someone heard children crying. Before we get to the door, you're going to have already gone in. When you find the children, you let us know—then we'll pretend to hear a kid scream and enter under what we call exigent circumstances."

Keith nodded. "Give me five minutes. I can't go great distances, but I can move fast."

"Perfect. Thank you."

They parked in front of the expansive property, and Keith drifted on out. Luke glanced at Daniel and then looked down at his phone, as if he were reading from a file.

"Just in case someone is looking out," Luke said.

"Of course. I wonder if whoever answers the door is going to do so with a gun."

"Couldn't that someone be in trouble just for having a gun?" Luke asked.

Daniel laughed. "Not if he just shoots us first."

"Ah, well, they won't know we're armed—and like Keith, I can move damned fast."

Daniel leaned back for a minute. "We've got to give him time…"

"We are doing so," Luke assured him. Finally, he opened his door and looked at Daniel.

"Two cottages were bought by the same person—or entity. If legend or archeological suspicion is right, they are all attached. Maybe as a way for the workers to move about more easily? Who knows. No one even knows where the original plans are for the chapel," Daniel said. "I hope we're right!" he added, almost in a whisper.

He got out of the car, too, staring at the cottage for a long moment. Luke did the same, taking in the stonework, the old chimney and the windows, which didn't appear to have been redone in a long, long time.

Then they walked up to the front door. There was no bell, just a huge lion-shaped door knocker.

Luke banged it several times.

A man opened the door. He was in his early thirties, dark-haired and dark-eyed, with stern facial features.

"What is it?" he demanded with annoyance.

As Luke had said he would do, he let Daniel do the talking.

"Sir, we're here to investigate rumors that are circulating in the area. It's been reported that screams are coming from this house, screams that are issuing from the lips of children."

"Impossible!" the man exploded.

"Sir—"

"It's those annoying preservationists or whatever, the idiots who want to dig up this place. They will say anything!"

His accent wasn't Scottish, but not American, either.

Luke couldn't quite place it; he believed the man had a full knowledge of the English language, but it was a second language for him.

"I'm sorry, sir," Daniel said. "We still need to investigate."

Keith came running up behind the man. "They're here!" he exclaimed excitedly. "Basement leads to tunnels, and they're in the first room of the tunnel. But not just two, there are four children down there, three little girls and a boy."

"I heard it!" Luke exclaimed.

"Heard what?" the man demanded.

"That scream!"

Obviously the man hadn't heard anything, but he dropped any pretense and reached behind his back for a gun.

Luke was faster, and Daniel drew on the man as well.

"Drop it!" he ordered.

The man shook his head and Luke heard the click of a safety.

He fired, and the man went down, screaming and clutching his right upper chest. Luke kicked the man's weapon far out of the way and shouted to Daniel, "Take care, there may be others here—"

But Keith spoke up. "No one is up here. There is a woman in the tunnels. It is a small place, two bedrooms and a kitchen, parlor, entryway and steps below in the kitchen. I don't believe the woman is armed, but I hurried back up when I heard you at the door."

The man on the floor was groaning in pain. "Call Campbell—have the troops come out along with an ambulance for him."

He had his own phone out. Carly answered quickly.

"Hey!" she said cheerfully, like a good bar patron, feeling the effects of a different kind of spirit.

"We've got the children," he told her, remembering to add, "alive!"

Nine

Marjory wouldn't need to be phoning in the fact that an inebriated woman was leaving the bar that night.

The man who had been seen with Lila Strom was there; just as Keith said, he must have been there the night Lila had been killed.

Maybe they didn't trust Marjory to manage what was asked of her—even if she was desperately trying to keep her children alive.

But the children were safe now. MacDuff would be planning to get Marjory out of the place as soon as possible.

"Soon?" She asked the question while twirling the liquid in her glass, as if she were murmuring about a refill.

"You hold it well!" Emily Dougherty said.

"Feeling a little dizzy, but then again, I don't get many nights on my own," Carly told her.

Not a lie. She was always with someone, which was wonderful since that someone was Luke. However, it would be nice to just spend some of that "together time" by a pool…with maybe a piña colada she could sip slowly while basking in the sun.

"I'm probably going to take off soon," she told Emily.

"Well, you know what is going on here, so you must take grave care, lassie. No pun intended!" Emily told her.

"Of course. And what about you? Will someone meet you, how do—"

Emily broke her off with laughter. "Ah, I look too old to have someone, eh?"

"No!"

"Brody is yonder with his old business mates," Emily told her. "Married fifty-plus years, we are. I like to sit and meet people, and he enjoys his friends. I'm in good company, lass, and thank you for your concern. Now… on the other hand…"

"I'll be fine," Carly assured her.

"I saw the news today. Young lasses should not be out alone!"

"Seriously, I'll be fine," Carly repeated. As she did so, she heard Jordan's voice coming through her earbuds.

"I don't know how long you can play it, Carly. Luke and Daniel are now on the way back—the children are being cared for. And thanks to them being found, we know about another game the killers have been playing. Two of the little girls have parents in Edinburgh. We'll be finding them now, too. A good evening it's been. Play it out a bit longer."

"Are you all right, lass? You seem a bit distant," Emily said.

"I'm fine, thank you. Just thinking about all the things I want to do here."

Emily sipped her own drink. "Well, considering the circumstances now, there's truly a strange display, if you're of a…slightly twisted mind."

"Oh? What's that?"

"Dolls," Emily said. "Dolls, in the Edinburgh Museum. There are eight of them. They were discovered in the park, and eight of them were given to the museum in the early 1900s. People believe they represent the victims of Burke and Hare. But no one knows why they exist or who made them, though it's quite possible—because of the way the little coffins that they lie in were made—that a cobbler created them. Burke was a cobbler. Did he make them himself? Or perhaps they represented sailors lost at sea. No one knows, but the suspicion was so strong that an attempt was made to compare DNA from Burke's bones to DNA from the boxes…but the results were inconclusive. Just something to see if you happen to be at the museum."

"Oh," Carly said.

Marjory made another round and stopped before the two of them.

"How lovely!" she said. "The two of you getting along so well! Now, may I bring either of you another?"

"I do believe I shall imbibe one more!" Emily told her.

"And I shall, too," Carly said, curious as to what Marjory would do, considering Emily's drinks had come from the bottle in the well.

"Of course," Marjory murmured.

She took two glasses and filled one from the bottle in the well as she had through the evening for Emily, and then pretended that she'd been summoned from the other side. "Right back!" she said quickly.

She was quick, returning with both glasses full and placing them before Carly and Emily.

"Sorry, that bloke on the other side is a bit of a wanker!" she told them.

"Not to worry!" Carly assured her.

She was ready to pretend to finish her drink and leave, but she knew despite all that they had come to discover about the inebriation, the calls that a victim was ready and even the man who was watching from the bar, Marjory had to be safe.

The very next moment, William MacRay came sweeping round the bar, touching Marjory on the shoulder.

"Marjy, luv, manager needs to see you in the kitchen," he told her.

She was perplexed. "Why? William, I've been running—"

"Of course, of course. He isn't angry, I don't think, just whizzed by saying he wanted to thank you for something. Go on now. I've got this!" MacRay told her.

Marjory slid through the little door at the rear of the bar and headed toward another door that led to the kitchen.

Carly placed a few bills on the bar and smiled at Emily. "See that they get these, will you please? I think I need to head out now to meet a few friends. And I'll be fine. Please don't worry about me."

She slid from her stool, accepting a quick hug from the older woman, and hugged her in return.

She slipped through the crowd and walked on out to the street. She noticed Jordan was there and grinned inwardly.

It must have been a long, long night for him.

As she exited, he was talking to a man smoking a cigar as he leaned against the building.

She began her walk, retracing the steps they believed Lila Strom had taken on the night of her death. She neither walked too quickly nor too slowly and pretended to stumble just a bit now and then as she did so.

She was behind Greyfriars Kirkyard when she heard the footsteps close behind her. Then she found herself being hailed.

"Good evening, young lass! Forgive me. I saw you at the pub, but I didn't want to interrupt. That old dear seemed to be having such a lovely time with you!"

Carly turned and smiled. He was a good-looking man, tall, with a pleasant smile. Easy to see how he had been chosen for his role in this.

"She is lovely, Mrs. Dougherty," Carly said.

He was carrying a glass. Maybe, though she had appeared to drink through the night, he'd decided she might not be drunk enough.

Drunk enough to be easily pliable? To be swept up and dragged into a van or other vehicle? So far, the vehicle isn't visible on the street.

She laughed softly. "Are you supposed to leave the establishment with their glasses?" she asked him.

"Ah, I suppose not," he said. There was only a slight burr to his voice. He might have been Scottish, and yet the slight roll of his words came from time spent in several places. "But all night, I wanted nothing more than to meet you and buy you a drink."

"Carly," she told him, offering him her hand. "And you're…"

"Jared. Jared Stone. Please. I'm a bit late, but may I

buy you a drink? Well, as you can see, I have purchased one, and…"

"Ah!" she told him. "But I can't drink alone."

"Then together?" he asked.

She took the drink, pretended to sip it and handed it back to him. "Together!" she said.

He tried to smile, but she knew he wasn't all that happy. He took a sip.

"You're American," he said.

"I am. And you?"

"A citizen of the world. Born in the south of France, Italian mother, Norwegian father, lived all over and now…"

"What do you do that brings you here, to Edinburgh?" she asked him.

"I'm in investments," he told her. "And you?"

She smiled sweetly. "I'm in travel."

At last, a nondescript minivan made an appearance on the street.

"Ah, my friends are arriving. I can buy another drink, though sharing this one has been great fun. Please, come with me."

"I don't think so," Carly said.

"No, you will come with me!"

His manner changed; everything about him changed. It was time to act.

She wrenched her arm free, reached for her holster and found her Glock, aiming at him as the van came to a halt and another man stepped out, racing for them.

Armed himself, aiming at Carly.

He never came near her. She heard a shot ring out and saw Jordan slip out from behind a tree, followed by Luke and Daniel. The man who had called himself

Jared Stone threw his glass of whiskey aside and tried to draw his gun himself, but Luke walked up to him with his weapon in the man's face and jerked the gun out of his hand.

He spoke out loud and she knew MacDuff had to be listening on his earbuds as the men had been throughout her entire conversation with Jared Stone.

"Ambulance and patrol," Luke said.

Luke looked in the direction Jared had thrown the whiskey. "Super-charged, eh? I guess your victims are usually much more compliant," Luke told him. "But Carly wasn't really drinking, so..."

Jared shrugged. "Hey. I just wanted a date with a chick. What's your problem, man?"

"A date with a chick?" Luke said incredulously.

"You shot my friend!" Jared shouted defiantly.

"No, Jordan shot your friend. I was too afraid that if I shot at him for trying to help force her into the van, I'd kill you. And we need you alive," Luke said.

"You—you're an American! You are going to be in so much trouble for this—"

"I'm not an American," Jordan said. "Police Scotland, Edinburgh Division."

"National Crime Agency," Daniel said.

"You can't arrest me for trying to get a date!" Jared shouted again.

"I can and will arrest you for that gun," Jordan informed him. "And for murder, of course."

"I didn't kill anybody!" he protested.

"You probably didn't physically do the killing," Luke told him. "But being an accessory to murder, well... I think all your dates from now on are going to be behind prison walls! For the moment..."

Sirens were loud in the night. Police cars arrived, and Jordan greeted a friend and told him, "Take him! Campbell is going to want to meet this bloke himself. And the other..."

"Ambulance is here," Daniel noted.

And it was.

MacDuff arrived as well, nodding grimly to them and telling them, "Your work for the evening is done—there will be no victim tonight, I do believe we can rest assured on that. We'll begin again in the morning. For now..."

"More evidence," Luke said, indicating the broken glass of whiskey that Jared had tried to share with Carly.

"You and I will bring it to the lab. The glass is broken, but remnants will remain. No one goes anywhere alone, even now. We have a great deal of evidence that pertains to Marjory Alden's part in this, but this will also seal this fellow's involvement."

"The children are really all right?" Carly asked anxiously.

"They were not hurt," Luke told her. "They were frightened. But the woman who looked out for them was a prisoner, too. She was told to keep them healthy and well, or she'd be shot between the eyes herself. I think she cared about the children, so..."

"Where do they go from here?" Carly whispered.

"Protective custody right now, and we have Marjory Alden," MacDuff told her. "And Special Agent MacDonald, exceptional work this evening!"

"Thank you," she said. "But..."

"But?" MacDuff asked.

"But we might not have played it close enough to the vest," she said.

"What are you talking about, Carly?" Luke asked her. "We miraculously found the children, we have Marjory Alden, this man and the van driver. That's a success."

She hesitated. "Maybe I should have let them get me into the van and had you follow the van to wherever they were going—"

"Too risky," MacDuff said firmly. "This city...too easy to have lost the van, to have discovered that we couldn't follow with enough force. We have players in this wretched game now and one of them will give us something, something that we need. Tomorrow. We let them sit in cells tonight—or in surgery for the fellow who was shot. Tomorrow! Please do not forget that we have fine law enforcement in Scotland, and that our team is supported by all of it. Tonight, our plan worked, and taking it further could have been extremely dangerous and perhaps even yielded us nothing. Now, this team is officially off for the night. And Carly, you are worth far more to this investigation alive," he said firmly.

"Thank you," she murmured, still worried they hadn't really managed to end anything.

But Luke was watching her and she forced a smile. "Going back will be good. I didn't really drink anything and I feel as if..."

"You spent the night in a pub?" he offered.

She nodded.

"I say we walk back together now!" Daniel suggested.

"And we can tell you more, of course," Luke told her.

Her smile was genuine. She would get to hear the truth about everything that had happened, everything that had allowed them to save the children.

"We're heading out," Daniel announced, starting through all the support personnel who had arrived, politely excusing himself.

Carly and Luke followed.

They made it back to the Royal Mile. And when they were there, Daniel told her excitedly, "It was Keith, Carly. He found us on the way out before we were able to get to the car. We told him where we were headed. He insisted on coming—he knows so much about Rosslyn Chapel, the history of it and the layout and..."

"And besides that, he could walk through walls, tell us the only danger there was the armed man who opened the door and that the children were in the tunnel area, guarded by just the unarmed woman who was a prisoner as well," Luke told her.

"Wow. Keith is...wonderful!" she said.

"He is. Though he insists he did nothing. He said our investigation gave him what was really needed, the knowledge that the kids were near Rosslyn Chapel, that Marjory was involved and that we even knew—through Flora MacDonald—that the man calling himself Jared Stone was part of the killing machine," Daniel said. "Bloody hell, but I am so... I am so, so grateful to be able to speak with the dead and meet men like Keith!"

Carly smiled at him. He had been a good man, good at law enforcement, from the get-go. He was young, and she believed he would continue to have an amazing career. But it wouldn't be the career that mattered to him—it would be the good he was able to do for others.

"We always remember that we're lucky, that our abilities do allow us to do some things others might not manage," Carly said. "But no one is ever invited into the Krewe unless they have gone through the academy, unless…unless they do know how to investigate without help. We never count on the dead to solve situations for us."

"Of course not. But tonight…"

Luke glanced at Carly, grinning. It was great to see how much Daniel embraced the newfound depths of his ability.

She nodded to Luke.

"And you, Carly. Seriously!" Luke said. "There is no way in hell anyone would have endorsed you getting into that van."

"But—"

"But if you had entered the van, it would have been two to one. Those are bad odds. And we don't know the steps they take to kill their victims. All we know from the medical examiner is the victims were first inebriated, then asphyxiated and then disemboweled. They might have gone after you in the van—the killing part might be immediate."

"I really don't think so, not when the time for transplants—"

"I don't think so, either. But we don't let ourselves be killed while trying to save others," he reminded her.

"I know, I know, I guess that…"

"It's frustrating. We haven't gotten to the major players yet," Daniel said.

"We will," Luke told him.

"Someone from tonight will give us something," Carly assured him. "The police have the man calling himself Jared Stone in custody, along with Marjory

Alden—with her children safe. They have kids belonging to someone else in the community. And they have the man who was holding the kids and the man who was driving the van in custody as well, just undergoing surgery before they're brought in."

"Tomorrow is going to be a hell of a long day," Luke commented.

They reached the house and keyed their way in. They were the first to arrive since MacDuff and Jordan had gone on to bring the glass with whiskey in it to the lab.

But as it turned out, MacDuff and Jordan were right behind them; while Carly was more than ready to crash into bed, MacDuff wanted them to join Campbell around the table.

When they were gathered, he told them, "Brendan Campbell questioned Marjory Alden tonight, assuring her first that her children are well, and she'd be able to see them. Her ex-husband was informed that the kids had been found and were all right. But she had to help us. She was an accessory to murder, of course, but she might mitigate her circumstances by giving us every piece of information she has. The woman was hysterical at first. She said that these people could get anyone, but we convinced her we could keep her safe. She began spilling everything. But the problem is they keep everything separate. In other words, they kidnapped her children, sent her pictures of them on her phone so that she knew they really had them, and then told her if she didn't find young people who appeared to be in excellent health and inebriate them with the specially distilled whiskey, her children would be killed. We have the phone and, of course, it's a burner. She said she could give us the one contact she knew about—except that was Jared Stone and we have him. At this point, as far as she goes, we are seeing that she, and especially the children, are safe."

"So she's a dead end there," Jordan murmured.

"But we do have Jared Stone and the unknown man from the house. The van driver didn't make it through surgery," Campbell told them.

"We have something else," Carly said.

They all looked at her. "Flora MacDonald saw Jared Stone at the Connoly house. We need to find out what their involvement is in all this. And as far as the house by Rosslyn Chapel, we must be able to trace ownership on that—"

"The property is owned by a group doing their banking out of the Cayman Islands. Jackson and Angela and the team in the States are hunting down everything possible, and I do believe we'll have some answers on that soon." He paused, shaking his head. "This operation is for money, but they had to have had money to get it going."

"Burke and Hare," Luke murmured.

They all looked at him.

"These people may be more like that duo than just the comparison created by the press," Luke said. "Someone may have either found that a dying relative or friend or even stranger was available just when someone with real money discovered they needed a transplant. Maybe someone with millions ready to part with it for themselves or a loved one. Just like Burke and Hare, they discovered there was a tremendous market in dead bodies."

"But how do you involve so very many people?" Daniel asked thoughtfully.

"Bribery and threats," Jordan suggested. "We know how they coerced Marjory Alden."

"We need to have our tech people finding out everything they can about the Connoly family, even more so than before. I understand they looked fine on paper so far, but there must be something we're not seeing." She frowned. "We also needed to get started on lists— from across the world. Somewhere out there, someone received a life-saving transplant when they were low on the list."

"Oddly enough, the world is full of billionaires from across the globe. And there are countries around the world who aren't as fair and caring when it comes to who receives what," MacDuff said. "Why here?" he added angrily.

"The islands," Carly murmured. "There are three things we have to do. We need to find out where the operations are happening. We need to find the whiskey distiller who is making the special batches. And we need to find the head of the snake." Carly paused and then continued, "I think we should try at the hospital here again. Find out if anyone was fired or was coming in due to being on the organ waiting list—and then stopped coming."

"That's a good plan. I think Carly, MacDuff and Luke might want to interrogate Jared Stone first and see what you can learn from him. Then go to the hospital. We'll work on the fellow who was keeping the children. And I'd like to see what can be found out on the Connoly couple. By tomorrow night, I think we might want to make a call on them again."

"Right. We'll want to start early," Luke said, rising.

MacDuff nodded. "Clock's set for six. I think seven

a.m. will be a fine time for a chat with Mr. Jared Stone."
He hesitated. "Carly, I believe the man is something of
a misogynist, and you will be able to draw the greatest
reactions—including the truth—from him."

"Here's hoping," she said, rising. "It's so strange. I
barely pressed any of those glasses to my lips, and I
feel as if…"

"And it may just be exhaustion!" Daniel said lightly.
"Good night, all. Oh!"

He had risen with the others, but he started suddenly
and looked at MacDuff.

"We're not going to confront him with Flora, are we?
I can't help but feel that even with Jared Stone out of
the picture, she may be in danger."

MacDuff smiled at him. "We will not put the lass
in any danger," he promised. "Oh," he added lightly,
"we'll arrange for you to see her soon, since I know
that you're worried."

Daniel grinned at that. "Aye. Thanks."

Carly looked at Luke, smiling.

As they finally got into their room, she told him, "I
do think there's a budding romance growing there."

"And a difficult time for it," Luke agreed. "I had a
strange conversation with Daniel as we headed back
tonight, right before we reached the area where Jared
Stone made his move."

"Oh?"

"He wants to be part of the Krewe of Hunters, on
our international team."

"Poor thing, he must be conflicted at this moment.
Falling in love with a witness—though that was some
fast falling in love. Wanting to be with people who un-

derstand him, with whom he can be honest. But we won't always be in Scotland and—"

"Ah, but people have managed long-distance relationships," Luke said.

"True. And…"

"And we don't know where anything is going until all this is over," Luke said. "Except, I'm going to bed. But I know you. Ready to drop or not, you're going to the shower."

"I am."

He shrugged and grinned. "I guess I am, too!"

They showered. And showering led where it always did. But it was also always an incredibly beautiful piece of normalcy when it seemed that the world had gone off the rails.

She smiled, curling against Luke, feeling the warmth of his body and the simple security of lying with someone she trusted not just with her life, but with her heart and soul and entire being.

"How did we get so lucky?" she murmured.

"Being together, working together?" he asked softly.

"Yes. Makes me feel a tremendous empathy for poor Daniel!"

"I believe it will all work out for him. Somehow," Luke assured her. "He is a great teammate. I'd love him to continue working with us."

"But is that possible—"

"All kinds of things are possible," he assured her

He was staring up at the ceiling.

"What?"

He smiled dryly. "I try not to take it all with me when it's time to sleep, to let it go, refresh the mind, but…"

"But something is bothering you."

He nodded. "Lily Connolly."

"In what way?"

"She pretended such horror. And according to her husband, she never even saw the body. So either that's true, or she's the brains behind whatever part of the operation they might be. She could be an exceptional actress, throwing us off—and maybe even deceiving her husband—with her hysteria and horror over everything."

"She would really be an exceptional actress," Carly agreed. "And still…"

"Still?"

"Okay, percentagewise, most serial killers are men. But this isn't your usual serial-killer situation. And if you're talking to many, many law enforcement officials, they'll assure you that women can be the most vicious and manipulating criminals out there. Which brings me back to the hospital," Carly said thoughtfully.

"Do you really believe that a doctor—"

"No. I found Dr. Leith Forbes to be solid, a man in medicine because he does want to save lives. I think he's perplexed that anyone would do this. But…"

"We're back to a disgruntled doctor. Maybe someone who had their medical license ripped away from them."

"Possibly."

He smoothed her hair back.

"The morning will come. We need to…"

"Stop thinking."

"Sleep."

"Or fool around until we do."

Carly laughed softly. That wasn't such a bad idea.

MacDuff had pegged Jared Stone right—the man did believe the male of the species was superior to the female. He'd been brought to an interrogation room early, at six o'clock, Brendan Campbell told them when they arrived. And he had been left to sit for an hour.

Carly entered first and the man started to laugh. Luke, Campbell and MacDuff watched from the observation room.

"So, they send in the bait first? What a joke!" Stone declared.

"Ah, you'll spend the rest of your life behind bars. That's a joke?" Carly asked him.

"For what? Trying to get a female body into bed? You'd need to arrest half the world."

"Do you always pick up women with your friend in a van—after plying them with mega-charged whiskey? Well, maybe you do. Maybe that's the only way you ever get a date, but…"

He leaned toward her. "Honey, I can have any cow I want, anytime I want."

"Now, that's a laugh. A good joke."

He was furious; he tried to slam his fists on the table, but since he was cuffed there, all he did was jangle metal and cause a little bump.

"Yeah, that's you," Carly said, laughing softly.

"If I weren't chained here—"

"I'm willing to bet that my training is superior to yours, and that I could clock you within about ten seconds," Carly said sweetly. "Thing is, you're going down for accessory to murder at the very least—"

"Again! I was just picking up a bitch! Oh, yeah, you! So you know that I'm telling the truth. I just tried to get you some good whiskey, bar whore!"

"Sticks and stones, sticks and stones—oh, it's funny,

really funny, since you say your name is Stone. I wonder what it is, really. Who cares? I'm sorry, there's so much more. According to witnesses, you were seen in the vennel with Lila Strom—oh, right after you were seen with the woman in the street, forcing whiskey down her throat."

"Bull! And hey, what if I was drinking with her? That doesn't mean I killed her."

"Maybe you didn't kill her," Carly said with a shrug. "Maybe you just brought her to the people who killed her."

"All I did—"

"You were seen forcing her to drink, and—oh, yeah, you were also seen getting her into the van."

"Well, talk to Joe, then! Maybe he did something with her. Hey, all right. I'm a good-looking guy. Joe, not so much. I get women drunk so he can get laid."

Carly smiled very sweetly. "What a good friend you are!"

"Nah, that kind of thing is easy as pie."

Carly sat back, arms folded over her chest and smiled.

"Pity we don't really have such a witness," MacDuff murmured.

"I'll give her another minute, head in as if she's my superior. That will rile him a bit more and maybe…"

"When you're ready," MacDuff told him.

"I'm so sorry! Joe is dead," Carly told him.

"Another thing I can sue your asses for!" Stone exclaimed. "Shooting a man in cold blood!"

"Well, it's allowed in law enforcement when a person is about to shoot an officer," she said calmly. She leaned forward. "Buddy, you're fried. The only chance you have to help yourself is by helping us!"

Stone stared at her. Luke chose that moment and wandered in.

"Ma'am," he said, nodding with respect. "Campbell asked to speak with you for a moment—our witness wants a word with you."

"All right," Carly said. She smiled sweetly at Stone. "I'll be back," she promised.

She left the room and Luke sat wearily.

Stone stared at him. "How the hell do you do it? You take orders from a...from a bitch?" he demanded.

Luke shrugged. "I need my job. Besides, according to our bosses back in the States, she's the queen bee. Gets results, you know. Anyway, buddy, she was right about one thing: you're fried. Your only chance is to help us."

The man sat back, swallowing. "Hey, will it hurt her if you manage to get something when she couldn't?"

"Sure. It would help me a lot. Maybe I'd get out from under her thumb," Luke said, leaning forward hopefully. "And I will do everything in my power to make sure your part in this was totally innocent. You were just—as you said—helping a friend get laid. You had no clue your friend was taking people off to be murdered. Except—" Luke paused, frowning. "What about the male victims?"

"Oh, she did that all by herself," Stone said.

"She?" Luke said, surprised. "You mean, *you* were working for a bitch?"

"No, never working for—just working with," Stone said.

"All right, then, who the hell is she?" Luke asked.

He shook his head. "I don't know her name. She didn't know my name…"

"By any strange chance, was it Lily Connoly?" Luke asked.

"Lily? No," he said with a laugh.

"Why are you laughing?"

"Because I was only sleeping with Lily," Stone told her.

"But you were also seen dumping a body behind her house."

"Because I dumped a body doesn't mean that I killed anyone!" Stone protested. "I get texts, they tell me where to go, what to do—and when and where to dump a body. Actually, I became quite an artist! The last few…the women…they were beautiful, right?"

"They were dead," Luke said. "So… Hmm. You have nothing to give us. How the hell can I help you with nothing?"

Stone looked worried, suddenly. "Joe. Look into Joe. Joe was the one who…"

"Who?"

"He brought the women where they were supposed to be. Oh, and the men, too."

"We told you. Joe is dead."

"Right. Well…" Stone leaned forward. "Joe wasn't the only one. Just keep looking. They have a few of them."

"A few of them—what?"

"Minivans and drivers," Stone said.

"That's not enough. We didn't think that with something so incredibly detailed going on that you'd be their only gofer."

"Gofer?"

"Well, if you don't know anything at all…" Luke paused and shrugged, leaning forward. "You were in an even worse position than I was!"

"I had what they needed! Good looks and charm."

"That's not going to help you at trial."

"You never know."

"Hmm, not when they see the witnesses against you. And watch a few people sobbing their hearts out. You'd be surprised how stealing a person's life can upset their loved ones. Or what they're willing to do. A few of the victims actually had some money, too, I believe. Now their loved ones have that money, and even during a short stint in prison…"

"Say it!"

"Well, it's possible to die without law enforcement having anything to do with it. Anyway, okay, if you can't help me…" Luke let his words trail as he stood.

"Wait!"

"What is it?"

"All right, I'm not lying. Everything was kept on a need-to-know basis, but I was told where to dump the body. Joe wasn't my driver that night. I didn't know the guy in the van that night. And I don't know what the hell they're doing with people before they chop them up. Burke and Hare, selling bodies. Whatever. But I was told to dump the body in the vennel there because I know it."

"A different driver for the van. Can you work with a sketch artist?"

"I can. And I can tell you something else."

"What is that?"

"Okay, yes, I was at the Connoly house. I mean, I was just sleeping with Lily Connoly, but…"

"But?"

"But she was paying me for it. She has some kind of money that her husband knows nothing about. Hey, who knows? She could be the brains behind the whole thing!"

Ten

"We still didn't get anything worth having. Mrs. Connoly was willing to pay for a gigolo, great, and she may have an extra income. I can't arrest her for that," MacDuff said.

"But," Carly told him, "we can get him with a sketch artist. And we can see what else tech can find out about the Connoly family."

Brendan Campbell turned to look at her. "Thank you again, by the way. The man is an absolute...caveman! I am sorry that—"

"Sir! No problem. We use whatever methods we must. Now I'm thinking more and more about Lily Connoly. But—"

"We're going to need a real confession, written, from the wanker in that room!" MacDuff said. "Because so much of what he said is true. You can't send a man to trial for trying to get a date."

"You can for forcing people, which he did do. But I think that Luke will get him to confess. He's still in there with him now, and he's passing the paper to him to write it all down…you know. Luke has to win. That's how he gets out of working for a woman."

MacDuff and Campbell just shook their heads.

"We do what we need to do," Carly said. "I'm fine—Stone doesn't faze me in the least. We use what we have and what's legal when we need to."

"But no getting into a van," Campbell warned her.

"Yes, sir," she told him.

"And don't worry about the Connoly house, or them panicking or taking off or anything," MacDuff said. "They're being watched. So, if you still feel that another interview at the hospital would be helpful, now would be the time to do that."

"What about the children, sir? Not Marjory's children, the others we found. What about their parents? Have they been located?"

"We're having a bit of a problem with that," Campbell said.

"They don't know who their parents are?"

"The little girls are three and five," Campbell said.

"A five-year-old, though, she must know her full name, right?" Carly asked.

"Oh, aye, she knows it," Campbell said. He looked at Carly. "Smith. You think that you have a lot of people in the States named Smith? It's the most common surname here. The girls are Kenna, the five-year-old, and Skye, her little sister. They just know that they were sleeping and when they woke up, they were scared, and a lady tried to make them feel better. She gave them food and took care of them and told them stories."

"Let's go back. You said you found a woman with the children who was a prisoner, too. Who is she, where did they find her and what does she know?" Carly asked.

"Ameerah Abassi, a young woman from Pakistan. She studied here and was trying to gain her residency, and she was given a call and was assured that the college was setting things up for her. She was met at the airport by the man at the house who was pretending to be from the college—next thing she knew, she was locked up with the children and told to take care of them or she'd be killed," Campbell said. "And she's in protective custody now, too. She won't be able to give us anything more—she was taken in a car to the house and then she was forced down into the tunnel. She knows nothing else. Of course, we have people still tearing the house apart, and we're seeking the owners."

"The children know nothing about where they live?" Carly asked.

"We don't think they live in Edinburgh," MacDuff said. "Skye is three—seriously, she is very little help. Kenna told us that it's a big house with lots and lots of yard space for them to play. We're looking through missing persons reports, but so far…nothing."

"So, I will go back to the hospital. I'll try to find out who has disappeared off their lists—" Carly began.

"We checked records. No one was fired recently," Campbell told her.

"There's something that someone there must know," Carly said. "Again, not Dr. Forbes, and I doubt that any of the doctors on his team are involved. But…"

"Do you think that someone quit and was angry?" Campbell asked her.

"I don't know about anyone quitting! But I do know there is someone there that coworkers refer to as Nurse Ratched, so…"

"Nurse Ratched?" Campbell repeated.

"The tyrant character from *One Flew Over the Cuckoo's Nest*," Carly murmured.

"You saw that movie?" Campbell asked her.

"Streaming—you can see just about anything," Carly said. "I'll try to find out more about her—"

"Real name?" MacDuff asked.

"I don't know. I will find out!" Carly assured him. "Oh, wait, I was talking with one of the younger nurses, and she said that her name was Dorothy Norman. I'm thinking she must be a senior nurse, maybe irritated with young nurses making mistakes. But I didn't see anything that would suggest anyone was doing more than caring about their work."

"All right. Dorothy Norman. But take Luke with you this time. If the hospital is on the up and up, then it's not going to matter if anyone there knows you are law enforcement seeking help," Campbell said.

"They know that already—I had to give real information to get to see Dr. Forbes. As soon as Luke finishes with Jared Stone, we'll take off," she told him. "And Stone seems to be writing away!"

"Did you see this Dorothy Norman?" MacDuff asked.

"Maybe, but I'm not sure. There were two older women working when I was there—one might have been her. I don't know," Carly said.

"Get a look at her today, all right."

"Will do," Carly said. She looked through the one-way mirror again and said, "Jared Stone is still writing."

"He wants to prove that Luke was the best interrogator," Campbell said. "Even to his own detriment, the man has to practice his machismo."

"Hey, it worked," Carly said. "When I was at the

hospital before, the Douglases' son wasn't working—he didn't have office hours that day and wasn't at the hospital. I want to speak with him, too."

"Right. Until we have some real answers, we cannot discount the neighbors or a *Doctor* Douglas," Campbell said.

"And…look! Jared Stone is finally finishing up!"

She smiled and walked out of the observation room followed by MacDuff and Campbell. They met Luke in the hall, and Luke gave Campbell the man's written confession to his part in the abductions.

"We'll be going to the Connoly house?"

"We will. This evening. Tech departments are still searching financials, and I want to have possible ammunition when we go in there," Campbell told him. "As I told Carly, they're being watched, and they are not going anywhere."

"And I still want to get to the hospital," Carly told him.

"Let's do it," Luke agreed.

Carly had a good sense for people. Luke wasn't surprised to agree with her assessment of Dr. Leith Forbes. He was naturally disturbed to consider even the remote idea that someone who worked so diligently on his staff could be involved, but he understood their need to explore every possibility.

"We're not really thinking someone on your staff is involved," Luke assured him, "but whoever is doing this must be accomplished enough to manage these surgeries. Someone who might have tried for a job but quit for one reason or another. Our departments have gone through public records looking for someone who might have been fired, but we don't know much about everyone who might have worked here in the past and moved on for whatever reason. Or perhaps someone who wanted to work here, but was never hired," Luke suggested.

"That's possible," Forbes said thoughtfully. "I'm very careful about hiring staff—conditions here must be as sterile as possible. We have hired many men and women as nurses—we've had both as surgeons operating here…" His words broke off and he concentrated for a minute. "There was one man who came in saying he'd worked at a key hospital in Miami, but I didn't like his attitude. He seemed to be so full of himself. Despite the assumption that many doctors think they're gods, most good doctors do not. And it's as annoying to the rest of the medical community as it is to patients when one of our number behaves so. I'll see to it that you're given the information that I have on him."

"Thank you!" Carly told him. "And on anyone else that gave you a hard time in any way."

"Believe it or not, I do have a list of those people we didn't take on. We have a tremendous reputation and doctors, nurses and orderlies all seek positions here. Even kitchen staff," Forbes told them.

"And other operations take place here, too, right? Well, not just surgeries, other medical treatments?" Luke asked.

"Yes, it's a major hospital. We're a part of it all," Forbes told them.

Carly glanced at him, leaning forward. "Do you know Dr. Douglas?"

"Which one?" Forbes asked her. "You do realize the name Douglas—"

"Is akin to Smith," Carly said. "I'm sorry. Dr. Westin Douglas?"

"I do, indeed. He is a fine pediatrician. He works in the hospital and through his office in the city. He is a young man but dedicated. I've been impressed by his work." He frowned. "Dear Lord, you can't begin to believe that Westin…"

"No, I'd just like to meet him," Carly said. "We were with his parents. I don't think that it was publicized, but the press discovers everything. His parents own one of the fine manors in front of the vennel where one of the victims was discovered."

"You would just like to meet him?" Forbes said skeptically.

"Doctor—" Luke began, but before he could continue, Forbes waved a hand in the air.

"It's all right, I understand. You are just doing your jobs. I'll see if he can come up for a minute."

He picked up his desk phone and dialed a number, greeting the man and asking him if he could spare a few minutes.

Apparently, Dr. Douglas said yes.

Forbes ended the call and folded his hands on his desk.

"Harold Gleason," he said suddenly.

"I'm sorry?" Luke said.

"That's the name of the man I refused to hire who had such a horrific attitude. I'll have my assistant go back and find the application he filled out and make sure you get it," Forbes said. He was thoughtful. "There was one other man… Just the opposite. I didn't think he had enough confidence in himself. If you're hesitant when you are speaking about surgery, you might as well be hesitant while doing it. And in the middle of surgery, you must know what you're doing, know how to stop a bleeder..."

He broke off when there was a tap on his door.

It opened and a man in a doctor's white coat stuck his head in. "Leith, you wanted to see me?" he asked.

"Come in, come in, please, Americans with an international force after our murderers want to meet you," Forbes said flatly.

Carly and Luke both stood, offering their hands to the young man who didn't seem surprised to see them. He didn't resemble either of his parents but was about six-one with smoothed-back dark hair, features that were well-contoured, and amber and green eyes.

"Hello!" he said, offering them both firm handshakes and a nod. "I've heard about you, of course, so I'm going to assume you are Special Agents MacDonald and Kendrick?"

"Carly and Luke," Carly said, smiling. "And, of course, you are Dr. Westin Douglas."

"I am. How can I help you? Ah, wait, never mind. People are being killed, and it's suspected since they have been gutted that a doctor must be guilty. Personally, you know, I never thought Jack the Ripper was a doctor or a medical man, though that supposition went around."

He seemed relaxed, not offended by them. His handshake was that of a man who had both confidence and a willingness to listen to others. Of course, it was impossible to judge any human being quickly, but there was something about his understanding of why he might fall under suspicion that seemed to slant him toward being innocent.

"Sit, everyone, please," Forbes said. He glanced at his watch. "I need to prepare for surgery soon, but this office is the best place for us to talk."

They took seats, Forbes behind his desk, Carly and Luke returning to the seats they'd been in, and Westin Douglas perching on the edge of Forbes's desk. "I don't live with my parents," he told them. "I have a place on Canongate. But my family is close—my sister and I both watch out for my folks. They're in good shape and they're not that old, but..." He trailed off, shrugging. "They were good parents. We try to be good kids in turn."

"That's great. We're lucky. We have good families, too," Carly told him. She glanced at Luke, not looking for his approval but his agreement. And he did agree. With this, they could just be honest. "And, I'm sorry, but yes. When a body was found in the vennel that borders your parents' house, and with you being a medical man, well we did need to meet you."

"And I am not resentful or offended," Westin Douglas assured them. "I'll be honest, too. Leith told me you were here, and you're trying to investigate by truly understanding the needs of transplant patients. I'm a pediatrician and honestly, I deal with more colds and flus than anything else—tonsillectomies and illnesses that often plague children. The most heartbreaking, for me, tends to be the occasional horrendous accident or cancer. But I did go to medical school, and I have a sound knowledge of anatomy. So...a doctor in the family, a body in the vennel. Trust me, I understand. But I swear to you, I am innocent. I don't believe I have any way to prove it, but..."

Luke shook his head and assured him, "Innocent

until proven guilty is still the norm. And quite frankly, we believe you. But we did need to speak with you. And we hope that you, just as Dr. Forbes has done, might give us any help that you can."

"Of course! We are sworn to save lives, not to take them!" Westin Douglas said.

"Exactly," Carly murmured. "There's something else, though. We've discovered people involved with helping to send victims out alone while inebriated. And they were being forced to participate. If someone suddenly doesn't show up for work, disappears…anything of the like, can you please make sure to alert us immediately?"

Westin Douglas and Leith Forbes spoke at the same time. "Aye!"

They looked at each other and shook their heads, and Westin Douglas said, "I think it would be difficult to find a person truly dedicated to healing who would take part in this—especially at risk to their own life."

"These people were holding children and threatening them with a slow torturous death if their mother didn't cooperate. That could be done to anyone—professional, nonprofessional—anyone," Luke said.

"Wait!" Forbes said. "Westin, I was telling him about the man who was here, applying for a job, the man that I didn't hire. You saw him when he left my office, and I know I said something to you about having just met one of the most obnoxious human beings."

"I do remember," Westin Douglas said. "He pushed me and looked at me as if I was a piece of dirt as he left. I thought…"

"What?"

Douglas shrugged. "I thought he might be someone furious because he wasn't high on the list for one kind of transplant or another. Then Leith told me the man was angry he didn't fall on his knees, cross himself and thank him for walking in."

"Did he have credentials?" Carly asked.

"He had the right papers. I never verified them because…because I would never hire him to work on any team of mine," Forbes told them. "I will get all that information for you. I have surgery and I need to prep, but I'll see to it Selina gets that information to you."

"I need to get back, too," Douglas said. He produced his card. "You may call me day or night if I can help you in any way."

"Thank you, and here's ours," Luke told him, producing a card in turn. "One more quick question—what do you know about your parents' neighbors?"

"The, uh, Connoly family?" Douglas asked.

"Yes," Carly said.

Douglas shrugged. "They, uh…they're nice enough. Ewan Connoly likes to come over for morning tea with my dad. Lily is a bit…"

"A bit?"

"High-strung, I guess you'd say. I've warned her she needs to watch out for her blood pressure since she can get so upset. My mom told me she's been the proverbial basket case ever since the body was found. But… as far as I know, they're just…normal people," Douglas said, shrugging.

"Did you ever see them behave suspiciously in any way?"

"To be honest, I haven't lived at my parents' home in fifteen years. College, medical school, interning… and now having my own position. I haven't seen much of the Connoly couple in years," he said. "I remember when they came, though. I must have been about seven or eight years old. Old Mr. Connoly was a great guy, a storyteller, and we kids loved him. When he passed on, the house went to the couple who are there now. They came over from America, and..."

Carly interrupted him. "I know he said that he'd spent time over there when his father was working in the States. I had the impression she was Scottish."

Douglas shrugged. "You can meet a good Scottish woman in the States," he told her lightly. "Let's see, you are Special Agent *MacDonald*."

"Of course," Carly said. "Well, thank you! We'll let you both go. We do not want to take you away from your patients!"

"Let me give Selina a heads-up; she'll get what information we have for you. You'll find her at the nurses' station."

"Thank you," Luke said. "And we'll get out of your hair." He and Carly both rose, nodded a second silent thank-you and went out of the office.

"Nurses' station," Carly murmured. "Luke, do you think this person that Dr. Forbes was talking about could be...?"

"It wouldn't be surprising. There are a few ways this might be happening. Either, yes, it's someone at the helm who has a huge medical chip on his or her shoulder, or someone who is being forced to comply, just as Marjory Alden was forced. Very few people could simply refuse to do something if their children's lives were in jeopardy."

"True. Hopefully, they'll be able to hunt down the *Smith* family that those two girls belong to," Carly said.

She was looking at him, and he knew the entire episode with Marjory Alden disturbed her.

"She will have to pay for her part," he said quietly. "But I do believe she will be given special consideration because of the circumstances."

An attractive young brunette in uniform was standing at the nurses' station when they reached it, apparently waiting for them.

"Hi, Carly," the young woman said, producing a stack of papers. "Dr. Forbes said you needed these."

"Thank you!" Carly told her, and of course, Luke realized Carly had met the young woman on her first trip to the hospital. "And—"

Carly didn't get to finish the introduction. The young woman looked at Luke and said, "I'm sorry, hi!"

"Hi, I'm Luke," he said. "And thank you! That was fast."

"I'm Selina, and of course. Modern technology and a really decent printer! I was thinking I could have just sent them all digitally, but I didn't know your email address, so…"

"This is great," Luke told her. "We can figure it all out from here. Even in this day and age, we can still read off paper!"

Selina smiled, but then her smile faded and she looked around swiftly as if afraid of being overheard.

"I'm guessing you think the killer stalking the city might be in this group," she said.

Luke glanced at Carly, but he was sure she hadn't explained anything about their investigation to the young woman. It was all probably fairly obvious; if law enforcement was asking questions, there was suspicion regarding someone, even if Carly had just been "re-searching" medical information.

"It never hurts to know all that we can," he said.

Selina wasn't ready to let them go.

"Please! This is all so horrible. I'm even afraid when I leave here at night... What's happening, it's just..."

"You've seen the news conferences, I'm sure. Just be careful not to be alone and not to accept any drinks from strangers," Luke said, glancing at Carly.

She glanced back and smiled at Selina. "One more thing: if you do go out, go out with friends, stay with friends and I suggest you drink out of cans that only you open."

"Cans...so that..."

"Simple. So that a drink can't be spiked," Luke said.

"Of course," Selina agreed. She drew in a deep breath. "Truthfully, I haven't gone out. I go home and lock myself in. I broke up with my boyfriend a month or so ago, and now I'm wishing I'd been a lot more patient with him and that we were still living together. I can't go home—home is in Stirling, not so far, but not a great commute to the hospital on a daily basis."

"Just be very careful. And if you do go out, stay with a group," Carly told her.

Selina nodded and they thanked her and headed for the elevator.

On the way, another nurse paused, looking at Carly. She looked to be in her mid- to late thirties, a petite blonde woman.

"Hi, you're back!" she said to Carly.

"We are," Carly said. "Luke, this is Milly Blair. Milly, Luke Kendrick."

"Milly, how do you do?"

"Ah, tough day, we have a number of people in recovery!" Milly said. She frowned again, looking at Carly. "Are you thinking of coming here for medical help? You are so lovely, sweet lass, I hope that—"

"No, no, and thank you, I'm quite well. Just asking for others," Carly assured her.

"Right," Milly said, shaking her head. "And you're coppers, eh?"

Carly laughed. "Something like that."

The elevator door opened, and Milly glanced around and slid into the elevator with them.

"If you're looking for someone mean enough to be involved, it's Nurse Ratched!"

"Dorothy Norman, right? She's the one who makes everything so hard on others?" Carly asked her.

Milly nodded. "I think she's been here since the dawn of time. She seems to feel she owns the place, and it should be lovely all the time. We have a young fellow working here as a nurse, and she's especially hard on him. A bit opposite from what we strive for these days. Dorothy seems to think only men should be doctors, and only women should be nurses. Of course, Dr. Forbes just cares about good, knowledgeable and hard-working people—he could care less if a doctor or a nurse is a man or a woman. If it were me… Well, it's not. But I do believe he is considering replacing her. She's good—she's excellent at nursing. But she makes those around her miserable, and I know he is weighing the possibilities of replacing her."

"Interesting," Luke said, glancing at Carly. "Perhaps we should have a chat with her before we leave."

"I'm sorry, Dorothy isn't here today. I believe she called in sick, or I don't really know. I just know she

didn't come in. But you might want to check up on her!"
Milly said seriously. "Oh! And please! I need this job,
so—"

"Not a word, Milly," Luke promised her. "We'll see
what we can find out."

The elevator reached the ground floor and they
stepped out.

"Oh!"

Another young woman in a nurse's uniform, a brunette with a wealth of dark hair carefully knotted up
beneath her cap, was waiting to step on.

"Uh—hi!" she said to Carly.

"Hi!" Carly said.

Milly laughed. "I don't believe you met formally—or
informally!" she said. "We three did have a swift chat
the other day. But I was rude and I forgot to introduce
you to my friend. Janelle, please meet Carly and Luke.
Carly and Luke, Janelle."

"Nice to meet you," Janelle murmured nervously,
glancing at Milly.

"It's okay, they're good." She laughed and whispered,
"They did not come to report us for talking trash about
Nurse Ratched!"

The brunette managed to smile. "Hey. Sorry. I'm
afraid I'm a wee bit late and need the elevator!"

"Of course!" Carly said, and she and Luke stepped
off.

"Good day," Luke added, nodding as the elevator
doors closed.

"Let's get out of here," he said quietly to her, catching her hand and hurrying them both out the doors. On
the street, heading for the car Campbell had given them
to use, he glanced at her and said, "So. *Nurse Ratched*

isn't here today. Either she's just an old grouch who decided to take a day, or she's off helping chop people up. You didn't meet her the other day?"

Carly shook her head. "No, but one way or the other, we should get tech looking into her. And now we have the papers that might lead us to the person who is the snake's head," she said.

"I'll give Campbell a call."

He did so, telling Campbell what they had gained from the hospital, assuring him they'd be right in with the sheets for the tech team. For now, they had two names to start with—Dorothy Norman, known around the hospital as Nurse Ratched—who hadn't shown up for work today—and Harold Gleason, M.D., turned down for a job at the hospital because of his arrogance and attitude.

"We're on it," Campbell told him, and then he said, "All right, pause on the one of them, bit of a wee problem there."

"What is it?"

"There's not much we'll be able to blame on Nurse Dorothy Norman."

"Why—"

"Her head was just discovered in a bin outside of Greyfriars Kirkyard."

"Her head—"

"Just her head. Decapitated from the rest of her body. Lord, Almighty! Just her head. Meet us at the scene, I'll send you coordinates."

Eleven

Campbell hadn't lied.

It was a head. Just a head.

It was discovered by a worker when he came to clean out the bin.

When Carly and Luke arrived, the scene was already chaotic. Police and the forensic crew were trying to work, seeking to find any evidence. The medical examiner was arranging to have the head—and the bin—returned to the station so authorities could find whatever they possibly could.

She'd been quickly and easily identified because her work badge was in the bin as well.

"I believe the badge was tossed in the bin on purpose," Campbell said. "Whoever did this wants the world to know who she was...whose head was in the trash."

Gloved members of the forensic team were ready to take the bin with the medical examiner's approval when Campbell asked them to hold for just a minute.

Carly wasn't sure she wanted to see the head in the bin, but she followed Luke. They went and observed what they could.

The bin was shaded by a tree and sat off one of the streets that offered many businesses—including restaurants and pubs. It had probably been placed to accommodate those who left such an establishment and realized they were carrying trash, perhaps a plastic cup or other, chewing gum…any such little bits of trash.

The head was perched atop a pile of old newspapers, cups and ripped-up receipts. It leaned back against the rubble.

The eyes were open.

Staring.

"And…no body to be found anywhere?" Carly asked.

"Not as yet," Campbell told her. "And…"

"What, sir?" she asked.

He shook his head. "This is different. Perhaps we're even looking at something else entirely. She wouldn't be the right victim for our Burke and Hare murderers. She was well over fifty, and all of their victims have been more than a decade younger and in great physical condition."

"Sir, I think it's too convenient she was someone we were about to investigate, and she wound up being killed," Luke said. "But…"

"You think she was involved, and the killers got nervous?" Campbell asked.

"That is, of course, possible. But from what we've heard, she was a tyrant, but a good nurse. I'm thinking maybe she discovered something about someone, and that's why she had to be silenced."

"Well…" Campbell breathed, exhaling.

MacDuff had been overseeing an examination of the area near the bin. He walked over to join them. "Like usual, we're not finding anything. Of course, there are no witnesses. Whoever did this must have come through here right around three thirty in the morning. At that time, there are no tours at the kirkyard, bars and pubs are long closed, and early morning crews of any kind have yet to get started."

"But there are patrols in the area—" Carly began.

"Carly!" MacDuff said, dismayed. "Every twenty minutes someone is through here. But whoever did this watched and waited and…in all the UK, I don't think we could patrol every square inch of the city at every moment!"

"Of course not, sir, I'm sorry!" she said quickly. "It's just—"

"Frustrating as all damned bloody hell?" Campbell queried.

She nodded and looked at Luke. "We need to get on the other name Forbes and Douglas gave us this morning. Sir—"

Campbell gave her a nod. "He's being researched as we speak."

"Have we gotten anything else on the distilleries or the islands?" Luke asked.

"We have some reports. They're being sent to you," MacDuff said. "Jordan and Daniel are back at the house studying what we do have."

"All right. I believe Carly and I should join them. And have we anything new on the financial reports on the Connoly couple? Anything that will help if we stop by to see them?" Luke asked.

"They're still investigating online," Campbell said. "Hopefully, we'll have something by this evening."

"We should find out if they have had any interactions with…" Carly began. She almost said *Nurse Ratched.*

Under the circumstances, it seemed proper to be more respectful.

"Nurse Dorothy Norman," she finished.

"We can add that to our investigations," Campbell said.

"Maybe we should grab a quick bite or have some food ordered and delivered to the house," Luke mused.

Carly stared at him.

He smiled. "Yeah, I know," he said quietly. "We just stared at a human head with…tendons or sinew or whatever. But—"

"Let's get out of here," she murmured. "Maybe my appetite will improve."

"I was hoping Keith might come and find us," he whispered back to her.

"Maybe he will. Let's start walking."

They did. Keith didn't find them, but they had barely gone the length of a football field when their phones buzzed.

They looked at each other, arching their brows, and then looked at their phones.

"Well," Luke murmured, "we don't have to worry about food or getting to the house. Daniel and Jordan should be coming along any minute because they've found something in the water just off one of the little islands, and we're heading to a boat to get out there while Campbell works on the warrant."

"And there they are. So incredibly efficient and well-timed," Carly murmured.

They hurried off the pedestrian stretch where they'd been walking to the car. Daniel was driving with Jordan in the passenger seat, and he had pulled to the side of the road. Carly and Luke hurried to the car, surprised no one had honked yet.

Maybe drivers in Edinburgh were just more courteous!

"The coast guard has been searching as directed," Daniel explained as they closed the doors and he eased back into traffic. "Apparently, they found a plastic container that was filled with blood along with several empty needle canisters and needles floating just offshore from a little place called Arthur's Isle. It's a small island and sold just three years ago to another corporation, out of Switzerland this time. It will take us about thirty minutes to reach it once we're on board. Campbell intends to have a warrant for us by the time we reach the marina. The islet is one of the small places that has gone up for sale many times through the years. Apparently, whoever named it first was fond of Arthur's Seat at Holyrood. It's mostly a hill and takes a climb up to the medieval cottage at the top. I guess for many people, the getting up and down was a bit too much and the charm of owning one's own isle wears off easily. Electricity bills have been paid by something called the Donner Association. As I said, their banking is in Switzerland. And who knows what we're going to find."

"Were they able to freeze the assets by any wild chance?" Carly asked.

He glanced at her through the rearview mirror and shook his head. "Carly, the law, remember? We don't even have a warrant yet—"

"Or we may by now," Jordan offered. "When Campbell wants something… Well, he's good at getting it quickly."

"Aye, that he is," Daniel agreed.

"It seems strange to me, though, that these objects were just out floating," Carly murmured.

"Everybody makes a mistake sometimes. And getting rid of medical waste is not easy—certainly not in the United Kingdom," Jordan said. "Of course…"

"It could have all floated in from somewhere else?" Luke asked.

"This could be an exercise in futility," Daniel said. "But…"

"It may not. We are following our leads. And while it still seems incredibly frustrating, we are moving forward. Any part of this enterprise we crack puts them off and brings us closer," Luke assured him. "And, Jordan, after last night—"

"You're talking about the fact I discharged my weapon, and the man wound up dying?" Jordan asked.

"Yeah," Luke said.

"Campbell again. I turned in my weapon and now have a new one. But you shot the fellow at the cottage by Rosslyn Chapel, the bloke who survived his surgery!"

"Campbell again, and the fact I'm part of an international agency," Luke told him.

"Good. I don't want any of us taking chances on this island. The coast guard found the items, but we're heading out with a small craft belonging to the Royal Navy. Our coast guard is usually a rescue force, and most often composed of volunteers. The Royal Navy—"

"Is what we need now, though one can hope we find someone to rescue," Carly said.

She had no idea where they were going—never during the many times she had visited had she left Edinburgh to visit any of the islands.

She could remember asking her grandmother if they

could go swimming while they were visiting, and her grandmother had laughed. "Ah, dearie sweet thing, can ye imagine the cold o' the water?"

Her mother had assured her she could swim in the hotel's heated pool.

But it wouldn't have mattered if she'd thought she'd known where she was going; they pulled down a small road and she quickly realized they were headed to a private dock.

They were met by Captain Rory McDermott. He was, Carly thought, what one might call an "old sea dog." He was a big man, apparently strong, with a shaved head beneath his cap and weathered features.

"McDermott," he told them, shaking their hands. "We've received the warrant. I have four fine sailors aboard, all ready to meet whatever the occasion demands. We've been briefed on the operation. Now, of course, we may meet a lovely old couple just enjoying their later years, but…"

"Doubtful when a corporation bought the place," Luke finished. "Sir, we thank you."

"Now, Arthur's Isle, like Arthur's Seat, takes a bit of hiking—"

"And we're all fine with that," Carly assured him. "If we have the warrant…"

"Climb aboard!" McDermott told them. "We'll be heading out the Firth of Forth, Fife on the north, Lothian on the South. We will get you as swiftly to the destination as humanly possible!"

The craft Captain McDermott was navigating seemed perfect for what they needed. She believed larger navy vessels plied the North Sea, but this little craft with a decent-sized deck, helm, galley and sleeping quarters below was perfect for swiftly and easily moving across the water.

They met the sailors even as McDermott revved the motor on the craft.

They were Rodgers, Simmons and Macklemore, but to their friends, they were Duckie, Mouse and Hound-dog. As they all met and the men explained their nick-names, McDermott rolled his eyes but accepted it all with good humor.

As they started out, Daniel joined the men at the galley table, watching as Hound-dog and Duckie went after one another in a game of chess.

Jordan stood, studying a few of the maps that were available behind the helm. Luke joined him, then see-ing Carly was just staring straight ahead, came over to join her.

The ride seemed fine enough through the Firth of Forth; the water began to chop and wave once they reached the North Sea.

"Not quite the Gulf, eh?" Luke teased her, watch-ing from just behind Captain McDermott at the helm.

The boat took a serious swerve and she crashed against him.

"Ah, no, not quite the Gulf—unless a hurricane is brewing, you know," she told him.

"My king!" Duckie called out. "Hey, you didnae take me king! He's just flying about over there."

It had landed near Carly's feet. She quickly picked it up to return it.

"Thanks so much, lass. I may win this thing yet!" Duckie told her.

She grinned and left them. She balanced carefully as they caught another huge wave.

"Ah, well, the North Sea is notorious for being rough. Personally, I prefer the islands on the other side of Scotland. Sometimes, the currents bring lovely weather and water that may be the weest bit warm! But—" McDermott turned to look at them "—in truth, my friends, not a bad day. Trust me, it can be much—much—worse!"

Luckily, it didn't take long to reach the small island that seemed to stick out of the water like a large green snow cone.

There was a small weathered dock, but no boats.

"Has anyone seen any boats here recently?" Carly asked as they stepped onto the dock.

"Who knows? Fishermen come out. The islands appear to be sparse and far apart, but there are so many," Duckie said, standing by her side. "And it's not easy to find out what fishermen or pleasure cruisers might have been out at a given time. And if you did find them, they might not know what islands they saw and if there were or weren't boats at their docks."

McDermott came to stand by her, too, having seen his craft was secured.

"And," he added, "there are a few of these islands where the occupants don't own their own boats. As in much of the rest of the world, they seldom leave, so they have supplies delivered to them."

"I suppose for some that would be a great and private way to live," Carly murmured.

"Then," Hound-dog supplied, "there are some islands where two to ten families, say, may live. They keep one craft and take turns with errands, work and all."

"I think I'd like living in Edinburgh best," Carly said.

"Aye, absolutely!" Jordan agreed.

"We should start," Luke said, looking up at the

foliage-laden hill before them. "I am assuming there is a path…"

"There is. We shall begin the hike," McDermott said.

He led the way.

And there was a trail. It was, to say the least, rugged, composed of dirt and rock with bits of weed protruding here and there. Carly frowned, trying to imagine someone carrying a body up the steep slope or even the equipment needed for surgery.

Luke was apparently thinking the same thing.

"There's a lift," he said.

She turned to him, frowning. "If there was a lift, I'm sure we'd be taking it," she told him.

He shook his head. "We're going to find a charming cottage with a few bedrooms, kitchen, a window with a view perhaps. And somewhere, hidden, there's going to be a lift. Look at the size of this place. The hill, I mean. And think of the centuries and the many, many things that have gone below the ground not just here, but other places."

"If there is an underground," Carly said, "there must also be an exit near the dock as well, else how would anyone get the people—and everything needed—down below?"

"Well, we'll soon see," he said.

"Now, this may be quite a goose chase!" McDermott warned as they climbed the hill and finally reached the flatland leading toward the entry to the cottage.

"It may, but…" Luke said.

"We follow every lead," Daniel said.

When they reached the door, McDermott turned to Luke, arching a brow. "Your operation, sir," he told him.

He nodded and banged on the door. "Law enforcement! Open up, please!"

They waited. There was no response.

"Shall we?" Duckie asked.

"We shall," Luke assured him.

"Wait!" Carly said. She twisted the old knob on the door.

It opened inward.

McDermott tried to hide his laughter. "Ah, well, that is the easier way! Far gentler upon the shoulders, lads!"

They entered.

Just as Luke had said, the cottage appeared to be a small and charming place with old stuffed sofas in the parlor area, no television, just tables with fiction novels and little wooden holders filled with magazines.

Small hallways went to the right and to the left while a dining table sat at the back, and Carly assumed the kitchen was just behind the wall.

"I'll go left," Jordan said.

"I will take the right," Daniel told them.

"Kitchen," Carly said and Luke nodded.

"We'll divide and follow rather than conquer," Hound-dog offered.

They split up.

The dining table, like the parlor furniture, appeared to be about fifty years old, dating back to the '70s maybe, Carly thought.

The table there was large worn mahogany. The chairs around it matched and were equally as aged.

They moved on into the kitchen.

"Furnished circa 1965, 1970?" Luke murmured.

The kitchen appliances also seemed to have been there for many years.

"I don't see any kind of a stairway leading to a basement," Carly murmured.

"I don't, either," Luke admitted. He wandered through the kitchen, opening cabinets. At first, all of them appeared to be empty.

Then he paused, murmuring, "Well, here's something. This brand of crackers hasn't been around for fifty or more years…these are new. Not in a box…just the tail end of a wrapper." He turned to look at her. "Check the refrigerator," he said.

She did so.

"Empty," she told him.

"And old. Look, under that little table. An ice chest. An ice chest and an empty refrigerator. Hey! Grab that edge."

"Edge of—?"

"The refrigerator!"

She did so. They pulled together and as the appliance was empty—and unconnected—it was easy enough to drag out.

And Luke was right.

There was a door behind the appliance, a short door—no taller than five and a half feet. But when Luke found the knob and pulled it open, they saw that it did lead to a staircase.

All they could see from where they were was darkness.

"Told you," Luke said.

"Yes, you did. Well, we still don't know—"

"Bedroom empty on my side!" Jordan shouted, coming back around.

"My side, too!" Daniel called. "I found some old

clothes, dusty, not touched in years and years in the closet. Maybe this corporation—"

He reached the entry to the kitchen and stopped speaking as he stared at the pushed-aside refrigerator and the open door leading to darkness.

"Oh," he said simply.

By then McDermott, Duckie, Hound-dog and Mouse were also at the door to the kitchen, standing right behind Daniel and Jordan.

"There is something below," McDermott murmured. "Not a shock, mind ye—"

Luke pulled out his penlight. "I'll start—two should stay topside."

"The rest of us will be behind you," Jordan said.

Carly pulled out her own light.

Even she had to stoop as Luke did to begin moving down the flight of stairs.

There were at least twenty steps downward until they came to a landing. At first, it looked like little more than an empty basement with decaying stone walls.

"Door! There's a door," Carly said.

She hurried over to it, knowing Luke was right behind her along with Jordan, Daniel, McDermott and Duckie.

All had their flashlights out and glowing and their arms ready.

She took hold of the knob, drawing back as she opened it. As she did so, she stared at the faces of the men.

They all lowered their arms.

Curiously, she came around and gasped softly.

The room they had discovered was a far cry from what they had seen so far...

At first look, there was one bed, covered in a white sheet, showing a great deal of stains—bloodstains. A partition separated it from something else, and Luke walked through quickly, drawing back the canvas.

There was a second bed. This one offered a table by its side, along with a stand for IV drips. A few instruments remained on a nearby silver tray on a small table.

Each were covered in what appeared to be bloodstains as well.

"Someone has been operating here," Luke said.

"But it appears they're gone now, and that they left in a hurry," Carly said.

McDermott was looking at the discovery and cursing beneath his breath. "Bloody bastards!" he announced curtly as he walked through.

"Captain," Luke said. "We need to get a forensic team out here—"

"No one to save, so it seems," McDermott replied.

"But we need to know who was here," Luke said quietly.

"Of course, of course. And then…" He paused, puzzled. "There must be more. How were they getting people in and out? We're still, even here below, only halfway up the hill. An able-bodied man or woman can manage that kind of walk easily enough, but a prisoner…someone not able-bodied…"

"We need to find it!" Luke called. "No one touch anything in here—let's start looking. There's a door somewhere. Stairs or a lift."

"Aye, sir!" Duckie called.

Carly paused, looking around the room where they stood. She closed her eyes and opened them again.

The victim, she surmised, had lain in the first bed—the one that was stained so deeply with blood.

No one would care about that blood. It would have come from a victim already dead.

The second bed was the one that had mattered. But of course, it would have been important then that the area was sterile, that everything was pristine lest infection set in and all would have been for naught.

But…

Had those who received transplants been here while the person next to them had been asphyxiated? Burked? Were the donors killed before they ever reached this level? Or perhaps, the receivers were sedated before anything had begun?

"They only pulled out of here a day or two ago," Luke noted. "And they did so quickly. Except I don't believe they ever thought we'd find the lair here—just that we'd find an empty cottage," he murmured, looking around. "There must be more here. The recipients couldn't have been sent out into the world so quickly. There had to have been a place for recovery."

"You're right," she muttered. "And yet…"

"Their last victim wasn't discovered that long ago. They had to have taken someone out of here who was still recovering from having received a transplant. I'm wondering if that person could have survived the waters around here."

"And where did they go and how did they manage to carry a person in recovery like that without being seen by anyone?" Carly murmured.

"Waterfront house on the Firth of Forth or thereabouts," Luke murmured. "Or perhaps another island. I'm thinking this scheme has been in the works for a while. Time to form dummy corporations, time to arrange a setup like this…"

Carly frowned. "I was thinking…they might have gotten away with this much longer if they'd just tossed the bodies into the North Sea."

"There must be a strange arrogance involved. Maybe our enraged doctor who wasn't given a job. Maybe this is his way of proving he was the best, but why embrace the whole Burke and Hare thing the way that he—or they—did? Because I agree—this would have been easier for them if they'd tossed the bodies. By the time they were discovered—if they ever were—it would be truly difficult to discern just what had happened to the victims and when."

"Found it!" Daniel suddenly shouted from beyond the room.

Carly looked at Luke and they hurried out together.

At first, they didn't even see Daniel or any of the others. Then Luke's penlight showed them what appeared to be a solid wall with a break in it.

Luke pressed the wall at the breakpoint and it moved inward.

They discovered another large room, this one looking as if Mr. Clean had been through it recently. It offered just one bed with a table and a silver stand for an IV.

Daniel was there with Captain McDermott. "Sorry, the wall swung back," the bigger man murmured.

"Recovery room!" Daniel announced. "And another just behind with a few beds—not so sterile. Must be where the doctors—if they are real doctors—slept."

"What about an elevator—a lift?" Luke asked.

Another shout greeted them, sounding like it was coming from the depths of the earth.

Maybe it was.

"Come! Scoot around the right wall. There's a lift just behind it!" Jordan shouted up to them. "You have to work the ropes—I think there was maybe electricity at one time, but it's off now!"

They hurried out of the back room, following Jordan's directions.

There was a lift.

And a pulley system allowed them to take it down.

Down and down. And as they reached the bottom, they found Jordan and Duckie standing in what appeared to be a second, deeper basement.

Empty of everything.

"There's the break!" Luke said.

And he was right. Again, the wall appeared to be seamless—almost. And this time, it was a little more visible because daylight, just a sliver of it, was seeping through.

Luke stepped forward.

The hidden door swung outward as he pushed it. He held it open, showing them they were outside. The dock wasn't far from them at all, but the secret door was hidden by the branches of an overgrown fir tree and the heavy growth of bushes around it.

"This is how they managed," Daniel murmured. "Patients came in by boat—victims came in by boat. And since they seemed to know someone was onto this place…"

"They deserted it," Duckie said.

McDermott swore again, adding, "Aye, if we'd just heard something, seen something, a day or two earlier… This is horrible. Horrible. I am so sorry. We've brought you out here, and it's been a waste of your time, had we just gone in—"

"Captain!" Carly said quickly. "This hasn't been a waste of time at all. When a forensic team comes in here, they will find prints and trace evidence. We can see from what they left behind that they were in a huge hurry and that means something important can be found. We may even discover who has been involved with everything that went on here, at the least!"

"Of course, of course," McDermott murmured. "For now—"

"I'm calling Brendan Campbell, Captain," Luke told him. "He'll see to it a forensic team gets out here quickly."

He pulled out his phone and stepped aside.

That was when Carly saw the white fabric wedged beneath the bushes near the fir tree. Frowning, she headed over and moved a branch.

"Oh, my God!" she murmured.

"What is it?" Luke shouted to her instantly.

She held onto the branch but looked back at Luke and the others.

"I believe we've also discovered the rest of Nurse Dorothy Norman," she told them.

Twelve

The day stretched long as one of Campbell's forensic teams arrived at the island along with the same medical examiner who had looked at the head.

Luke pondered the situation, interested beyond a doubt in returning to the Connoly house, except all they could do as of yet was ask Lily Connoly about Jared Stone.

He wasn't sure where he thought the killers might have taken their surgery unit when they left Arthur's Isle, whether it was another island, or perhaps one of the properties on the water. Again, it was frustrating; it had to have been a major operation, moving so much medical equipment and the people who had the ability to use it and use it well.

The medical examiner wouldn't tell them with positive certainty until he'd done a few tests, but in his educated opinion and having studied the head—and hoping there weren't other detached bodies around—yes, it appeared this body was the rest of Dorothy Norman.

At last, they returned to the mainland. Campbell ordered them to stop long enough to have a luncheon, supper, dinner—a meal. He was still hoping to find something on Lily Connoly's financials—wherever her money was, she was certainly hiding it well.

Carly just wanted to return to the house and have dinner sent in. Jordan and Daniel agreed. MacDuff was staying with Campbell at the island a while longer, so it was just the four of them. It might be Scotland, but they all agreed on ordering in from an Italian restaurant.

As they sat at the table, Jordan asked, "What are we doing when we go to visit Ewan and Lily Connoly? I mean, we don't have solid evidence that they're involved. Jared Stone didn't say Lily was part of the greater picture, just that she'd paid him to sleep with her. So…"

"We probably need Ewan to like us until we do know more. So if we don't have more, my suggestion is we just ask her what she knows about Jared Stone and tell them witnesses saw him entering the house."

"Won't we put Flora MacDonald in greater danger?" Daniel worried.

"No, we can say a witness on the street identified him, that the witness recognized him from having been at Filigree," Luke said. "When she went into protective custody at the safe house, we had her call Lily and say she had to resign her position because she had a sick relative down in London. She knows nothing about Flora being in touch with us."

"Unless Jared Stone told her he'd run when we came up to Flora," Carly mused.

"I don't think there was a decent enough time gap. He did see Flora, but she might have gone on to London right after meeting with us. Again, we need to get their reaction. We will tell them Jared is in our custody, being charged, and we're trying to get him to tell us more to help himself. And if Lily knew anything about him, it would help us tremendously."

"If she is involved..." Carly mused.

"What?" Luke asked.

"She wasted her talents—she could have been a star. She was behaving so hysterically," Carly said.

"And in acting?" Luke queried. "How about Shakespeare? 'The lady doth protest too much, methinks!'"

"Hamlet," Daniel murmured. "But maybe so true."

"More than possible."

Their food arrived and they busied themselves setting up the table to eat. They continued to muse on the events of the day when MacDuff arrived at last.

All were happy that they had ordered plenty of food since they did have a full kitchen and could reheat everything.

But once he had a plate before him and managed a few mouthfuls, he told them, "I just received some strange information from Jackson Crow and Angela back in the States."

Luke looked over at Carly; they were both surprised Jackson hadn't contacted them first.

But MacDuff went on to tell them, "I called him in frustration. They're still working on just what went on. But the man who applied at the hospital, Harold Gleason, was a doctor in Miami. One who left the hospital where he was working about five years ago. The hospital couldn't help them, but in searching all kinds of records, Angela found a death certificate for the man. According to official records, Harold Gleason has been dead several years, killed in an automobile accident in Cairo. They are still trying to determine the authenticity of the death certificate. Also, they're tracing down his family, but he wasn't married and didn't have children. They are having trouble trying to find out who might have been his next of kin."

"So, the Harold Gleason who applied at the hospital here stole a dead man's identity—or he is the dead man, and he didn't really die in Cairo," Carly said. "Surely, it will be easy enough to determine if Gleason is Gleason or an identity thief. Facial recognition, DNA… There must be traces of the real man out there somewhere."

"Aye, there must be," MacDuff said. "But I got Jackson and Angela in the middle of their investigation. That's why you haven't heard from them yet—they like to be thorough before passing on information. Our people discovered that he had worked in Miami, but little more. Angela is tracking every possible lead with your people, and she'll leave no stone unturned. But you two know that!"

Luke nodded. "Right. So, we're looking for a ghost," he murmured.

Daniel made a strange sound, and Luke lowered his head to smile.

"We're collecting the players. We must be making movements in the right direction," MacDuff said. "Aye, and Italian was a great idea tonight! Regrettably… Campbell has informed the Connoly couple that we'll be coming by tonight to seek more help from them, is what he's said."

"And they didn't disappear or refuse to see us," Carly murmured.

"I told you we had people watching them. No, they have made no attempt to flee. Possibly because they know we're watching. Possibly because the woman just had extra money and wanted a young lover," he said.

"Are we all to go? Isn't that a bit of overkill?" Jordan asked.

"I'd like to split. Just as they've moved their surgery unit and supplies from Arthur's Isle elsewhere, I believe they've changed their modus for finding victims," MacDuff said.

"Sir, you know how many pubs, restaurants and bars there are in Edinburgh," Jordan reminded him.

"Right. But when Lila Strom left Filigree, we knew that she was headed to Kevin's," Luke said, looking at MacDuff, who nodded.

"Half of us to Kevin's to try to ascertain if he has his other players in place there," MacDuff murmured, "and half of us to the Connoly house."

"I will happily go to Kevin's. Of course, Kevin and his people do know who I am," Carly reminded MacDuff.

"But if there's a new charming young man—as in a second Jared Stone learning to work the ropes, inebriate young women and lure them to a van—he won't," Jordan said thoughtfully. "Maybe I should be with Carly. My city, I know Edinburgh well."

"And that is true. Luke, I'd like it if you were with me at the Connoly house." He shrugged. "You're an American. You might be able to get away with more."

"Whatever you want."

Daniel looked at them all thoughtfully. "I should hang at Kevin's," he said. "Because if they're already starting out again…"

"Strange, though," Carly murmured. "I talked to Kevin; instinct tells me he's a decent man. And Catherine, the bartender, was extremely helpful. I don't think either of them is holding on to super-charged whiskey and slipping it to people."

"And maybe they don't care how drunk they have people anymore. All they need to do is get them to the van," Luke noted. "And we need to remember the first two victims were men."

"Well, I'm charming, right?" Daniel said.

Jordan groaned, but the others laughed.

"Jordan," Carly assured him. "Don't worry, you're charming, too!"

MacDuff had finished his food. The man probably hadn't eaten all day, but then again Luke knew all too well how easily that happened.

"But, regrettably, enough food. Luke, you're with me. Carly, Jordan, Daniel, as always, be charming but take the greatest care."

Luke rose. It was time to go. He looked at Carly and nodded. Professionals. He still couldn't help but wish that he would be the backup headed out with her.

Then again…

The island had been deserted. Jared Stone was in custody, one van driver was dead and the man who had held prisoners at the old cottage near Rosslyn Chapel was in a hospital bed.

He sincerely doubted Nurse Dorothy Norman had been involved.

But she had known something. She had been executed—decapitated. She hadn't been killed for money or her organs. He was convinced she had known something and been a liability.

Did that mean they were running scared?

"Luke?" MacDuff asked.

"Right along, sir."

Carly, of course, knew he wasn't happy about their split. "We'll toss the paper and put away the leftovers."

"I've got this!" Jordan said, starting to pick up plates.

"With my charming help," Daniel told him, grinning.

"I'll be right back to add in my own help!" Carly promised, and she followed Luke as he headed to the door, stopping him for a minute and speaking softly for his ears only, she said, "Remember, in every species, the female may be far more cunning and devious and deadly."

He grinned. "Are you talking about Lily Connoly or yourself?"

She shrugged. "Maybe both. I'll be fine. Have faith in Daniel and Jordan. And me."

"I do," he promised her. "I would pit you against the finest agent, male or female, across the globe. But—"

"That's a little dramatic," she teased.

"Some of our finest agents have fallen in the line of duty."

"Right. So, you be careful, too," she said.

"We'll both be careful," he promised.

"Luke?"

MacDuff was out down the walk, ready to head into the car.

Carly indicated the door, and he grinned and strode on out to meet MacDuff.

It didn't take long to reach the Connoly house. They went through the front, and it was Lily who answered when they keyed in the number to say they were at the gate.

"Aye, we knew you were coming," Lily murmured. "And, of course, we've been waiting."

The gate opened; when they reached the front door,

the woman was waiting for them. Again, she was anxious, looking at them worriedly and saying, "Dear Lord, please do not tell me there's another body. I saw on the news. Oh, my, things are getting worse and worse. Now they are reporting that a nurse has been killed. This must be ended!"

She had made herself angry.

"Mrs. Connoly—" MacDuff began.

"What are you? Entirely incompetent?" she demanded.

Obviously, that didn't sit well with MacDuff. Luke stepped in quickly.

"Mrs. Connoly, please, we've made several arrests in the matter at hand, it's something of a frightening scope, I do assure you. But as you know, Brendan Campbell spoke with your husband because we need your help on a certain matter. One man was killed in a kidnapping attempt, which was supposed to lead to murder and organ removal, and another is under arrest."

She backed away then just as her husband arrived at the entry, frowning. "Come in. I spoke with Brendan Campbell, and he said you needed more information from us," he told them, looking curiously at his wife. "Lily, please, ask our guests in."

"There are more dead people, more and more! What is going on?" she demanded.

"We were thinking you might be able to help us with that," Luke said pleasantly.

"Aye," MacDuff said. He forced a smile. "You see, Mrs. Connoly, we had a wee bit of a sting operation going on the other night. I'm afraid one man was killed—"

"Who? Do you have a name? Who was it?" she asked.

"We're still working on that," Luke told her. "But

here's our question. We have a picture of this man—I can show it to you—and witnesses on the street out here saw him entering your house. He has identified himself to us as being Jared Stone. Do you know him, and can you tell us what he was doing here and anything else you might know about him?"

"Let me see the picture!" Ewan Connoly said, frowning.

Luke pulled out his phone and keyed up a picture of Jared Stone, which had been taken when he'd been brought into the station.

Ewan Connoly looked at the picture, frowning. He looked truly puzzled.

"I've never seen him before," he said. "Lily?"

Luke showed Lily Connoly the image on the phone.

She recognizes the man, I'm certain. And she's dismayed.

She might have hoped that Jared Stone was the man who had been killed.

She looked at Luke.

"I've never seen him before," she said.

"Look again, please—"

"Your witness is lying!" Lily said angrily.

"I'm sorry, Mrs. Connoly," he said politely, "but several people saw him come here," he told her. He was lying, of course. But despite Jared Stone being involved in the heinous murders, Luke didn't believe he had been lying about his association with the woman.

"Lily?" Ewan said worriedly.

"Ewan! Stop, please. I don't know who or what these people think they saw—"

"Perhaps someone with a cleaning crew, with our internet…to fix appliances. My luv, try to think. They are here to get this stopped. If we can help in any way…"

"Well, you didn't see him, did you?" Lily demanded.

"I'm often out, at the bank—"

"Over with Ian, working, something!" she snapped. "And I'm here. And no, I don't care what people told you! I don't know him!"

Her temper was growing. Ewan just looked lost.

"Get out! Get out of my house and leave me—leave us—alone!" she cried.

"All right, we can do that," MacDuff said. "But I'm afraid you'll have to come with us to the station."

"What? No—why?" she demanded.

MacDuff looked at Luke. Luke shrugged and MacDuff nodded.

"We believe you do know this man, Mrs. Connoly. In fact, according to him, ma'am, you know him very well," Luke said, his tone low and regretful.

"He's lying!" Lily cried. "Liars! They're all liars! Ewan! Make them stop this. Order them off our property."

"Lily, if this man says he knows you, let's just do whatever it is they want to get it all straightened out," Ewan said.

"Ewan! No!"

"Lily, please. Why are you so upset and angry?" Ewan sounded truly baffled. "Aye, a wee bit of annoyance, but if we see this man—"

"I'm to be forced to face a liar?" she demanded.

"I'm afraid with his statement and the witnesses, we do need to understand just who is and who isn't lying," Luke told her.

"Straighten it out!"

"We'll straighten it all out, Mrs. Connoly. You can come with us willingly, or…" MacDuff said.

"You can straighten it out yourselves!" Lily raged at them.

But Luke ignored her and continued where MacDuff had left off. "Or…we can put the cuffs on you and escort you out forcefully."

She stared at him furiously and tried to slam the door on them.

Her husband stopped her.

"Lily, please!"

"You are worthless, not a man!" she raged at him, and she pushed past Luke, running wildly—and ridiculously—out to the yard.

Luke glanced at MacDuff, shook his head and took off after her. He caught her just as she reached the gate. She flailed at him furiously with her fists flying.

He caught her wrists and drew them behind her back.

"Sadly, Mrs. Connoly, it's going to be the cuffs. And we're afraid that what we're going to need to know is did you just pay a man for an illicit affair—or are you the very heart of a murder conspiracy?"

Kevin of "Kevin's" and his bartender, Catherine, were both behind the bar when Carly, Jordan and Daniel arrived.

They'd split up on the street so they wouldn't appear to be together. Of course, Kevin knew Carly, and she intended to explain to him—without alarming him, she hoped—that they were afraid his pub might be next in line as a place for the killers to scout out victims.

Luckily, there were still seats at the bar. Carly was able to slide onto a stool with no one beside her. She left Daniel and Jordan to find their places. Daniel was around the bar to the left, between a young man in a leather jacket and a dark-haired woman of about thirty. Jordan was around the bar to the right, taking the one empty chair by two young women, the empty stool being right next to a pretty young blonde girl.

Kevin was good; he saw her, and he seemed to realize she didn't want to be addressed by her professional title in any way. She was just a customer that night.

He was careful to speak with her as if she were any customer, as if he were just a good and jovial bartender meeting a new patron for the first time, asking her what she'd like to drink before lowering his voice and making it appear as if they were just casually speaking.

"You're welcome here, and grateful I am. What is going on here...the news grows worse and worse. Another woman was found, but not...not ripped up. But a news reporter stated it was a decapitation. Are these the same killers? Why kill now without a reason? Lord, help us! How many monsters may there be?"

"We don't know, but we are drawing some of those involved into custody. We will not stop until we have them all, whatever their part in the operation."

"Aye, that you must. And I'm glad to have you here. But I'll have ye know, I check every bottle of liquor that comes to the bar. I make certain that it's sealed and the labels are right. And we will not serve anyone to the brink of inebriation."

"That's responsible and wonderful of you," Carly assured him. She discreetly pointed out Daniel and Jordan.

Jordan was around the other side of the bar. He was already chatting with a young and attractive woman.

Doing his job, she thought with some amusement.

"Catherine is also the best," Kevin said. He lowered his voice, barely whispering. "She has been watching out, we've all been watching out. With what's going on…"

"Thank you."

"I'll fix you up with a bit of apple juice in a glass; it will appear you are sipping a whiskey. And I'll leave you, I assume…"

"Thank you," she told him.

It was not long before the stool next to her was taken. This time, it was by an older man, white-haired, polite and pleasant.

He welcomed her to the country after discovering that she was American and suggested many things to do in the city and in the surrounding areas.

He enjoyed his one drink and left. Jordan was laughing with the blonde woman, enjoying himself. It seemed to be fine with her dark-haired friend, because another young man had taken a seat next to her. They all seemed to be enjoying the night.

Daniel was engaged in conversation with another young woman. She was very attractive with shoulder-length burnished red hair and soft, lovely features.

She was watching him when she felt someone behind her. For a second, chills ran up her spine. Then she lowered her head and smiled.

She realized the spirit of Keith MacDonald was behind her. He slid into the stool next to her.

"This will be the next place?" he whispered.

Carly lowered her head to reply softly, "We aren't sure—we suspect it's also in a good area."

Keith nodded. "I'd like ye to know, I'll have my eyes on all that happens."

"Thank you!"

He nodded, and quickly slid from the stool. Carly saw that a pair of young men were about to take the two stools to her right.

Catherine came around the bar, asking them what they'd like. They ordered whiskeys. The man closest to Carly turned to her, asking, "Luv, can we get you another? Ah, pardon me, too forward? I'll introduce myself. Robbie Landon."

"Hello," Carly said. "Carly. Carly MacDonald."

"Now, there you go! American, eh?"

Carly nodded. "Is it that evident?"

He was a handsome man, early thirties, clean-shaven, with a quick smile, a strong jaw and sculpted cheekbones. *Accustomed to being liked*, she thought.

Just like Jared Stone?

"We like to be welcoming here in Edinburgh," he told her.

"I'm quite fine right now, but thank you," Carly told him.

His friend, about his same age, with light blue dancing eyes and dark hair, leaned across him from the farther stool, grinning at her. "Oh, aye, miss, you are quite fine!" he said, grinning. "Me mate forgot to introduce me. Cullen, miss, Cullen Darien."

"Nice to meet you, too, Cullen. And thank you," Carly said.

"So, first time to Scotland?" Robbie asked her.

"Oh, no. My grandparents were born here. I've been many times," she said honestly.

"Hmm, of course," Robbie said. "But you came with your grandparents or parents or...?"

"Both at different times," she said.

"And now you're on your own? First time?" Cullen asked.

She shook her head. "No, I come now and then."

"Ah," Cullen said, giving Robbie a punch in the shoulder. "There you go. We can't tempt her with showing her the wonderful sights to be seen!"

"Ah, but she hasn't seen them all, surely," Robbie said.

Cullen sighed. "He may be referring to himself. He is a sight, eh?"

Carly laughed softly.

But Robbie suddenly became grave and serious. "All in all, luv, you shouldn't be out here alone. I'd like to think you were just a lovely lass, one we could share a few laughs with at the bar, and then all go on...safe and sound. But I can't believe you haven't seen the news here. You really must be extremely careful. Horrible things are going on. You do know, right? I hope you saw the news conference given by the National Crime Agency bloke. It's truly lovely that you're here, but you must be careful!"

She nodded. "Thank you. I will be careful."

Are they going to suggest that they should walk me back to my lodging? Maybe two are involved now?

"I have some friends in the city. We'll meet up," she said.

This time, Robbie punched Cullen in the shoulder. "See? She has friends in the city—she doesn't need our help."

"Ah, but maybe her friends haven't been to every museum!" Robbie said.

Carly laughed softly and sipped her apple juice, the perfect foil for a real drink.

Robbie and Cullen were friendly and polite, suggesting places and falling into a serious discussion about the museums she shouldn't miss.

She was paying attention to them and trying to keep an eye on Daniel and Jordan. And as Robbie and Cullen argued about the museums, telling her she needed to come for more of the festivals, she noted Jordan was getting up. He smiled at the one girl who had been right next to him, telling her something as her dark-haired friend rose from her stool and interrupted the two of them, laughing and apparently telling them to have fun.

The dark-haired girl started down the hall to the restroom, leaving her blonde friend with Jordan.

Jordan and the blonde stood also.

Jordan set money on the bar and casually put an arm around the girl's shoulder. They started for the door.

Daniel was already excusing himself to his companions.

And Carly knew she needed to do the same. She smiled at her new friends, thanked them for a great time and rose.

"Wait! You could be in danger. The bloke on the news said no one should be alone," Cullen warned seriously.

"I just realized one of my friends is right there," she said, pointing to Daniel. "I'm going to get him to walk me back. Thanks for the conversation!" she told them.

Daniel was headed out the door. It was important, of course, for them to follow. But they needed to follow safely and give nothing away—but be close enough if something was about to happen.

She caught up with Daniel, who looked at her with surprise.

"Are you supposed to know me?" he asked her.

"There's no one on the street. I told the fellows at the bar that you were my friend here in Scotland," she told him.

"Do you think that a woman could really be involved in luring men to their deaths?" Daniel asked, then noted, "They turned just ahead."

"As will we," she murmured. "And yes. Two men were killed first. Who else might have lured them to a dark place to be killed? And while there may not be a worker at Kevin's who is involved with getting anyone inebriated—Kevin is keeping close watch on the bottles of alcohol himself—a woman can still lure a man away."

They took the turn that brought them behind the kirkyard.

The streetlights seemed especially pale. The weathered stones of Scotland's ancient city walls seemed to add a strange miasma to the night.

Of course, there was nothing wrong with the night. But the darkness did seem deeper. And even in the darkness, shadows seemed to loom.

"Ahead!" Carly said, as she saw there seemed to be a large lump on the ground ahead of them.

They heard a strange groaning, strange in the silence of the night that seemed as heavy as the darkness.

"Where are they?" Carly murmured, "and what is that? No, no, *who* is that?"

She hurried forward, Daniel close behind.

"Jordan!" she exclaimed, dropping down beside the man. She quickly felt for a pulse; he was alive. His eyes were closed. A strange soft sound escaped him again, a groan.

"Jordan?" she whispered urgently again.

Carly glanced at Daniel, who was searching in the

distance for a glimpse of the girl. What was going on? Had she been sent out to lure another male to the killers? But why leave him as he was, knocked out on the ground?

"Maybe she saw us, maybe she knew we were following," Daniel muttered.

"We need an ambulance for him," Carly said, pulling out her phone.

Jordan opened his eyes and looked at her at last. "Fiona...must..."

"Did she do this to you, Jordan? Did she attack you?" Carly asked anxiously.

"No...no...go!"

"Jordan, what are you saying? Did she attack you? If so, why did she leave you?"

He struggled for speech, wincing, but he managed at last to form words. "No...lying in wait...ahead of us, man in a ski mask...lying in wait... Never saw... He has her... Hit me, iron pole...golf club...caught me back of the head...grabbed Fiona..."

"She didn't scream! You didn't cry out. We were right behind you!" Carly reminded him.

"So fast. Something on a handkerchief...over her face. She started to scream...the world...dark, dark descended... Must go save her, must go..."

Carly rose, staring at Daniel. "Stay with him, I'm going—"

"Not alone, and hurry!"

She whirled around.

The spirit of Keith MacDonald was back with them. "He didn't have a chance, Jordan didn't have a chance. I didn't even know he was already in the bushes, waiting...striking...but he's ahead at the cross street. A van will come, and he had the young woman knocked out. Please, hurry!"

"We can't leave Jordan alone," Carly said. "Daniel, stay—"

"But, Carly, not alone!" Daniel protested.

On the ground, Jordan was still groaning. But he managed, "Not alone, not alone, not alone!"

"She won't be alone!" Keith announced. "She will be with me!"

Carly was up. They had to move.

They had a chance, just minutes…

Daniel had his phone out. He looked at Carly and said, "Putting all coppers on call, getting to Brendan Campbell…the street goes out to main streets. We must do this—"

"You are oh, so right!" she agreed fervently.

She nodded quickly to Daniel. And she began to run into the darkness, determined to stop whoever had hurt Jordan.

Whoever now had Fiona…

Thirteen

Lily Connoly ranted and raved in the car to the station with such fury and ferocity that her husband begged her to stop.

He apologized to MacDuff, telling him the whole thing had been so upsetting to his wife that apparently she had gone off the rails.

MacDuff reminded her she could call for legal counsel.

Ewan, baffled by everything, said they'd just get there and solve the entire nasty pack of lies. Just because someone said something, didn't make it true. He was happy to confront any statement and dispute it irrevocably himself.

"Sir," MacDuff reminded him, "we do need to know what is going on. Perhaps, when Mrs. Connoly isn't so upset, she'll remember something that will help us."

"They are liars!" Lily Connoly exploded again.

She didn't stop when they reached the station. MacDuff asked Ewan to stay with his wife—he would act as her counsel for the moment.

Despite her screaming, they managed to get the two

of them in one interrogation room and Jared Stone in another, with the observation room being between the two.

Brendan Campbell took up a position in the observation room.

"Luke," MacDuff said, "with your agreement, I will have you speak with our screaming virago, and I will have a nice chat with Jared Stone."

"Fine," Luke said.

Once he was seated across from Lily and Ewan, Luke let her go on and on until she was finally winded.

"When do I face my accusers?" she demanded.

He frowned. "You want to see this man, Jared Stone?" he asked. "You want to face him?"

"I want to call him a liar to his face, yes," she told him.

"You don't remember he might have been at your home in a work capacity, again, maybe as a repairman, maybe even as a deliveryman?"

"No!" Lily snapped. "He is a liar, and I have never seen him!"

Ewan Connoly looked as if he'd suddenly received a silent revelation.

"Wait!" he exclaimed. "If anyone let him in at any time, it had to be Flora MacDonald!" He turned to his wife. "Is it possible? Maybe she let him in."

Lily didn't answer, and Ewan looked at Luke.

"If she wants to face this man, we can perhaps discover the truth of this abhorrent situation of lie after lie!"

He was either an extremely talented liar himself, or he was earnestly trying to comprehend what was going on, Luke determined.

He nodded grimly to Ewan and rose.

"Let me confer and see if this is possible," he told them. Rising, he headed out and into the observation room.

"What do you think?" he asked Campbell.

Campbell sighed. "Well, see for yourself. MacDuff is having an interesting time in there. Stone keeps insisting he is no liar, and Lily Connoly is a dangerous woman. He insists she is cunning and vicious—that when she paid him, she demanded everything she wanted. She promised him she could make life hell on earth for him if he ever breathed a word of what they were doing."

"I think I'll join MacDuff for a minute, see if there is anything that can prove this situation one way or another. We know he was in the house—Flora MacDonald was terrified and anxious to get to us and equally anxious for protection," Luke said.

"Be my guest. Go join MacDuff," Campbell told him.

Luke nodded, left the observation room, and headed in to join MacDuff and Stone.

Stone looked up at him. He'd been caught; he knew he was caught.

"Ah, the American has arrived! Mr. Kendrick, no... Special Agent Luke Kendrick. I remember a little ditty from some movie or show that was on years ago... streaming now, I believe. Had a great song!" He grinned and sang, "Secret agent man..."

"Mr. Stone. You seem to be in decent spirits," Luke said.

"Mr. Stone has spoken with his counsel. He is happy to speak with us now. He's been advised and has chosen to plead guilty to certain charges and hopes to cooperate with us in any way," MacDuff told Luke.

"This is true?" Luke asked Jared Stone.

"I've been cooperating—I will continue to do so," Stone said.

"Even if the charges include conspiracy to commit murder?" Luke asked.

"I did no killing," Stone assured him. "I don't have the stomach for it."

"Accessories to murder don't need to wield the knife," Luke reminded him.

"But my full cooperation will help at my sentencing. I'm a changed man," Stone assured him. "As you can see, I am here. I am willing to say everything I can that might help you in any way."

"And you are aware Lily Connoly is here, calling you a liar, swearing you were never in that house," Luke said.

Stone started to laugh. "I can describe the house down to a tee. I can describe the woman's bedroom. Oh, did you know? They keep separate bedrooms. She claims he snores like a yeti, or something like that, and she needs her personal space when it comes to sleeping." He shrugged. "She also told me she doesn't mind being his wife at all, and her sexcapades are simply because he isn't capable of getting it up, and he does nothing else to appease her needs. She also told me that surely I could tell she is an extremely sensual woman."

"And now she says you're a liar," MacDuff reminded him.

"Paper," Stone said. "I'll draw her bedroom for her— and write about unusual details of the house."

"That can be arranged," MacDuff said.

He left the room and quickly returned with paper.

"She is something!" Stone muttered as he drew.

When he was done, Luke could see the complete placement of furnishings in the room and more. He described everything in her bathroom—and in a top drawer.

"Lots of sex toys!" he told Luke.

Luke nodded. "I'll bring this and show it to the two of them and see their reaction."

MacDuff nodded and Luke left. He brought the paper to the room where Lily was now sobbing and clinging to her husband, who kept trying to soothe her and assure her the wretched criminal would be proved a liar, and they would be out of it once and for all.

However, once Luke entered the room and placed the drawing on the table for both Lily and Ewan to see, Ewan drew back.

"The man drew this?" he demanded. He pulled away from his wife. "Lily, how—"

"Ewan! Don't, don't, I... I don't know how—"

"Lily! He's seen the house, he's seen your room!" Ewan told her, baffled.

But Lily quickly responded, gasping and saying, "That girl! That horrid, horrid girl! She's the one! Arrest that little witch, that deceitful vixen! She did this—oh! She is in conspiracy with this man, creating nothing but trouble for us while we were nothing but kind to her. That's it, Ewan, that explains how this man was in our house. Oh! In my room, in my things! She must be arrested. It's her! She's been working with this horrible man to discredit my husband and me, and I can't even begin to fathom why!"

There was a tap on the one-way mirror.

Luke excused himself again. He entered the observation room. Campbell was waiting, shaking his head.

"Intriguing couple. They are among the...wealthier landed members of the gentry, or so it appears on paper. Mrs. Connoly has been from the beginning, as is my understanding, rather hysterical about everything. Either we're about to send the poor woman to a mental institution through no fault of her own, or…anyway. Jared Stone has insisted to MacDuff he can prove everything that he's saying. He wants to see you again."

"MacDuff is in there with him—"

"Changing places," Campbell told him.

As Campbell spoke, he saw MacDuff was walking into the interrogation room where Ewan and Lily were sitting.

Ewan had moved his chair; his body language seemed to be speaking loud and clear. He was doubtful of Lily now himself.

"All right, then," Luke murmured, heading in to speak with Jared Stone again.

He took the chair, looking at the man. "You know Lily is now claiming you were working with Flora Mac-Donald. You two are in a conspiracy together."

Stone burst out laughing. "That's just sad." He leaned forward. "You know, one might just think of Lily Connoly as a sad and lonely older woman, disappointed in life, seeking any diversion. But lovely young Flora Mac-Donald would never need to pay for…attention. I am quite sure you know that to be true. And our dear Lily made sure our…communications all occurred when dear Flora was out of the house. That—"

"Mr. Stone," Luke said. "You said you have some means of proof?"

"You want something on paper again?" Stone asked.

Several sheets remained on the table along with a pencil. For a brief moment, Luke feared their suspect might intend to do himself harm, such as stabbing himself with the pencil.

Such things had happened.

But there was nothing suicidal about Jared Stone. It seemed he believed his cooperation with them would heavily reduce his sentence.

At first, Luke wasn't sure what the man was drawing.

Then he realized it was the human body. A woman's body.

A woman's naked body.

He began shading areas and then writing next to each of the marks he made.

"Birth mark on the dear lady's upper thigh. Marks from a caesarean birth here…and a strange mole just above the groin, here. Surgery scar, maybe? Oh, and an old scar close to the…well, you know. Show her this— and tell her I am not a liar." He started to laugh. "Now, I do understand one might not want to own up to being a horrendous murderer, but she denies being quite the animal in bed! Ah, poor Ewan. So deceived. So tragically deceived!"

"Well, we shall see," Luke murmured. He started to rise again.

"Wait!" Stone said.

"What is it?"

Jared Stone leaned forward. "I heard her on the phone. And I noted she was listening to someone and becoming testy, saying that things needed to be on time. That was the very night I led Lila Strom from the bar to be met by the van driver who your friend killed."

"She might have been talking about anything," Luke said.

"But I was able to see her phone. I saw the number

on it. It was the same number from which I received orders on what to do, what nights to do it…if a man or a woman was needed," Stone said. He shrugged. "Now, that I cannot prove. They changed phones frequently. And in fact…" He paused, frowning. "In fact, it was one of the burner phones through which I received a call regarding an older woman seeking companionship. Seriously," he said, grimacing. "Do I look like a bloke who would normally run in the same circles as the Connoly couple?"

"But you think Lily might be involved but not her husband?"

"Poor cuckold! Now, can't say I know the bloke. As you can imagine and have seen, I was never summoned to the house when Mr. Connoly was home."

"All right, thank you," Luke said.

Again, it was time to change rooms. He decided he'd confer with Brendan Campbell before heading back to Ewan and Lily.

He knew he could have taken it right away—but this was Scotland. And he wanted Campbell aware and approving of his actions.

"Crazy waters run deep, eh?" Campbell said, shaking his head. "So…is it more? Take it as you will. This is not a good day for Lily Connoly, one way or another. Either she is just a straying wife—most likely on the serious outs now with her husband—or it gets much, much worse."

"Anything odd yet on her financials?" Luke asked.

"Nothing we can pin. Seems like she had cash with which she paid Mr. Stone for his—services," Campbell said.

Luke nodded and left Campbell, this time joining MacDuff as he sat with Ewan and Lily Connoly.

"Well," he said. "We have another interesting aspect of what you say are lies being created by Mr. Stone," he told Lily, taking a seat.

"He is a liar, a murderer, a con artist—" Lily began.

"But he did draw this," Luke said, tossing the sketch of Lily's naked body on the table.

Ewan stared at the picture and then at his wife.

It was evident from Ewan's expression that Jared Stone had done an accurate depiction of Lily's body. With all its little imperfections.

It was equally evident that Lily was desperately considering her next words.

"I don't know… I mean, I have no idea… I can't explain…" Lily began, looking at her husband.

"Strangely, I do!" Ewan announced. He stood. "I must get out of this room!" he said.

"Ewan, no! I'm being set up! It's all… I don't know how or… Ewan!"

Her words had no effect. MacDuff opened the door for Ewan, who was quickly out of the room, before giving Luke a nod of silent encouragement to continue his interrogation and following after the aggrieved husband.

Lily stared stubbornly at Luke. Then she moved forward, as if she would leap across the table, and told him furiously, "We welcomed you into our home. We tried to help. And you…you are nothing but an American monster seeking any way to look good, ready to blame anyone so you don't appear to be so horribly, horribly incompetent! And what is this? What do you think you can hold me on? A lie? A liar saying he slept with me, that…"

She leaned back suddenly. "That girl."

"Flora MacDonald?"

"Aye—her!"

"You slept with Flora MacDonald?" he asked.

"No! No, but the only way they could concoct this ridiculous lie is if she saw me, if…as if she hid in a closet while I showered and changed. That's it. I know that's it. Why do you think she's now disappeared?"

"Fear. She'd be a perfect victim," Luke said.

"Victim, my arse!" she exclaimed furiously. "She… she planned this!"

"How did you meet Jared Stone? He believes you and he were in contact with the same number, and you were able to hire him through this number. A number belonging to someone who contacted you both—or someone you specifically contacted."

"What? Oh, that's a lie. I was never in contact with people who Jared Stone would know, who would… Oh, wait. Don't you think you're going to trap me. That is not how I was in contact with Jared Stone!"

"So how were you in contact with him?"

"What, wait, no! I was never in contact with him."

"What you're telling me is Flora MacDonald hid in a closet to see you naked so she could describe every nuance of your body to Jared Stone so that he could then set you up? And that, of course, you knew nothing about anything he was doing for others?"

"Yes! Don't let her fool you. The lass is not a good person. She had me fooled. But there is no way the man, that the horrible man, could describe me—"

"I'm afraid he also described your house and your room—and even what might be found in several of your drawers."

"But that's it—she prowled around. She was into

everything. Of course she might know what was in my room—she cleaned it!"

Lily Connoly stood. "I am leaving. My husband was a nitwit to bring us in here from the get-go. You have nothing on me, and I believe I will sue for the anguish and strain you have put upon me and, therefore, on my husband. You bastard! Now Ewan will doubt me, and I have never been anything but a faithful and loving wife!"

She started to walk out of the room but Luke told her, "Sit down!"

"You can't hold me."

"I admit I'm not familiar with the subtle differences in our legal systems, but..."

MacDuff entered the room and sat. "We will be holding you for a few hours, Mrs. Connoly. Please, settle down."

"A few hours—"

"We're searching your home."

"You need a warrant!" Lily exclaimed.

"Well, actually, no, we don't," MacDuff told her. "Your husband has offered us his complete cooperation."

"No! He can't! I won't allow it. It's my home, too—" Lily argued.

"But on paper, the house and grounds belong to your husband, Mrs. Connoly," MacDuff said, and he rose. "Special Agent Kendrick...if you'll join me."

"You're just going to leave me here?" Lily raged. "No, I will not stand for it!"

"Then stay seated," Luke told her dryly.

And like MacDuff, he headed for the door, and it closed and locked behind them.

Even then, they could still hear Lily ranting.

"How much is true?" MacDuff murmured to Luke.

Campbell joined them in the hall. "I intend to be part of the search team heading to the Connoly home. MacDuff, I'll have you join me. Luke, I got a call from Daniel. He just got an emergency vehicle and medical personnel out to the road you've been taking out of Kevin's pub by the kirkyard. Jordan was walking with a young woman, and Carly and Daniel came upon his unconscious body. Head straight out of Kevin's and to the right, is what he told me. If you could join Daniel—"

"Daniel is with Carly," Luke said.

"She went in pursuit while he stayed. He is now in the progress of catching up with her. The young woman has disappeared. It appears that Jordan was ambushed."

"But—" Luke began, a sinking feeling in his heart.

"No, no, Jordan is alive. We don't know how badly he was hurt, but Daniel said he has a pulse, and it's strong. Jordan is a strong man. He will be fine, I'm confident. But—"

"I'll join Daniel immediately."

MacDuff called for a car to pick him up.

Once they arrived, Luke asked that the patrol car remain, watching every avenue of the street.

He quickly hurried to the point where Jordan was just being taken away on a stretcher.

The man's eyes opened and he saw Luke.

"Go, go, they have her… He was waiting. My fault, I should have been prepared. We thought she was luring me, but he was there…came out of the darkness and hit me and… Go!"

"Take care of yourself right now, buddy," Luke said. He looked at the EMT.

The man nodded at him. Jordan had been hurt, assuredly. Blood had dried on his temple.

But it was possible he had suffered a concussion and nothing worse.

"Thank you," Luke said.

"That way!" Jordan whispered. "Carly... Daniel... That way!"

Luke started out. He'd barely gotten a hundred yards down the dark street when he saw a shadow sweeping through the darkness toward him.

Then the shadow was before him in human form.

It was Keith MacDonald, anxious, breathless, if such a thing could be said of a spirit.

"Hurry, hurry! Carly is talking, talking away, but he has a woman...he has a knife at her throat. Carly is aiming at him but...the girl, she could die. He is ready to slit her throat!"

Luke took off running, Keith sweeping along at his side.

"Careful, careful... Here, we can go around," Keith said.

"Go around—through a wall? Keith, I can't—"

"No, it's deceptive! Follow me."

It was another of those strange places unique to the city where it appeared that a wall was one piece, but it really wasn't. A very narrow alleyway opened, allowing the passage of one person at a time through the opening and down a hundred feet or so.

Luke paused when he reached the end, looking around as Keith urged him onward.

Then he saw the tableau that had been described.

There was a man against a high stretch of stone wall.

He had a pretty blonde girl with him, one arm around her, holding her prisoner.

With the other hand, he held a knife.

And that knife was pressed so tightly against her throat that a slim line of blood had already appeared.

Carly was across from him, and Daniel was a few feet back.

Both had their weapons ready, but Carly was talking.

And Luke knew why.

No matter how good a shot she was, she risked two things: the man being able to slice the woman's vein or artery as he went down, or…the man could move in a flash and Carly's bullet could hit the terrified young woman.

He assessed the situation as he listened.

"Please! Think about this. Yes, you can kill her. But if you kill her, you won't have fulfilled your orders. If you kill her, you know you will die. These people aren't worth dying for! So far, you've not done anything that can't be alleviated. Listen to me, please."

"If I don't die now…" the man said.

Luke studied him. Young. This person seemed to be from somewhere in the Middle East, dark hair, shaggy, a bit of an accent…

The killers seemed to be able to recruit their ground men from those who were either greedy or desperate.

They chose those they could threaten or bribe.

"They will kill me if you don't!"

The man's words had a sad finality about them. He was so terrified of those who had hired him or forced him to do what he was doing that he might well consider death to be something easier than having to face them again.

Luke waited, listening to Carly.

He could pull out his gun and try to fire, but the same scenario played out in his head again. He knew he would be taking the same risks Carly or Daniel might be forced to take, which might make the fellow twitch with the knife…

And watch the young woman bleed to death before them.

And if he missed…

Hit the young woman as the man jerked away or used her instantly as a shield.

And again…

Watch the young woman bleed to death before them.

There wasn't a good answer here.

"Warn Carly and Daniel I'm going to walk out," Luke said to the spirit of Keith MacDonald.

"Just—walk out?" the ghost replied, confused.

"Whistling," Luke said.

"Just walking out…whistling?" MacDonald asked.

"Different tactic," Luke told him.

As Luke had asked, Keith moved. In the night, he was like a whirl of shadow, sweeping first to Carly and then over to Daniel.

He apparently startled Carly; she gave a little shiver.

"You need to let me go. Let me just take her and go," the man said.

"We can't do that—you know we can't do that," Carly told him quietly with regret.

"Then we both die," the man said.

"No, no!" Carly protested. "They don't deserve your life. I don't know what they did, how they threatened you, but we are powerful, too. We can protect you—"

"And throw me back to Iran," he said. "You don't

understand. I will be killed if I return to my own country. I was part of a protest—"

"And you're a good human being. I can promise you won't be thrown back," Carly told him. "Please, please, don't die for such horrible people. They have no ideals, no beliefs! They would kill this girl for money and nothing more. It's a business, not a belief. And innocents are dying—"

"Good lives are being saved."

"And they can be saved the right way. But we're not gods—we don't have that right. Some will die of disease, and sometimes that can be stopped, sometimes it can't. But life is our greatest gift! Life can't be stolen from others. You know how wrong it is. I believe you're a good man. You know what you're doing is terribly, terribly wrong—"

"I just needed to bring her to…the street. I didn't kill anyone, I was careful just to knock the fellow she was with out of his senses. But I was wrong, he is in on it."

"He's in on it?"

"Yes, yes, yes! Don't believe what he says! I was to watch for such a man and woman leaving Kevin's, then I would take the woman. And I should have thought… that man was guilty! He was guilty of getting her drunk and bringing her to me. But I didn't kill him. I'm not a killer. I just… He's a killer, he's one of them."

"You're confused. Jordan is no killer, my friend. He's with Police Scotland."

The man started to laugh.

"All the better for him! You don't think the coppers get into things? You talk to your man. He's guilty, guilty, guilty. I didn't kill anyone!"

"No, but you don't understand. You just deliver people where they're supposed to be. You do this for the killers. That makes you just as guilty. And you don't need to do this. We can help you."

"Yes, yes, they let you know…some people die easy! They never know…they go straight to heaven and live sweet lives in the clouds. Some…some die hard! They make them die hard. Because you can't threaten them, if you're a threat, you die and you die hard, so hard! But—"

Carly spoke again. "No. Stop right there. They aren't infallible. Their empire is crumbling. Don't die for these people! We can and will protect you."

The man was listening to her and hesitating, but he was growing nervous. The blonde was sobbing, and in doing so, she was shaking…

Bringing the knife closer against her own throat.

It could go either way, but the time had come to put himself into the action.

Luke began to whistle. Just as if he were nonchalantly about to head into the street.

He did so, moving out with his hands in his pockets.

He stopped suddenly, as if startled by the scene in the street.

"Hey…wow, buddy, what's going on here?"

He walked over to the man, staring at him.

"What's going on here?" he asked. "Are you guys filming some kind of a movie? Oh, wow, if so, I'm sorry if I messed up any kind of a shot!"

"Go away!" the man roared.

"Okay, not a movie," Luke said. "Ah, come on! She's bleeding!" Luke said pleasantly as if he had, perhaps, just broken up a domestic fight taking place out on the street, as if they were throwing barbs at one another rather than the man holding a knife to a woman's throat.

He hoped his assessments of the person and his strengths were correct.

But they had to act.

And they were in the best situation to do so.

He sprang forward, instantly grabbing the man's wrist, tearing it away from the woman's throat. She screamed and slumped forward.

Then the man instinctively tried to fight.

But Luke slammed the man's hand against the stone wall, crushing bones.

The knife fell. But the man wasn't to be undone easily. He roared with pain and frustration and swung at Luke with his other arm, crushing the captive blonde between them. Luke pulled the young woman to him, then ducked and missed the blow.

The man swung around, and Luke pushed him hard against the stone.

"Stop! Stop now—you don't need to fight and be hurt!"

And the man began to weep and cry.

"I am not a killer—I couldn't have killed her. I am afraid. I am so afraid. When they are angry... I saw the news. I saw what they did because that nurse asked questions. They tortured her, they tortured her and cut her head off slowly while she lived and screamed."

He turned around, looking at Luke, shaking his head in horror.

He seemed to crumple into Luke's arms. The pretty blonde was free and screaming. She raced across the short distance to throw herself into Carly's arms.

Daniel was already dialing it in. The patrol car would bring in their new "procurer."

Luke looked back at Carly, who was holding the

blonde, trying to soothe her, and assuring them both that the necklace of red around the woman's neck was superficial.

Then Carly looked back at him.

And he knew she was thinking the same.

Another night. Another night in which they'd been successful. And yet he had to wonder...

They had saved a life. The blonde was going to live. EMTs would be here any minute. They would bring this fellow in, question him again.

But they wouldn't get the answers they needed, though they were gaining information all the time. Threats were being used severely on those who were vulnerable.

So...

They had saved a life. They had another captive.

They also had Lily Connoly in custody; and if Jared Stone hadn't been fabricating a greater story than the sad truth of the situation, she just might be part of the upper hierarchy in what was happening.

But why?

That remained to be seen.

The night was going to be long.

Very, very long.

And, looking at one another while sirens again blazed in the night, they both knew it.

But...

There was something worse. An accusation. An accusation against one of their own. A ridiculous accusation and yet...

Now it was there. And if he didn't tell MacDuff and Campbell about the incident...

Daniel would. And, of course, it didn't matter. They would quickly find Jordan innocent of any wrongdoing.

Wouldn't they?

Or was it just as possible that someone in law enforcement was involved, and that was why they knew they were looking for an island...

And perhaps knew that they were investigating Dorothy Norman...

And they were changing their operation to watch what was going on at Kevin's.

But Jordan?

Ridiculous!

And yet, he knew.

They could leave no stone unturned.

And they would not.

Fourteen

It was late. Carly didn't feel the hours that often, but tonight, she was exhausted.

She was grateful Luke had arrived when he had. While the man was listening to her, she'd been afraid that in his fragile state he might twitch so hard he would have killed the young woman. But she was alive, and he was alive.

Daniel walked over to them. "Campbell says we are to go back to the house and get some sleep. He even ordered MacDuff home. And…" He paused, looking at Luke. "He's still holding Lily Connoly. They found everything—and I do mean everything—Jared Stone described in the woman's bedroom. They're running DNA on a few of her, uh…"

"Sex toys," Luke said flatly, shrugging to Carly.

"At any rate, he believes they will find she did, indeed, hire Jared Stone as a, uh…"

He broke off again, looking awkwardly at Carly.

"Gigolo?" Carly suggested.

He grimaced and nodded. "And if they find his DNA… well, it proves Jared Stone wasn't lying about that. They also found a few different cell phones—all burners—beyond the one that's on the same plan as her husband's. They will be investigating what they can find on those."

"What has Ewan Connoly had to say?" Luke asked.

"He is being quiet. Campbell thinks Ewan is astounded, furious…and a little bit broken. He allowed them free rein of his place, sitting in the dining room with his head in his hands the whole time. I don't think Lily would want to go home, even if she were released. She demanded counsel now, but she can't be arraigned until the morning and it's unlikely she'll get bail."

"Maybe the woman will regret that she overplayed it."

Carly was so tired she had almost forgotten Keith was still with them.

She turned to him. "Hey, you brought Luke out here, right? Thank you!"

"I wish all this led to more. We have another man in custody. Never saw a van tonight—and the bloke screamed about Jordan being involved," Keith said, shaking his head. He frowned then. "It couldn't be, right?"

"I don't believe it for a minute," Carly said.

"But it is possible that someone who… I mean we don't want to think that many things may be possible, and yet they are. Doctors study to save lives, and law enforcement is out there to save lives. But…" Daniel said unhappily.

"I'm not buying it, either," Luke said. "But I take it we're supposed to be questioning him."

"Not us. Campbell is going to the hospital himself," Daniel told them. "We're to go home. Patrol has taken the man in, they'll get an ID at the station and hold him until morning. The blonde has been taken to the hospital to see how badly she's injured. Campbell is going to speak with her, and… Oh, yeah, one more thing. We need to do the incident reports, but he's said we can write them up at the house and email them in."

"Then let's go," Carly said. "Keith, again, thank you!" she told the spirit.

"If only it was enough," he said quietly.

"Step by step," Luke told him. "We've thwarted a few things now."

"A few, and yet…" Keith said. The three of them looked at him, waiting. "Dorothy Norman," he said at last. "This fellow knew what was done to her. How? Was he there, was he warned? It's so frustrating!"

"Want to walk with us back to the house?" Carly asked him. "You're welcome with us at any time, you know. There's a great TV in the living room or parlor or…whatever one calls it in that house," she assured him.

"I think I will wander about a bit," Keith said. "Maybe clear my head, see what I can see…maybe head to the station and listen if anyone speaks to himself—or herself."

"Thanks," Luke told him. "Well—"

"You're flesh and blood and full of human needs and weaknesses. Go!" Keith commanded.

Grinning, the three of them turned to obey him.

It was a bit of a walk home. And as they traveled back to the Royal Mile, Carly noted that despite all that was happening, despite the hour, the streets were still busy.

But it was good to see no one seemed to be alone. Couples were walking hand in hand and groups of three or four were common.

At last, they reached the house. MacDuff had just beat them there. He looked worn.

"I guess, despite the evening—or because of the evening—I'm going to bed," he told them, and he paused. "They're wrong. Everything that man said is—wrong. I know Jordan. Jordan is my man. He is not guilty of anything."

"Well, the accusation has no standing whatsoever," Carly told him.

"No, but it was there, and in a situation like this… his place is being searched even as he lies in a hospital bed," MacDuff said.

"But he's been staying here, he's been with one of us all the time," Carly said.

"We have to do everything by the book," MacDuff said.

"Well, there's no problem with that," Luke said. "We haven't known Jordan long, but even in that, I don't believe it—a wild accusation by a man holding a knife against a woman's throat. There's not much in that. Anyway, let's head to bed ourselves if our hands are tied for the night. We can bet on the fact that something else will happen tomorrow. Because we are getting closer."

"The hospital," Carly said thoughtfully.

"You still think someone from there is involved?" Luke asked.

"I never met Dorothy Norman, I merely heard them call her Nurse Ratched. But from that, I imagine she was hard on people, demanding the truth and maybe demanding to know about someone's time if they didn't show up for work. How else could she have come under the scope of these people and wind up—if this man tonight was right—tortured before she was beheaded?

And I imagine because she was older, whoever did it didn't even want to bother with her organs. They wanted her head in that bin as a warning to anyone else. And it seems to have worked. The people we have managed to corral are all just about ready to die rather than take a chance that someone decides they're worthy of the same fate as Dorothy."

"Great thinking," Luke said, shrugging. "I was just going to agree with you for the same reasons."

"Do we all go tomorrow? You know, this is ridiculous. We're down a man. First, Jordan takes a whack to the head. Then he's accused of being part of this thing."

"Daniel, you and Carly get to the hospital together. I'll meet you there—I want to question Lily Connolly again. The DNA will all be in. Once it's been proven that she's been with Jared Stone, she may start to sing a different tune."

"I'll work with Campbell and Luke at the station," MacDuff said. "We're still trying to track down this doctor who gave Forbes such a hard time when he wasn't hired for the unit here."

"Whoever he is, it's likely he just might be a part in it. He may even be a major player," Daniel said. "And we could still get some help if we find the distillery with the super-charged whiskey."

"They're not using it anymore, so it seems," MacDuff said.

"Maybe they've decided they just don't need to because using the whiskey would mean that they need to threaten and/or bribe another bartender," Carly said.

"Still, if we knew…"

"It would help, yes," MacDuff agreed. "Good night!"

He walked to his room. Daniel grimaced. "'Night, all," he said, disappearing behind his door as well.

Carly walked into the room she and Luke shared. It was late, well past midnight. She wanted a shower, she wanted to play, she wanted to shake it off and enjoy the little time that was truly theirs to be together. The time that made it all right to deal with everything else.

She set her Glock down and paused for a minute then lay down on the bed and told Luke, "Shower. Getting up in two minutes."

She never did.

She fell asleep more quickly than she had ever done before.

Sleep was good. She wasn't troubled by nightmares. It was…finally interrupted as she heard Luke's phone ring.

He answered it and instantly protested. "I still don't believe it! He's being set up, framed! All right, we'll be in soon."

Carly realized that he'd drawn the covers up around her during the night. She moved them quickly, sitting up and asking, "What happened?"

"They found a cooler in Jordan's home. And they've already tested it."

"For what? Many people have coolers."

"Not with blood in them," Luke said.

"No!"

"He's being arrested and held for conspiracy."

"It's bull!"

"I agree," Luke assured her. "But now instead of someone proving he's guilty, we're going to have to prove he's innocent."

* * *

"We have you dead to rights," Luke said quietly, sitting across the table again from Lily Connoly. "Jared Stone can't be lying since his DNA was discovered on your sex toys."

She stared at him, silent. She didn't rant.

She didn't reply.

"Mrs. Connoly—"

"So," she said at last, "you've proven that I had an affair—"

"Paid a man for his services," Luke said, grimacing.

She inhaled deeply, something very hard in her eyes as she looked at him. "So, proud of yourself? My husband has had medical problems. I love the man but have a few needs he can't fulfill. Human needs. I paid for them rather than disrupt our relationship. And for that, you've ruined our lives."

"No, ma'am. You ruined your lives—"

"With a human need?" she demanded coldly. "You sleep with that bitch of a partner of yours, and you'd deny a purely physical need to another human being? What a hypocrite!"

"You ruined yourself when you lied to us," Luke said.

"Well, sir, in truth, it was not a conversation I wished to have in front of my husband!" she snapped.

"We needed to know what you knew about Jared Stone. And when you denied even knowing him, well…" Luke let his sentence hang, staring at her sadly.

"So, now you've proven I slept with a man who happened to be a criminal. I didn't do anything criminal, and my solicitor will be here soon, and you will let me go."

"And you'll head home into the loving arms of your husband?" Luke asked politely.

"I'll get my things and spend the next days fighting for my belongings and my share of our goods," she said, "since you have totally destroyed a good marriage."

"I'm afraid it's a little more difficult than that. I believe you will be charged with being an accessory to murder," Luke told her.

"That's absurd!"

"No, not really. Because Jared Stone is going to testify that you contacted him through the same burner phone he used when he connected with the people who ordered him to bring a woman to a van so she might be killed and her organs taken for transplant."

"No!"

"Well, that's where it gets tricky again. We found your extra phones when we found your sex toys. And we've done traces on them, and you communicate with that number frequently. Of course, the number is no longer in service. It was a disposable phone, but you did talk to someone at the end of that number often. We have physical proof."

He was surprised at the way she seemed to freeze then. Strange. He hadn't thought her stupid, but she hadn't managed to toss the phones that just might be the nails on the lid of her legal coffin.

"My solicitor will get me out of here within a few hours," she said at last.

"I don't think it will be quite that easy. Now, if you wanted to tell us who was at the other end of that number—"

"You think I know?" she said.

"Oh, yes, I think you know much more than you are saying."

"What you think doesn't concern me in the least," she assured him. "Like I said, my solicitor will be here soon. And you will be sorry!"

Luke shrugged. "I don't think so. You can help yourself—"

"Worry about you. I intend to use the law against you and all your little friends from here and from America. You will pay!"

"I am not particularly worried. I think you'd have difficulty suing people for the fact that you paid for sex and it was discovered. And in that discovery, more was proven against you."

"What was proven against me?" she asked, looking especially vicious as she leaned closer to him.

"There's proof you called a number—many times. You called a number that went to a person who was ordering others to supply him—or her—with human beings to murder. That is being an accessory."

"Wait, wait, wait! That's ridiculous. The phones... the phones were planted by Flora!"

"Just like a man's DNA—oddly comingled with yours—was planted?" he asked her.

"I didn't give you my DNA."

"Your husband helped us. He gave up your toothbrush and a few other things," Luke told her.

"Get out," she told him.

"I'm sorry?"

"Get out. I'm not going to talk to you. What? Is American law so far behind? No more conversation without my solicitor."

"All right. Just one last thing. Someone in this group

was enchanted with the press referring to the murders as the revival of Burke and Hare. Suddenly, the corpses were positioned in beautiful poses, as if the killer wanted the world to know their organs were stolen. That they had been murdered for monetary gain. Now, if you look back, Hare walked away from the whole thing. He walked away by giving testimony against Burke. Now you have a chance here to be Hare. Tell us who is the brains behind the operation, and you just might get a far reduced sentence," Luke told her.

"Someone else might be the brains?" she snapped.

"Oh. So, I wasn't expecting that. Are you admitting to being the brains behind the situation?" Luke asked.

He thought she was going to spit at him.

She managed to contain herself. "I said nothing of the kind! Whatever brains are out there, they are most evidently far superior to yours. I am innocent. I will not say another word until my solicitor arrives!"

There was a tap against the one-way mirror.

Brendan Campbell wanted him out. And he knew he needed to get up and leave Mrs. Connoly to herself.

There was no reason to jeopardize the case against the woman in any way.

He met Campbell in the observation room. MacDuff was in the second interrogation room with the man who had attacked Jordan the night before.

"Sorry, but she has asked for her solicitor."

"I know. Sir, I know that woman is more involved than she'll admit."

"Aye, she is. But we have a legal system."

"Right. And in there…"

"The man's name is Abdiel Hassam. He was an Iranian national. He was against the government, and voiced his opposition too loudly. He managed to escape the country before he was caught. Got here with nothing in his pockets, fell, was taken to the hospital and had someone help him fill out papers for asylum. Soon after that, he was out on the street. He is a practicing Muslim and doesn't drink—something that was on his papers at the hospital. So when one of the orderlies offered to buy him a drink when he left the hospital, the man said no. Next thing he knew there was a hood over his head, and he was being threatened with torture and death. When MacDuff asked him why he didn't go to the police, he said it's because he was told he would die an even worse death and that the police were involved."

"I still don't believe it, and I don't believe Jordan was involved no matter what was in his house. He hasn't been in his own home, sir—he's been with us. And we've been more or less with one another since this began. He's being set up," Luke said.

"They set him up well," Campbell said. "There was no sign of a break-in at his house whatsoever."

"And are his prints on the cooler?" Luke asked. "I'll bet not. It was put there to make him appear guilty, so the police investigation would center on him. Nor do I believe anyone is transporting human organs in a cooler. They've found another place, and we discovered that Arthur's Isle had been abandoned. We started to figure that this time they may have found a place right on the Firth of Forth, which is easily accessible for those who need to receive the organs and those who are about to provide them. We need to investigate—"

"Luke, you know we can't just go house to house

and demand to know if they have a makeshift surgery within," Campbell reminded him.

"I'm aware of that. But we can start watching. And something else…"

He paused, angry with himself. With all of them, really.

"And what's that?" Campbell pressed.

"I can get Angela on it," Luke said. "We need a list of those coming into the UK and Edinburgh who are on donor lists around the world. Especially those with money."

"Discerning just who has the money to pay for a human organ might not be easy," Campbell warned.

"I'll give this one to Angela. At the very least, she can get us a list. If we find someone who is here, seeking a donor organ…"

"If we find them." Campbell shook his head. "Then what do we do—arrest them because we believe they're here for an illegal transplant?" he asked skeptically.

"We follow them," Luke said flatly. "Sir, if it's all right with you, I'd like to head back to the hospital. Join Carly and Daniel there. And with your blessing, I want to talk to Jordan if he's still there."

"He is—they want to keep him a second night for observation."

Luke nodded, going silent for a minute and listening to the hum of conversation going on between MacDuff and the man they had arrested the night before.

"I needed…help. Desperately," Abdiel Hassam was saying. He was truly wretched, sitting hunched over, his head low. "You don't understand. I can't go back."

"Well, you won't be returning too quickly from an English prison," MacDuff said. "But we can work with you. The woman you were setting up is alive. You never reached your destination. Aye, son, you are guilty of assault and attempted kidnapping. But help us more. Why were you accusing Jordan of being a part of the scheme?" MacDuff demanded.

Hassam groaned. "You ask over and over, and I can only give you the same answer. I was told the police were in on it. That a cop might just be the one to walk a girl out of the pub."

"But you didn't have a name?" MacDuff persisted.

"No."

"So, it wasn't necessarily the cop you knocked out, right?"

"No, no…"

Watching from the room, Luke turned to Campbell, feeling his anger grow. "Jordan was set up. Whoever is doing this knows Jordan is a cop, chosen specifically for this team. They knew he was local. He was targeted, Campbell, surely you can see that, sir."

"I can see it. But we have to prove it," Campbell said.

Luke nodded. His anger had grown to the point where he needed to leave. Because he wanted to burst into the interrogation room and shake Hassam until he admitted that what he had said was what he had heard— and it meant nothing.

But the cooler was found in Jordan's house. After he was knocked out and sent to the hospital. But there were several days before that when someone clever enough could have gotten into the home and set the man up.

Luke waved a hand in the air and said, "Okay, I'm out of here. You know how to find me."

He'd driven himself in and he strode out quickly.

Within a few minutes, he reached the hospital, parked

and showed his credentials so that he was given permission to get in to see Jordan.

Two guards stood outside the door, but they recognized Luke and nodded and allowed him access without any inquiry at all.

He had the feeling Police Scotland was not at all pleased with the events—or the accusations.

When he entered, Jordan was sitting up in the bed and staring at the television—which wasn't on. He turned to see Luke and he gave him a look of gratitude.

"Luke. Luke. This is absurd. I've been with the team. There was no time I could have been involved with any of this. I swear to you on the lives of my family—I am not involved in this!" he said desperately.

"Jordan, I believe you. Our entire team believes you. But Campbell is right—if we don't follow procedure to prove it, the whole of law enforcement here will come under suspicion. And the public won't have trust in us. These murderers have been using people right and left, they find the down-and-out, terrified people, and they play vicious games with the lives of those they target and encounter."

"Why me?" he whispered.

"Because you have a home here. Because they could break into it, because they could plant evidence," Luke told him.

"How do we prove I had nothing to do with it?" he asked.

"We find the puppet master." Luke lowered his voice. "We believe there is a hospital connection. Someone who perhaps called in sick. Someone who did something that made Dorothy Norman suspicious—and because of that, she had to be killed. And in a gruesome manner. That got rid of her possibly calling out someone involved, and it was a damned terrifying warning to any of those, like Hassam, who might disobey their demands."

"What about Lily Connoly?" he asked.

"I left the station when she demanded I don't talk to her anymore without her solicitor. We have enough on her association with Jared Stone to hold her in custody. I suppose with a wild card, she could be charged with other crimes in order to hold her longer. But she will make bail soon enough. We're still hoping she'll break. We know she knows something. Just what, we don't know. But we found her phones, and she's blaming them on Flora MacDonald."

"Flora is lucky she's alive," Jordan said quietly. "With her suspicions against that woman...she could have been a victim. But I doubt they would have wasted her organs."

"We're working at this from half a dozen angles, Jordan. Have faith, we will find the truth."

"Aye," Jordan said quietly. "Luke, thank you. You have given me faith."

Luke gave him a thumbs-up and headed out. He knew Carly would be speaking with Dr. Forbes again, so he caught the elevator to the doctor's floor.

Nurses and orderlies were moving about, carrying trays, going from room to room. He found himself watching them all, as if somehow he might see them wearing some sign that they were killers.

He headed to the nurses' station, glad to see the doctor's key nursing assistant, Selina Caine, was at the desk. She smiled when she saw him.

"Special Agent Kendrick," she said. "Your friends...

sorry, associates? Anyway, they are here. But you know that."

He nodded. "We're searching for any help we can get again," he said. "Because I understand the employees here were not so fond of her, but—"

"Dorothy," she said. "So, so, terrible. She was hard, truly hard, but she was good—she just expected nothing less from those beneath her. We wanted to smack her now and then, but never, never something like this…so, so… Oh, Lord above us, what was done to her. The news is saying that she was decapitated. But they say, too, that her body was found, and her organs hadn't been removed. Do we even know… Oh. You think that one of us might have done something so horrible."

Luke shook his head. Best not to let anyone here know that yes, someone might well be involved and whether that someone had done the chopping or not was something not known as of yet.

"No, please don't worry on that account. We're just trying to discern if anyone here has thought of anything else," Luke assured her.

"Well, I do believe Carly has spoken with several people. And the young fellow she's with…Daniel. He also spoke with several people."

"You never know," Luke said. "Someone here could remember a patient not at the top of the list…or someone who came through here or even someone working on another floor who happened to show up here now and then. At any rate, I was just going to meet up with Carly and Daniel."

"They're in Dr. Forbes's office. I can take you—"

"I know where it is—I just wanted to check in and see if it was all right."

"Absolutely," she assured him.

He smiled and turned to make his way toward the doctor's office. As he did so, he almost ran straight into an orderly. By instinct, he studied the man. Late twenties, early thirties. Strong enough to push a heavy bed around, lift a patient if necessary…reddish-blond hair cut short, green eyes, good smile as he apologized for their near collision.

"My fault," Luke assured him.

As he walked to the office, he noticed three more of the men working. All were about the same age, maybe one in his twenties.

All appeared to spend time in a gym. Strong enough…

For what, exactly?

Capturing people, getting them into a van. Carrying corpses around. Lighter corpses…with their organs removed. Medical equipment… All that needed to be transported from an island to a boat and onto an island again.

Most of the nurses were women. A few were men. And the mole in the hospital could be either. Because someone not at the hospital could be doing the heavy lifting.

He walked into the office and found Carly and Daniel deep in conversation seated in chairs before the empty desk.

"Luke!" Carly said. "Anything more—"

"I saw Jordan, and I'm more convinced than ever he was set up. We must figure out a way to prove it."

"What about Lily Connoly and the man, Abdiel?" Carly asked.

"Abdiel, as you can imagine, was threatened with torture and death. He believes this person has the power to see to it that he's forced back to Iran where he would also be tortured and killed. And as for Lily Connoly... I left her when she called for her solicitor. But I do think she's far more involved than she will admit. They found the phones. They're doing their best trying to trace numbers and find out who is purchasing the burners. That's where I am. Anything here?" he asked.

"We talked to people," Carly said.

"So I heard. Anything?"

Daniel laughed. "Everything. They all admitted to having serious problems with Dorothy Norman. But not to the point of killing her. They think what happened to her was horrible. They just wanted to see her disappear—not die. But..."

"But," Carly continued, "there was an orderly. I saw him when I was here the first time, but I didn't give him—or anyone, really, at that time—serious consideration."

"And what about this orderly?" Luke persisted.

"He..." Carly began, and she looked at Daniel, trying to express her feeling on the matter. "He just seemed... overly upset."

"Just like Lily? 'Thou doth protest too much, methinks'?" Luke asked.

"Right. Except..." Daniel murmured.

"He's good. He had real tears in his eyes. He said she was hard as nails, but he'd learned beneath her as he might not have learned from anyone who wasn't as strict and determined."

"Has he not shown up for any of his shifts?" Luke asked.

"Yeah, we had it checked out," Daniel said.

"And?"

"He was off the day Dorothy Norman was killed," Carly said. "His name is Rusty Teller. He's thirty-five, a native of the Isle of Man. We want to have him followed."

At that moment, Dr. Forbes walked into the room. "You're here," he said. "Thank God! I have news for you. I'm sorry… I was in surgery. But right before I went in, I got a call from one of our security guards and…and he was back! He was seen in front of the hospital in a dark sedan watching the place, as if looking for someone or waiting for someone!"

"He—who?" Carly asked.

"Gleason! Harold Gleason. Head to security, the security guard is Winston Culpepper, and he's good. He knew I didn't ever want to see the man at this hospital again, and he called me as soon as he saw him. But even as he did so, the man drove away. If anyone around here has the coldness and…psychopathic personality strong enough to mastermind something like this, I would say that it is Harold Gleason!"

"There's been a bulletin out on the man pretending to be Gleason," Luke said.

"It all just happened—apparently he drove away before anything could be done, noticed he might have been seen and took off," Forbes said.

Luke stood. "Did security say which way he drove?"

"East."

Luke was already out the door.

Eastward. Possibly toward a line of rich homes along the Firth of Forth, right where logic indicated human beings and medical equipment might have been transported from the abandoned Arthur's Isle.

The man was surely involved.

Or was he? Was it just too obvious?

Whoever he was, he was guilty of stealing a dead man's ID.

And maybe what was too obvious was just so because it was the truth.

"Luke!"

He'd stepped into an elevator. He realized Carly was hurrying after him.

"Remember me?" Carly asked, hurrying in.

He started to hit the button to get them to the ground level but Carly stopped him.

"Daniel will be coming ASAP," she said. "He was getting more information on the car."

"Right. I'm sorry," he said. But he felt a surge of anger flow from him. They were too late; they'd never find the man. He had driven far from the hospital by now. It didn't matter. They were too late from the time Forbes rushed into the room to tell them the man had been seen.

"Luke, chill, I know you're frustrated that we find out about things too late," Carly said.

Luke shook his head. "I just… I don't understand. How has this man been here—and not been seen by anyone in law enforcement?" he asked.

"Luke, think about it. This may be his first excursion out. Maybe he has been inside somewhere all this time," Carly suggested. She stared at him, making him realize his comment might have sounded demeaning regarding the very people upon whom they were so dependent, and who were working as hard as they were.

"Wow. I'm sorry, and you're right," Luke said. "Of course. This so-called Harold Gleason has been out of sight, ordering others to do his bidding. He was most probably on the island. And when it was abandoned, he went to the new *surgery* they were creating. But..."

He broke off. Someone not on their team was now with them.

"What?" Carly asked. She was facing him so she hadn't realized that while they were holding the elevator for Daniel, a nurse had walked onto it.

She spun around. "Milly!" she said. "How are you?"

"Well, you know, moving along," the young woman said. "And you—you're back!"

"Always checking on what's going on," she murmured.

Daniel came in along with the nurse. "Sorry!" he told the others, and he smiled at Milly. "I'm holding everyone up. Milly and I were just talking about Dorothy. She didn't have any family, so the staff is going to get together to arrange a service and burial for her."

Milly nodded. "I don't know. We all complained and whined about her and even joked that maybe she'd trip on a rock and fall and die. And then this...but she taught us all. She taught us all so much. Anyway... Anything on what happened? Whoever did such a terrible, terrible thing?" she asked anxiously.

Luke shrugged. "Ongoing investigation," he told her.

"Of course, of course," Milly said.

They'd reached the ground floor. She gave them a wave and walked on back toward the cafeteria.

"We will never catch up with this person—a car could have gone anywhere by now. We need more information on the car," he said. "And it was in front. Maybe there's video surveillance. Let's head to security."

Carly and Daniel kept in step with him as he followed the signs that led to the security room.

It wouldn't be difficult to find the officer who had called Dr. Forbes. There were only two men in the room.

Luke instantly asked about the car and if there was footage of the car being directly in front of the hospital.

"If we had just seen it in time..." the one man said.

"The car was sitting there, cars do just sit there. If they begin to block others, we go out to move them. But we didn't get a good look at the man inside at first. In fact, Carl was about to go out and tell them they had to move—"

"And that's when we saw his face. But by then he was already moving, and I called Dr. Forbes—"

"But not the police," Luke murmured.

"Well, he'd moved, and we knew Dr. Forbes was the man who..." Carl began.

"Didn't want him around," his coworker said. "We don't get everything the men and women at Police Scotland get daily."

"And it was weird. I thought it was him when I started out to tell him to move," Carl said. "Then he ducked his head and looked up, and I wasn't certain anymore."

"Do you have footage?" Luke asked.

"We do!"

Carl hurried behind a computer. He was good with it thankfully. The car came into view. It was a dark green sedan with a parking insignia stuck to the front window.

"Carl, zoom in on that insignia, please."

The man did so.

"Do you know what that is for?" Carly asked him.

"I do. It's used by an exclusive community of the Firth of Forth," Carl said. "An enclave with houses on the water and very expensive. I think it holds just short of fifty homes in the area."

"Great. Thank you. Now the face."

Again, Carl played with the video.

"Hmm, I guess I caused a massive problem for nothing. I thought it just might be the same man who came in here as Harold Gleason, but now it doesn't look like him so much; it's a younger man. A better looking guy, good for him."

Carly inhaled sharply at Luke's side.

He turned to look at her.

"I don't know if that's the man who changed his appearance when he came here as Harold Gleason or not, but…"

"But?" Luke asked.

She turned to him. "I could swear that he is the man who was sitting next to me at the bar at Kevin's last night."

Fifteen

They left the hospital and headed back to the house, once again trying to put all the pieces they had together.

First, they knew the real Harold Gleason had died. But Angela had discovered that after a deep dig, so if Dr. Forbes had decided there was no way he was hiring such an aggressive and obnoxious individual, it might not have been discovered when his job application was checked. He had to be traveling with an American passport that was a damned good forgery.

Whoever he was, he was changing his appearance at will. So...

Had she met him at the bar the night before? Had she been his personal target? If she hadn't gone racing after Jordan, might he have tried to lure her out to the darkness?

She sat at the table with Daniel and Luke as they tried to determine their next moves.

"We do have people looking for the car," Daniel said.

"Right. And thanks to the security tape, we know the car—if not the man in it—belongs in a certain enclosed community," Luke commented.

"Should we—" Daniel began.

"Go door to door and ask people if they own the car?" Carly queried. "Is that within the law?"

"Just knocking on a door and asking a question is," Daniel said.

"But if the car isn't visible, we'd need a warrant to ask what kind of vehicle was being kept in a garage," Luke said. "And, of course, these people will lie."

"And we're getting nowhere with the phones we've taken from the Burke and Hare ground crew, right?" Daniel asked.

"The only real connection we have there is Lily Connoly. And while Campbell and MacDuff have managed to keep her in custody, she does have a solicitor. She's now claiming that she merely found a number for a man who would supply connections for sex workers," Luke said. "We have no proof she was corresponding with someone who is chopping people up."

"It's the world over," Daniel commented dryly. "The technological age allows us so much, great possibilities on facial recognition, DNA, fingerprints. And then when you have a burner phone, you're just at a dead end."

"They're still trying to determine where all the burner phones were purchased," Luke said. He looked at Carly and said, "I think I may take another go at Lily Connoly, even with her solicitor present. There has to be a way to crack her. And something Keith MacDonald said may help me with that. Lily is mean, stubborn, deceitful and so much more. But she also has pride and a sense of superiority. I may work on that."

"All right," Carly said. "And I may work on this Rusty Teller person and try to use some of the tech Daniel is talking about."

"No moves without telling me what is going on," Luke warned her. "Lily knows something—we must find out what it is. I'll be at the station."

Daniel nodded. "I'll go with—"

"No, it's daytime and I'm heading straight into the station. MacDuff and Campbell are there, stay with Carly."

Carly laughed softly. "Luke, we're in a house that has the most sensitive alarms known to man."

"Right. But you won't stay here—I know you. So, the two of you stick together," he said.

She had her phone out even as she watched him go. Daniel watched her in turn as she called Angela and told her about the orderly, Rusty Teller.

"I saw him, along with other people, the first time I went to the hospital. But when we talked to him today about Dorothy Norman, I just thought his supposed emotion was over the top. We can't go by death threats. Apparently, people working with her respected her for what she did, but they also hated her."

"All right. Rusty Teller. On it. We're still trying to figure out who might be playing the role of Harold Gleason," Angela told her.

"Well, he's a changeling, for one," Carly said. "They thought he was in a car in front of the hospital today, but when security went out to talk to him, he appeared to be someone else. Angela, I'm going to get the security tape to you. Do you think—"

"I can try with no problem," Angela assured her.

Daniel, of course, was listening to the conversation.

"I'm calling security at the hospital," he said. "We will get that tape immediately, and you can get it to Angela."

"We should have it momentarily," Carly told her.

She went on to tell Angela the latest on Lily Connoly and also that Jordan was now being held because evidence had been found in his Edinburgh home.

"But we don't believe it for a second. He's been here—with us—when certain things regarding this case were happening," Carly told her.

"But this Burke and Hare case has many, many players," Angela reminded her.

"True. But I trust my instinct, Angela. Gut feelings. Can they be wrong? Yes, but they are usually right. Anyway, at this moment, Luke is trying to find out what more he can get from Lily Connoly. Daniel and I are here, at our headquarters house, trying to put some pieces together."

When she ended the call, she looked at Daniel.

He looked back at her. "Lily Connoly, Rusty Teller, the people who were…"

"His pawns?"

"Aye. Take Abdiel. I think, for him, the concept of being forced back into a situation where he might be endlessly tortured was the catalyst. Terror for her children drove Marjory Alden. Jared Stone is a bit of a different story, but according to him, he doesn't know more. He gave us Lily, but the way he is in interrogation… He was in it to get paid. He doesn't have a great sense of empathy for others, but now in order to save his own skin, I think he'd give someone up if he knew how. He was just a procurer. We keep stopping the pawns in the game, but the king and queen are still on the board," Daniel said.

"Luke is hoping he can trip up Lily Connoly," Carly said.

"I can't just sit here," Daniel murmured. "There must be…something we can do, somewhere we can go."

"I was at that exhibit a few days back, studying the skeleton of William Burke. Do you want to see what's going on over there?" Carly suggested. "That will take us for a walk through the Royal Mile and..."

"The streets behind St. Giles' after, or maybe a stroll through the cemetery, or...why not dinner at Kevin's?" Daniel suggested. "And maybe by then, something will break. And maybe we'll find Keith MacDonald, and he'll have made a discovery behind a few doors we can't just shift through."

"There's a plan for you!" Carly said. "Let's do it!"

They left the house and walked down the Royal Mile. Even now, the streets were busy with people. It was technically early for dinnertime, but it seemed that the many restaurants were full and the day was active and bright.

They reached the exhibit, and Carly found her way back to the display that featured the skeleton of William Burke.

"How fitting!" Daniel said. "He killed people for dissection. He was killed—and dissected. But..."

"I think I know what you're talking about," Carly told him. "According to Keith, and we have no reason to doubt him, Hare was the real aggressor. I mean, Burke might have been, hmm, needy enough to think that murder was okay. After they sold the corpse of the fellow who died of natural causes...apparently the next victim was ill, and they were afraid his illness would spread, possibly ruin their business as a guesthouse. Since the fellow had one foot in the grave, that probably didn't take much. I don't know. Maybe Burke really was the cold-hearted bastard who was just capable of being a fine entertainer when he chose, but he was inwardly devious."

"What about Hare?" Daniel asked.

"Well," Carly said. "Hare was, again according to Keith, a rough and rude idiot who might have done the most horrible things. Yet, he walked away free."

"Because of his testimony," Daniel said.

"Kind of appalling, but from what I learned as a kid, the law wanted someone to pay and that was one way to at least get one of them. Hare's life was ruined—" Carly said.

"But he had a life."

"True. And apparently, Dr. Knox's life was ruined, too—" Carly began.

"And the wives had to know about it! But they left court with the verdict of *not proven*, which doesn't mean not guilty or guilty, just that they couldn't prove it. It just all seems so very, very wrong."

"Well, killing people is wrong. I wonder if what you're saying is what Luke is using with Lily Connoly. He may be trying to convince her that someone will pay while someone else walks away," Carly murmured thoughtfully. "Or…"

"Or? She is stubborn and proud, so proud. Maybe he's going to use that. Maybe. All right, we've stared at bones long enough. Dinner?" Daniel asked.

"Kevin's? It's a plan."

"And…though I really do like you a lot, I think you should sit by yourself."

"Hey! I was about to say the same thing!" Carly assured him.

"A plan in action," Daniel said, smiling.

"I'll let Luke know. I won't call him as he may be in

with Lily Connoly. I'll give MacDuff a heads-up of where we're going to be."

She did so. And the two of them headed for Kevin's for dinner.

Arriving at the police station, Luke was let in to a pleasant surprise. Mason Carter and Della Hamilton had finished working in France.

They had just arrived in Scotland and made it to the station before he had headed in to see Lily. They met with him, MacDuff and Campbell in the observation room.

They were down a man, Jordan Dowell, and getting Jordan out of his situation had been added to the plate. But now there were two Krewe members with them. Mason was acting field supervisor for the Blackbird division of the Krewe of Hunters, and Della was his second-in-command. Mason was a man of Luke's own height, cutting a strong presence just by standing there. Della, at his side, was a brilliant agent, trained to be powerful in movement and with her mind.

Luke explained quickly where they'd gotten that morning. Angela was working on digging out facts regarding suspicious people, while Daniel and Carly were working to put the puzzle pieces together.

"And you're going to speak with Mrs. Connoly again. Do you think you can get something out of her?" Mason asked.

"I think I know how to play her," Luke said flatly. "She's proud. She's an elitist, and she truly thinks herself above all others. She's a hell of an actress, except we've blown through her act already. So…local police are working on finding the car that may or may not

have been driven by our obnoxious, dead doctor imper-
sonator. They found a parking emblem on the car, and
they're patrolling the area looking for it."

"Maybe we would be most useful looking for the
surgery you believe is now in one of those houses,"
Della told Mason.

"If you're good here, we'll get on that," Mason told
Luke. "We'll catch you up on the lingering events in
France from our last case later."

"If we can find that surgery, we can cut it down. Although when they're angered, these people ensure very
bad things happen that aren't part of the money-making
plan," Luke said. "Police Scotland is on it, but they can't
just burst in on houses."

"A waiting game," Mason said.

Luke nodded. "And there were two other children
found with Marjory's kids. We can't find their parents.
I can't help but think their parents might have been in
medicine and they're prisoners, too. Or worse if they
might have discovered that the kids were no longer
being held. Campbell has seen that they are cared for
and will be until… Well, here's hoping the parents are
found."

"We know about the decapitation of the nurse,"
Mason assured him. "And about the kids. Jackson has
kept us up to date, of course. For now, we'll get moving. And we'll let you do the same."

They headed out.

Luke looked into the observation room where Lily
Connoly had been brought.

Lily Connoly had no problem speaking with Luke, as
long as her solicitor, Adam McCormick, was at her side.

The man was dignified to an extreme. He warned

Lily not to answer questions without consulting with him first. Then Lily snapped she had hired him, she'd tell him when he should speak. Luke sat back and let them hash it out. McCormick was trying to be calm and dignified; Lily was not giving a rip.

But eventually, they both fell silent and looked at him.

"I just want to give you every opportunity to help us in order to help yourself," Luke said.

Lily groaned. "We've talked and talked. I've told you I'm innocent."

"Yes, but you also told us you were innocent of having an affair. Sorry, of hiring a man just for sex. And that proved not to be true at all. We know you spoke with the same people—" Luke began.

"Proves nothing," McCormick assured him.

"I've already explained that. You ruined my life and my marriage. Yes, I hired the gigolo," Lily said. "And that's it!"

"But where did you get the number that you were calling?" Luke asked.

She stared at him. Then McCormick whispered to her, and she seemed to dismiss his words of warning, whatever he was saying.

She smiled sweetly at Luke. "Off a bathroom wall," she said.

"What bathroom wall?" Luke asked.

She let out a groan and waved her hand in the air. "What bathroom wall? Hmm. Let me think. I'm afraid that it was a long time ago. I don't remember."

"And you think a jury will believe that?" Luke asked.

"A jury?" McCormick said. "I'm telling you, when we speak with a judge, we will have Lily quickly out of here. These charges of conspiracy to commit murder are ridiculous. What you have done here is horrible. You're crucifying a woman because she had sexual needs and never wanted to hurt a husband who couldn't fulfill them, and so she hired a lover. I will see to it that she will not be railroaded!"

"I'm sorry. She has been charged, I'm afraid," Luke said.

"I will have her out shortly!" McCormick assured Luke.

Luke felt his phone vibrating in his pocket. He excused himself and looked at it. He'd received a group text from Angela, and it was a long one.

At Carly's request, she had traced the name Rusty Teller and through his picture on file with the hospital, she was able to put him through facial recognition.

Rusty Teller was *not* Rusty Teller. He was Vince Randolph, born and raised in Arkansas, arrested for armed robbery, sentenced to five years and part of an escape just two years into his sentence.

He then seemed to disappear from the face of the earth.

But that wasn't exactly the surprise part.

The surprise was that he was a second cousin to one Lillian Jefferson *Connoly*, who had wed Ewan Connoly in the United States. Like Vince Randolph, Lily had been born in Arkansas, in the same town as her cousin Vince, and while he had been much younger, she had known him and his family well before she had left America for Scotland.

Luke kept his head lowered, thinking with amusement that Lily must have very carefully cultivated her Scottish accent.

He kept reading.

Police Scotland would be picking him up. At the very least he was guilty of having entered the country under an assumed name.

He looked up at her. "How's your family, Lily?" he asked.

"My family?" She shook her head. "My husband has turned his back on me. When my son in the US finds out about this, he'll turn his back on me, too."

"I didn't mean them," Luke said. "What about the rest of them?"

"I don't know what you're talking about."

"Your family. The one you were born into—back in Arkansas."

She let out a long sigh. "Christmas cards, birthday cards... I have been gone from the United States a long, long time. I am a citizen of the United Kingdom."

"Well, have you seen your cousin?"

Her expression changed almost instantly. He had her.

But she held silent for a minute and feigned ignorance again. "I don't know what you're talking about," she told him.

"Ah, come on! Blood is always thicker than water," Luke said.

"I don't know what you're talking about!"

"Oh, no? Really? You know nothing about a man calling himself Rusty Teller and working at the hospital as an orderly?"

He could see it. She could act—but she also had a tell. Her facial expression changed.

"I do not know a man named Rusty Teller."

"Well, I think that you do. But maybe you're thinking of him as Vince Randolph."

"Still don't know what you're talking about," Lily told him.

"Oh, Mrs. Connoly, please," Luke said, shaking his head. "Suddenly, you don't know anything about your family back in Arkansas?"

She sat in silence for a minute. McCormick leaned over to whisper to her, and she pushed him away.

Luke let out a long breath. "I am so glad your solicitor is with you, Mrs. Connoly. Because there are things that we now know. You have been in contact with someone that Jared Stone was also in contact with. In fact, the person who told Jared Stone when to get a man or woman inebriated and out to the street so a van could come by and sweep up the victim for the purpose of murder. You got that number off a bathroom wall. Of course. Odd that it's the same number that calls for murder. Hmm. And now you have a relative from your hometown who is working here under an assumed name. But you know nothing about it?"

McCormick whispered to her again. She might not want to talk to Luke without her solicitor, but she didn't seem to want to listen to McCormick, either.

"What is he doing?" she asked at last. "I heard he was coming from America and then I heard nothing more."

"I don't think that's true," Luke said. He leaned closer to her. "I think he came here especially because you asked him to come. And I think he took that job as an orderly at the hospital specifically because you asked him to do so. And he reported to you from the hospital."

"Don't answer that," McCormick warned her.

Lily ignored him, staring at Luke with narrowed eyes.

"Vince was a horrid little child. He did not come here as an adult because of me in any way, shape or form. I did not know he was at the hospital—I didn't even know he was in the country—you know, I mean, I heard he was coming, but…um…" Lily told him, shrugging as if things just happened.

"Such a strange coincidence!" Luke said.

She shrugged. "Prove otherwise."

"Well, here's the thing. The police are picking him up right now. There's going to be a chance for one person, the one person who tells the truth about the other. Now, do I think your second cousin is the brains behind any of this? No. But then again… I don't think he's as cool under fire as you are, Lily. And I think he'll tell us all kinds of things. He is a strong enough looking young fellow, and maybe good at his job. And he's probably not bad with playing out a ruse—like the others working in the hospital, he whined about Dorothy Norman. And like the others, he was horribly upset about the way she died. He cried real tears. He hadn't liked her, but he'd have never, never wanted anything so brutal and heinous to have happened to her."

McCormick tried to speak to her again. Lily stretched out her arms, yawning.

"You are boring me. And if that boy comes out with anything against me, it's a lie."

"Why do you say that everyone else lies—and then it's proven that their lies are the truth?" Luke asked her.

"You haven't proved—"

"Oh, but we have, Lily!" Luke said. "I'm trying to help you here. I don't think you're the brains, the great manipulator, the murderer himself. I think you're a pawn, being used—"

"No one uses me!" she snapped.

"No one ever wants to believe or accept that they're

being used," Luke interrupted. "But we know a man claiming to be Harold Gleason—that's the name of a man who was an esteemed surgeon but died several years ago—is here, in Scotland. We know he used the dead man's name and pedigree when he applied for a job at the hospital. But despite those credentials, he was turned down for a job at the hospital because he had a true god complex. Now, we believe he's turned his fury against the establishment, and that spurned him into a murder-for-money scheme. Of course, he doesn't need to worry about the health of his donors since he kills them for whichever organ he needs, and he sells those organs on the black market. We think your cousin keeps you informed about events at the hospital, and you then inform your master."

"I answer to no master!" Lily snapped.

"Mrs. Connoly!" McCormick snapped.

"Don't you tell me what to do again!" she shouted to McCormick.

McCormick threw up his hands.

"I…quit," he said. "Mrs. Connoly, I seriously advise you to shut up and get a new counsel and don't talk anymore until you do!"

He stood and a guard opened the door for him and he walked out.

Luke stared at Lily.

He started to laugh and he leaned toward her again. "Do you know what I think?"

"Not really."

"Well, I'm going to let you know anyway. You want to think you're the power behind everything. And while you don't carry out any murders yourself, you want to believe you're the orchestra's conductor behind everything that happens. You want to think that, but you are not the brains behind the operation. You, like the others, follow the orders of the master."

"I follow no master!" she screamed, rising, slamming her hands down on the table. "I answer to no man, ever, not now, not ever! I am the brains!"

"No," he told her. "You were the money to get it off the ground. Now you're just a pathetic peon in a grand scheme that intends to leave you in the dust. You could do some good for yourself and give me the name of the puppet master, or…"

She began to backpedal quickly.

"I'm not the brains. I'm not the brains. I'm just too smart to blindly follow anyone else, and I didn't do a damned thing, and you will pay!"

Luke's phone buzzed again, and he sat back and looked at it.

He grinned at Lily Connoly.

"Well, well…cousin Vince is in the house! We're going to need to find out just what he can tell us. Are you the puppet or the puppet master? Somehow, I think we're about to find out!"

Sixteen

"Do you think Kevin could be involved in all of this?" Daniel asked as they walked.

"I sure don't want to," Carly said. She was looking at her phone; it had just buzzed again.

"They've picked up the orderly, Rusty Teller, aka Vince Randolph," she said. "That will give Luke plenty of ammunition against Lily Connolly."

"He will trip her up," Daniel said. "I just wish…"

"You're worried about Jordan."

"I am."

"We know that he's innocent," Carly assured him. "Hmm…"

"Hmm what?" Daniel asked.

"I was thinking. I mean, our Burke and Hare seemed to be able to bribe or threaten anyone. But I was also thinking our orderly might just be the one who made a point of setting Jordan up. But I don't know if he ever saw Jordan."

"Doesn't matter. Enough people knew about all of us," Daniel reminded her. "Any of us might have been the target for a setup. But Jordan lives here, has a home here, and that was the way to go. I really don't think that any law enforcement is involved. It was a way to throw a wrench into the efforts to stop it all."

"I think you're right."

They were nearing Kevin's.

"Get away from me!" Carly said, teasing yet serious. They didn't need to be seen together. While there were those who might recognize one of them, there were those who might not. And if anyone was seeking organs that night, the plan was always to work on one person.

So far.

But it seemed best.

"Yuck, yeah, get away from me!" Daniel replied.

They were both grinning as she walked ahead of him and entered Kevin's first.

There were a few empty stools dead center at the bar, and she noted there were a few more empty seats just around to the left side. Daniel would take one of them when he entered.

Kevin saw her. He wasn't surprised; once again, he played it as the friendly bartender and the pub owner who was determined to make all feel welcomed.

"Ah, so, I'm creating something that looks like whiskey but is not," he said, grinning as if they shared a great joke.

"I so appreciate you, Kevin!" she told him.

"No," he said very seriously. "We appreciate you."

He disappeared to create her drink. A minute later, Daniel came in and took the stool she had noted to the left.

There were people filling the tables. Couples, a few families and one lone man. Around to the right at the bar, there was a group that consisted of three young women and two young men who were apparently college students. She could hear them talking about a certain professor.

The seats by Daniel were taken first. Three young women had come in together. He offered to move so they could sit together.

They didn't want to bother him so one took the stool to his right while two took the stools to his left, laughing and chatting and drawing him in.

She lowered her head and grinned. Daniel could be very charming.

She felt a strange sensation at her back and realized Keith MacDonald was behind her again. His spirit took the stool next to her.

"I don't like this," he said.

Carly took her phone out and put her earbuds in so that she could pretend to talk on the phone.

"Keith, what don't you like?"

"This place."

"It seems a fine pub, Keith. And Kevin and Catherine have been helpful in ways they didn't need to be."

He shook his head, and then shrugged. "Last night, someone planned that setup. I think the fellow arrested after he had the knife to the woman's throat was intended to be sacrificed so that Jordan could be accused, and the public could make an outcry against the police. First, they were using Filigree, and now they are using this place."

Carly hesitated and said honestly, "Keith, that's what we're doing. We need to draw these people out. One of their van drivers wound up dead, but there's another. Maybe more. But anytime they do attack one of us, at least someone is saved."

Keith turned to look at her. "I don't want ye to be joining me too soon!" he told her.

She smiled, "I swear, I'm careful, I have great people behind me. I have you, Keith, and that makes me tremendously lucky and gives me an advantage others could never have."

"I can do so little!" he said.

She shook her head. "No, you have already done so much."

He turned suddenly and slid off the stool. She focused her attention to her phone, realizing that he had left because someone else had come in, and that person was going to take the seat.

"Ah, great, I am a lucky man!"

The man who slid onto the stool was the same man she had met the night before. The handsome man she thought to be in his early thirties, strong jaw, and quick and charming smile.

The same man who bore a resemblance to the person first suspected to have been the fake Harold Gleason.

But then different as the security guard approached him...

Much like the man sitting next to me again.

Possibly either the "Burke" or "Hare" pulling the strings on the operation.

"Hey!" she said.

"It's me, Robbie. Do you remember me?" he asked her.

"I do, of course. And you're alone tonight. Where's your friend?"

"Ah, me mate, Cullen, he had to work tonight. And what about you?"

"Oh, I am on my own. I don't think my friends are

going to make it, but...I do so love this place. They suggested it, of course—"

"But then you ran out so quickly," he said, eyes light and teasing. "I thought that...well, hmm. I'm on my own, you're on your own. I think fate intended this evening."

She smiled flirtatiously. "Fate. Maybe. So..."

"May I start by buying you a drink?" he asked.

"Well, that would be lovely. But I think I should finish this one first."

He laughed. "All right—but no running out on me!"

"I won't run out," she promised. "Except..."

"I'll not leave you alone here. I'll see that you get back to your lodgings safely, oh, aye!"

"That's very kind of you."

"Well, not to be too forward, but I was hoping we might get to know one another."

"Okay," Carly said, and turned in her chair, drink in hand, sipping through her straw as she watched him. "I get to start. What do you do for a living?" she asked him.

"I'm in the moving business," he told her. "Alas—mov*ing*. Not mov*ie*."

Carly laughed. "A legitimate business!" she assured him.

Is it? Tongue in cheek, he might well be talking about moving body parts from one human being to another.

She decided to answer in kind when it got to her. And it did. Swiftly.

"And what do you do, Miss Carly...MacDonald it was, eh?"

"MacDonald, yes, Scottish grandparents," she explained truthfully. Then she smiled. "Travel and research," she told him. "Reports…helping others find out what goes on in various places."

"Ah! And Edinburgh?"

"One of the most fantastic cities in the world, in my mind," she told him.

"And so it is!" he agreed. "Are you ready for that second drink yet?"

"Uh, yes, thank you. I believe I am."

He motioned to Kevin and ordered a whiskey for himself and said, "Another of whatever the young lady is drinking, too, please."

"Coming right up!" Kevin assured him. "I make a special drink for the lovely American, a bit of a mix of alcohols," Kevin said, lying easily.

"How long will you be here?" he asked her.

"My timeline is open-ended at the moment," Carly told him. "And you—this is your home?"

"It is for now," he told her, shrugging. "As long as business lasts here, as long as it works…and then, of course, if it doesn't, I will move on."

"Well, hmm. Would you consider moving anywhere?"

"Anywhere where my work—works," he assured her.

As long as you're able to procure bodies for their parts?

"*So*, we're both here for a bit at the least," she told him. "What do you do with your free time?"

"Ah, there is a great deal to do here, and so much that is very close. How much have you gotten to see?"

She was able to put a little truth in the conversation. "I love the city and I've been here several times."

"MacDonald is a good clan name," he assured her. "Family?"

"Yes."

"Any still here?"

"Not that I know about. My grandparents on my dad's side immigrated to the States about eighty years ago, so…"

"No distant cousins?"

"Not that I know about."

"So, you are all on your own and I can fix that!" he told her, grinning. "That is, if you're up to getting to know me."

"I say that we are making a start on that," she told him. "Hmm. Movies. It may not be your business, but do you like movies?"

"Depends on the movies, but if you'd like to see a movie, I would love the movies!"

She grinned. "Maybe. Then…museums! I love museums. And, of course, there is a fabulous exhibit going on right now by the castle. There's always something. Hmm…"

"Naturally, you've done the castle."

"I have. But I'm always willing to go back!"

"There is something new playing. I think it's an alien movie. Maybe an alien/horror movie. I'm not sure that's a first date kind of a thing, unless you love horror movies and strange…"

"Strange?"

He shrugged. "That it's opening now. Many people feel there is too much real-life horror going on right now. And you do, of course, need to be careful. Not tonight because I will see you safely to your lodging." He frowned suddenly. "Are you staying with your friends?"

"Oh, no," she lied. "I'm in a little bed-and-breakfast. And I must admit, I'm awfully glad that you're here tonight. It's not so far that one can't walk easily, but I might have been afraid to walk it alone. But with you helping me… Well, I'm quite lucky."

She realized Keith MacDonald's ghost was at the end of the bar, between her and Daniel.

Then, suddenly, he was gone.

She didn't know why.

But Daniel was still there having a wonderful time, or so it appeared as he continued to flirt with the three girls who had come in.

Of course, if she were to leave with this man, he would leave them and follow. No matter how much fun he was probably really having.

Kevin returned with fresh drinks.

"Okay, favorite sport!" Carly asked.

"That's easy. Soccer. You?"

She laughed. "Football—American football. Then again, I like tennis a lot, too."

They continued to laugh, talk, say the things that people say when they are getting to know one another.

Then they were flirting, seeking something more.

What if I'm wrong? What if he just drives a moving truck around the city and is simply happy to make the acquaintance of a young woman and flirt and have fun, truly determined to see me safely home?

But she couldn't forget the security footage. The hospital security officer was convinced at first that he had been the man calling himself Harold Gleason.

Footage that had seemed to show one man, and then another. A change that had even seemed to take years away. In a flash, just lowering his face, touching his face…

No matter; there had been something in the footage that had spoken of this man.

Could he be the one slicing up one person to sell the greatest gift, that of life, to others?

"Music!" he said.

And she played the game, flirting away, wondering if she was right...

Or wasting the evening with a friendly man who was determined to charm her?

She wouldn't know until it was time to leave, until they took the dark path that brought them behind Greyfriars Kirkyard and came to the area by the weathered old stone walls of Edinburgh where it seemed the body-collecting vans were soon to arrive.

It wouldn't be long...

He ordered them both a third drink.

And she kept laughing with him, not at all intoxicated but certainly appearing to be in the midst of a very nice buzz.

Campbell and MacDuff were both in the observation room when Luke entered the second interrogation room where "Rusty Teller," in truth Vince Randolph, had been brought.

The man was simply sitting there, staunchly silent, staring straight ahead.

"You!" he spat out, seeing Luke. "What the bloody hell is this?"

"I'm quite sure you were informed why you are being arrested," Luke told him. "I'm sorry, but it is illegal to enter the country under false pretenses."

"What false pretenses? I'm an orderly. A good one."

"But your name is Vince Randolph. You came in under a phony passport. And then there's another real crime."

"What's that?"

"We can start with you trying to feign that Scottish accent when you spent your life in small-town Arkansas."

The man looked down. He exhaled and spoke entreatingly as he looked at Luke again.

"Okay. I needed a move. I screwed up my younger life—" he said, dropping the accent.

"Not to mention breaking out of prison in the United States. I don't know if you face charges here first, if you're extradited—or if you'll face murder charges," Luke told him.

"I did not kill Dorothy Norman!" he snapped. He winced. "I mean, I swear, I did not kill her. I didn't like her. She was a total witch. But I didn't kill her."

"Maybe not physically. But, hmm, I think I know why you had to tell your cousin about her. She started grilling you about being late to work or not showing up period. You were busy planting evidence as ordered in the home of Jordan Dowell," Luke said.

The man sat back, staring at Luke.

He began to stutter. "I, uh, no. I was sick. Yes, I was sick. I needed the time off. Oh, yeah, she gave me a hard time for it. But—"

"Like I said. I don't think you killed her physically. But you did tell your cousin, Mrs. Lily Connoly, that she was getting suspicious and being a pain in the neck. In fact, she was so hard on you that you were growing worried she'd fire you. Then you couldn't tell your cousin who was coming, who was rich and needed a transplant, or maybe what the doctors were saying, if they were onto anything."

He shook his head strenuously. "No, no, no. I mean,

um, yes, I am a distant cousin of Lily's, but I don't call her—"

"Well, that's not true at all, is it? She already told us you reported to her on everything. Maybe she did tell you that you were going to need to take care of the situation yourself. I'm not sure how you got Dorothy Norman to accompany you anywhere, but you took her out to Arthur's Isle. And once you had her there, you hacked her head off. She was older, maybe suffering from a disease. She wasn't a planned kill, there was no one waiting for her organs. But you did hate her, and you were told that she needed to be a warning to others—and so you dumped her head."

"No! I didn't kill her."

Luke leaned forward, smiling grimly, and lied.

"Lily Connoly has already confessed to us that you killed her. She helped you get the false identity, helped you get out of the United States. In return, you had to tell her about things happening at the hospital. Then, when things started getting out of hand, you had to take care of Dorothy Norman."

"She told you that!" he exclaimed.

"She did. She said, though, that the whole thing was your idea."

"That horrible bitch! That's a lie. I didn't kill Dorothy. I swear it! I didn't even pick up Dorothy anywhere and take her to the island. That was Lily. I…" He stopped speaking, wincing, shaking his head in anger and disbelief. "All right, all right! She helped me get out of the States. Yes, she knew someone who could give me a new identity and the papers and history that went with it. And I had to talk to her, to tell her everything that went on at the hospital. And…"

He broke off. He appeared to be in tremendous pain.

"I should have finished out my time. I should have known she'd make me pay the debt. If I had just stayed and done my time...but I thought I would never get a job again. And if I came here, I could start over. I didn't know the price that I would have to pay."

Luke believed him. Oddly, he believed him. Lily had used him, just as others had been used.

But was she the impetus of all this? Because she hadn't been operating on people, disappearing for endless hours...

"Help me!" the man said suddenly. "Help me. I'll tell you anything I know!"

"All right. Do you know she has been behind the killings that have been going on?" Luke asked.

He let out a long breath. "I don't know exactly. But..."

"But?"

"She found out years ago she needed a kidney. Not here, she was on vacation in Thailand, and then she went to Pakistan..." He let his voice trail. He straightened and stared straight at Luke again. "She bought a kidney there. I don't think her husband ever knew. She lied and never told him that she was even sick. When she had the transplant, she told him she was on a family vacation, and she begged his forgiveness, saying that she'd left everything behind for him, and she needed some time with her own family. My mother helped her, then. I was still...really just a kid. When she helped me, I might have wanted to believe it was payback for what my mom had done for her by pretending that they were seeing many places in Asia. Time went by...my great-grandparents died, and I think she had some money.

I'm not sure. And when I came here… I swear, I didn't know what she was doing, but now…"

Luke knew Campbell and MacDuff were hearing everything he heard.

"I will do my best to help you, Vince, but you will do time. It will help in your sentencing—here or maybe in the United States."

He cried easily. There were tears in his eyes but he nodded.

"I'm ready to go home, even if home is prison."

"One more thing. How did you find out about Jordan Dowell, and how did you plant the evidence in his home?" Luke demanded.

Vince looked downward. "The dude doesn't have any kind of an alarm. I can pick just about any lock and leave no trace. I just walked in."

"Where did you get the cooler?"

He didn't even hesitate. He just shrugged. "She called me. Lily called me and told me to pick it up from the vennel behind her house. I didn't… I didn't open it. I didn't even know what was in it. I just did what she told me."

"Is that the truth?"

"Oh, the absolute truth," Vince said. "Please…"

"Your testimony will help with your sentencing," Luke told him. He rose then, gave the man a nod and headed into the observation room.

Campbell looked at him and told him, "Damned good job."

"Jordan Dowell is innocent of any wrongdoing. You heard that, right?"

"I never believed Jordan was guilty!" MacDuff said. "We just had to—"

"Follow proper procedures," Luke finished.

"Right. But we will see he is cleared of all charges immediately," MacDuff promised. "And, we've got her! We'll start getting on the records to prove everything that the man is saying. We've got her."

"From what he's said," Luke told them, "I believe when she bought her kidney, she realized what kind of money might be made in a scam like this. But she isn't the surgeon—"

"No," Campbell said. "It has to be our mysterious fake Dr. Gleason."

"And," Luke said, "I imagine we'll find the missing parents of the children who were kept with Marjory Alden's children. One or both of them was probably in the medical field, and they're being forced to assist in the surgeries."

"Quite possibly," MacDuff agreed. "So, we will add to her charges. I'd like to watch you let her know."

Luke nodded. He was going to be very happy to let the woman know.

He walked back into the interrogation room where Lily Connoly looked as if she were waiting with extreme irritation.

"Why am I just sitting here?" she demanded. "You are going to let me go, and you are going to let me go right now!"

"Ah!" Luke said, sitting in front of her and smiling. "No. No, I am not."

"This is outrageous—"

"Oh, no, Mrs. Connoly, in truth, all your actions have been outrageous. I'm afraid we have a truly solid witness who has told us a great deal about you. So. You needed a kidney. Simple enough for a woman of your talents. You faked a great vacation—and went and bought yourself a transplant. And when you did that—"

"That little bastard told you that? Lies!" she screamed.

"I'll keep going. You found out just how much money was involved. And you like money—that's how you buy your boy toys. You know, the men who help you with your needs while your poor husband walks about thinking you're the dear woman of his heart, tolerant of any of his problems, the mother of his child. Ah, well, that's beside the point. Somewhere along the line, you and the good Dr. Gleason met, and you realized how much money could be made in the illegal organ transplant trade. I mean, it's not as if you could just go to a store and steal what you needed for other incredibly rich people willing to pay the price as you did. So… hmm, I'm still guessing Gleason was the brains behind the enterprise. After all, he was the one with the talent as a surgeon—"

"No!" she screamed.

"Lily. We have you. Deny all you will. We needed proof. We have it."

"Proof from a lying little beggar. No, I don't know what he's saying—"

"Lily, it will be easy to prove you have had a transplant. What surprises me is we didn't find the pharmaceuticals you must now be on when we searched your house, but they were probably hidden better than your sex toys. We will find them. And we know you were warned that Nurse Dorothy Norman was becoming suspicious. And maybe she even had something, not on you perhaps, but on our mysterious doctor. Now, he is the brains—"

"No!" she screamed.

"Lily—"

"I am the brains! What are you, an idiot? I am the smart one. He is just a stupid and resentful man ready to do anything to get even with the world. He was kicked out of a hospital for killing a patient! I am the brains!"

Luke stood, shaking his head.

"Thanks for the confession."

"What?"

"You just confessed, Lily. The officers and courts will be taking care of you now. I'm going to suggest that you be really grateful the United Kingdom doesn't have the death penalty."

"Wait, no!" she cried. "I…didn't kill anyone!"

"No, Lily. You didn't physically kill them. You ordered their deaths. That's enough."

"No, no, no. I am not responsible."

"But you're the brains!"

"I… You go to hell! I will get a new solicitor. A good one. This will all be thrown out of court!"

Luke just shook his head, amazed she had managed to hide the depths of her truly malicious personality for so long.

"Good luck with that," he told her. "Now, of course, you can help yourself. You can tell us where to find the good Dr. Gleason. In fact, you can tell us who he really is, and most importantly, you can tell us where to find him and his new base of operations."

She sat back and crossed her arms over her chest.

"Lily, it could mean a lot to help you when this goes to court," he warned.

She lifted her head, and then for a minute she laughed. "You are not the brains of any operation!" she snapped at him.

"Oh? Because I'm suggesting you help yourself?"

"Because we were both too smart for me to know! I can't tell you anything, anything at all, because I didn't know whom they were going to kill. I just made the arrangements with those who needed a body part," she announced.

He smiled pleasantly at her, set his hands on the table and loomed over her.

"You're lying. But that's okay. We know it was moved to a home along the Firth of Forth with easy access from the water, maybe very easy for a few of the customers. You only get one chance, Lily. Which house?" Luke demanded.

She crossed her arms over her chest and turned her back on him.

There was a tap on the one-way mirror.

He left the room. Behind him, she was suddenly screaming at the top of her lungs again.

He ignored her and hurried in to find out what Campbell and MacDuff had to say.

"They think they have something," Campbell said. "Your teammates, Mason Carter and Della Hamilton. We're setting up with officers from Police Scotland, but they're not sure what they have. They believe they have found the car in the video surveillance from the hospital. They're about to go in."

"I'd like to be there. Is there time?"

"Go. Backup is being organized. The house is quiet. We don't have any new missing persons that we know about. Hopefully…" MacDuff said.

"Hopefully, we'll find our fake Dr. Gleason and the surgery," Luke said. "I need the address."

"Sending it to you now," Campbell assured him.

Luke hurried out to his car, set his GPS and drove as quickly as possible.

When he arrived, he saw police cars were gathering on the street. He parked his own behind them and quickly headed toward the house.

It was a fine manor house with a great property. And he saw what had alerted Mason and Della to the possibility they were in the right place.

Someone hadn't closed the garage doors carefully. And through the few feet of the opening, he could see a car of the make and color in the surveillance video from the hospital.

Moving quickly, he found Mason and Della.

He smiled. "Wow. You just got here and—"

"Oh, we had help," Della told him. "One of the officers noted the door. He alerted us, and we came. Of course, we can't be certain—"

"I can," Luke said. "This is a small community. There can't be more than one of these exact cars, color, year, make and model, even if we can't see the emblem from the street."

"Then let's do this," Mason said.

"Officer?" Luke called.

A man from Police Scotland joined them at the front door with other officers fanning out behind him, and with Luke, Mason and Della at his side.

He banged at the door and shouted, "Police Scotland. Open up!"

There was no response. He tried again. Nothing.

Then Luke frowned, thinking he heard something from within, someone...

Trying to cry out, not able to do so.

"Break it," he said.

An officer came forward with a ram. Using a heavy swing, he slammed against the door. Once, twice and then again.

The door shook and then splintered, and they broke in.

Luke knew what he had heard. Because there, in the middle of the large parlor floor, was a couple, bound at their wrists and ankles and tied together with more rope in such a way that if they had struggled, they might have strangled themselves. They were gagged as well.

"I've got them," Della said as she hurried over to the couple and was joined by an officer.

Luke glanced at Mason, and they turned and went in opposite directions. The kitchen and dining room appeared normal.

But there was another door to the right.

Closed. Locked.

Luke called the officer again, nodding.

The door was broken down. And in that room, they found the new surgery.

Beds... Trays with a surgeon's tools. IV stands, cabinets filled with pharmaceuticals, more...

And more.

"We've got it," Mason said.

Luke nodded in agreement as officers flooded the house. They could hear shouts.

"Clear!"

"Clear!"

"Clear."

And in a matter of minutes, they were back together, shaking their heads.

By then, Della and an officer had freed the couple who had been tied together on the floor. The woman, a young redhead, rushed forward with her husband, a tall thin blond man behind her with his hands on her shoulders.

"They're not here, they're both out!" she cried. "But you must help us, you can't be here! They have our children—if anything goes wrong, they promised us they'd kill them and do it slowly and horribly—"

"No, no, your children are safe! We have them!" Luke told her. "We found the children a few days ago. They are safe. We need to know—"

"We don't know where they went! I think they—"

She broke off, choking, tears in her eyes.

Her husband had to answer for her.

"We believe they are out to kidnap another victim. There's a boat due in tonight with—with a customer."

"All right," Luke said. "Please, help us now. *Who* are *they*?"

Seventeen

"You," the man calling himself Robbie said, "are fantastic. I really can't believe my luck, getting to spend such an evening with you tonight!"

"You're pretty cute yourself!" Carly told him. "And I guess I'm a lucky girl, getting to spend the evening with you, such a...such a stud to see me safely home!"

"Are you ready to go?" he asked her. "I suggest one more drink. I'd like one more. What do you say?"

He thought he was getting her inebriated. Kevin was playing his part well. She was sure that "Robbie" had no idea her drinks weren't alcoholic drinks at all.

"One more!" she said. With her elbow on the bar, she set her chin on her knuckles and stared into his eyes. "With you," she whispered, "one more!"

Robbie called for Kevin. Kevin cheerfully assured him he'd have two more drinks right over.

"A man who loves all the old Beatles tunes!" she said. "You know, I do meet a few people who barely know who they are!"

"And Bowie. You love Bowie," he said.

Kevin brought their drinks. "Now, lass, you're sure you're doing all right?" he asked.

"Oh, I am lovely. And I have this lovely gentleman to see me home!" she told him.

"And I'd love to pay up for the lady and myself," Robbie said. "We'll head out after this!"

"I'll get the counting," Kevin said.

Carly looked at Robbie and said, "I didn't mean for you to pay for my drinks all night! I can take a part of that bill—"

"No, luv! I'll be taking the bill!" he told her. "For the pleasure of your company, of course, I'll be taking the bill!"

She finished her drink quickly, glancing over at Daniel. He had played his own game all night. But he'd been watching.

Waiting.

She swallowed down the last drink quickly, causing Robbie to laugh softly. "I need a wee minute here!" he told her.

"As long as you like!" she assured him.

But after she spoke, she began to rise. She had flirted and fawned over him long enough. It was time to find out the truth. Of course, if she discovered he was just a nice guy trying to get a new conquest into bed, she was going to feel like a complete fool.

But…

No. There had just been something too similar in the video footage. The man had been staring at the hospital. Watching? Waiting? And when the security guard had approached…

He had done something. Slipped off an excellent

mask, rubbed away makeup—makeup and a facial prosthetic?

And come to look far too much like the man with me now.

She glanced in Daniel's direction. He had seen her rise.

"All right, we've paid the price!" Robbie said, placing bills on the bar.

She felt her phone vibrating but even as it did, he took her arm. There was no way she could reach the phone without him seeing whatever might be on it.

"You can walk all right?" he asked her, oh, so caringly!

She gave him a brilliant smile. "I can. With you by my side. And with all this terrible, terrible stuff going on, again, I am so lucky, so, so lucky to have such a strong and cool guy seeing me home!"

"It's nothing to help such a beautiful lass!" he assured her.

They stepped outside. He stopped about ten feet from the door, staring back into the pub.

She hoped Daniel wasn't obviously following them.

But he was not. Robbie seemed to be assured they were alone.

And it had grown late. The streets were quiet with only a few couples and groups moving about.

"I am glad you drank a lot," he murmured.

"Pardon?"

"I mean, I'm so glad you were free and easy and able to enjoy the evening," he said.

She suddenly felt someone at her side.

Keith.

"Lass, lass, he's turning you off the street. We'll be in the darkness behind the kirkyard, and then on to the small side street where the van comes. I've seen it! A gray van and driven by the bloke with him the other night, that Cullen fellow."

She couldn't answer him. She wanted to let him know Daniel would be coming behind them.

"Lass...that's the van just ahead," he told her.

It was. It might be time to drop the charade and pull out her Glock. But she still couldn't guarantee he was "Dr. Gleason."

And Daniel was behind her. Almost...almost. He just had to do something that would give him away...

Almost, almost, almost...

Luke arrived at Kevin's and hurried in. Carly hadn't responded to his call but Daniel had.

He'd let Daniel know they had discovered the house where surgery was now planned since the island "hospital" had been abandoned. They had confessions on tape from Lily Connoly and "Rusty Teller."

But they didn't have "Dr. Gleason" and an unnamed accomplice.

Daniel had informed Luke that he and Carly were at Kevin's, watching out for one another. Carly was with a man.

One she suspected. And she was playing the game.

Before Luke could reach the bar to speak with Kevin, he felt a strange touch on his shoulder. It was Keith.

"Come, come now! He is taking her along the street and the van is there, I saw it! He means to take her tonight."

"Does he suspect she's law enforcement?" Luke asked. If so, she could be in serious trouble. "Keith, we found their lair, their surgery. They can't go there—"

"But we don't know if they *burke* their victims right there in the van," Keith told him.

No, we don't.

"Daniel is following her," Luke told Keith. "And now we must do so. Show me the same route?" he asked.

Carly was good; she was competent. She was all right.

But the best cop or agent in the world could be taken. They both knew it.

"This way!"

Keith hurried along the street and then off it.

The great and ancient walls surrounding so much of Edinburgh seemed to be gray and miasmic with the night. Stars dotted the sky, but clouds covered the moon. Streetlights seemed distant.

They hurried along. Luke still couldn't see Carly with the man who might be the killer. But in another minute, they saw someone walking ahead and hurried to reach him.

Daniel swung around as they neared him, his weapon out.

He lowered it as he saw Luke and Keith.

"Where are they?" Luke asked Daniel.

"They must have taken a turn somewhere," Daniel said. "I couldn't follow too closely—he was watching. But he hadn't done anything yet! I think ahead, just ahead…there's a twist in the road and the walls that seem like solid walls and aren't quite on par…"

Luke let his strides grow longer. Carly could be in trouble.

* * *

"Ah, cool!" Robbie said. "See that? Me mate, Cullen, he's just ahead. We'll hop in the van, he'll give us a ride home."

"Stop!"

Carly was surprised to hear a female voice calling out.

She turned around as Robbie did, his arm around her now.

There was a woman standing behind them. In the darkness, Carly didn't recognize her at first.

And then she did.

It was Milly. Milly Blair.

Nurse Milly Blair.

Did she think she was a vigilante, and she could come out and save women from whoever was taking them?

"What the hell are you doing here?" Robbie demanded. His hold on Carly had grown fierce.

"Saving your arse!" Milly shouted in return.

"You're ruining a smooth operation," he told her furiously.

"No, no, listen to me! This has gone too far. Stan, she's FBI!"

"FBI?" He sounded disbelieving at first.

"FBI! She's been at the hospital talking to Forbes!"

It was over; no waiting on this. No choice. She dug in her purse for her Glock but even as she drew it out, Milly Blair aimed a weapon at Carly.

"You need to get this over with—fast! Get her off the street."

He still held Carly's one arm. Fiercely. She suddenly felt something against her side.

A knife.

"Do it!" Milly screamed.

"Do it? I'll shoot Milly, and I am a crack shot!" Carly snapped.

"So shoot her," the man who had now been called "Stan" by Milly turned to her with a broad smile. "FBI! So, well done! You played me, and I have been one hell of a player."

"Okay. I'll just shoot you," Carly said, aiming the Glock at him.

"Hmm. Think about it. Can I stab you right in an indispensable organ as you pull that trigger? Then again, you shoot me, Milly shoots you."

"What? After you told her to shoot me?" Milly demanded. "You shut up. Oh, yeah, you are the great Dr. Stanley Morton, thrown out of a hospital for letting too many living donors die when part of a liver or one kidney being given shouldn't have taken their lives. And you still think you're so hot—so hot that you had to play the part of Dr. Harold Gleason—who was a damned good surgeon until his death. You would let her shoot me? What an ass. Oh, Carly, you are going to die but…guess what? I'm no silly little nurse, and I should never have had to take any guff from that bitch, Dorothy Norman. Never. And now I see I've been working on this with a pure idiot! I have my medical degree—I received my license as a medical doctor, but this idiot wanted me to play the nurse. Guess what, Stan? I don't need you anymore. Because you're stupid—"

"Lily will never help an idiot like you!" Stan shouted. "You need me! She will only find customers for me!"

"But you've ruined everything tonight!" Milly raged. "And you know what, Carly FBI? You know how we got to be…who we are? People! They are idiots. The world needs more who are willing to donate their organs after death. You see, I have done a service—"

"I'm confused," Carly said, playing for time. Daniel was behind her. But...

What was he going to do? How would they end this? Milly was a wild card.

She had never fallen under suspicion!

Would she shoot to kill, perhaps kill Daniel before Carly could shoot her—and evade Stan's knife?

The question raged in her mind.

And then...

She hadn't seen him. Milly certainly hadn't seen him.

But Luke was behind Milly, the nose of his Glock pressed against her temple.

"Drop the weapon, Milly," he said.

Milly froze.

"You drop your weapon. I will shoot Carly."

"I don't think so. Carly will shoot you first."

"He'll stab her to death."

"No, he won't," Luke said. "He wants to live. He has an ego the size of the moon. He believes that as long as he's breathing, he will be clever enough to get himself out of prison and start it up all over again."

"Not true. Don't you understand? He was a surgeon, but I'm as talented and able as he is. I have been all along. All right, it was fun to be Burke and Hare, but that wasn't the point. He was in it just for the money. I wanted to save lives—"

"By taking lives?" Carly demanded incredulously.

"I took lives that didn't matter for those that did!"

"You did? I saved those people. You were only sometimes an able assistant!" Stan shouted.

"Not true!"

"You weren't even there half the time!"

"Because you used me!" Milly cried. "I was saving the right lives, you just wanted money! Burke and Hare—and I should have been—"

"I'm afraid you weren't either," Luke said. "Naturally, Lily Connoly considers herself to be Hare now, I believe. She'll start to tell everything—to make sure all the rest of you *hang* for the rest of your lives in prison."

"No!" Milly cried.

She raised her hand. She was going to shoot. "Donate any of my organs that are good!" she said suddenly. She twisted her gun to aim at herself.

"No! You don't have to do that!" Carly cried to her.

Luke moved to grab her gun, but it was too late.

Milly had aimed at her own temple.

And fired.

As she did, Carly twisted out of Stan's hold, her Glock directly on him.

He started to laugh.

"You're under arrest," Carly told him.

"Fine," he said with a shrug. "But you were right, so right. I will get out and I am a great surgeon! Unappreciated by some—adored by those I have saved!"

"And what about those you murdered?" Luke asked.

"Well, Milly was right about one thing. They really didn't matter. More important people needed what they had to offer."

There were sirens in the night. Luke kicked Milly's gun out of the way and walked toward Carly and the man who had apparently gone by Dr. Harold Gleason at one time and was now either Robbie or Stan.

"Drop the knife," he said.

The man shrugged and dropped the knife.

"Down on the ground. Hands behind your back. Carly, cover me."

Luke cuffed him and as he did so, Carly asked, "Luke, Daniel! He was behind me. Where is he? Nothing—"

"No, nothing happened to him. We had to split up. Daniel is after the man in the van," he said. As he stood over Stan, he told her, "The surgery has been found. It was empty—except for the parents we finally found of the children who had been with Marjory's children. It's over. Burke and Hare! This operation—at the upper level—was this fellow, Cullen, Milly, Vince and Lily Connoly. Burke and Hare and Hare and Hare and Hare. But it's a done deal. The money pipeline has been cut dry. This is finally finished."

Even as he spoke, Daniel appeared with the man she had been introduced to as Cullen. He'd been cuffed, and Daniel ordered him down on the ground with Stan.

"Mason and Della are here," Luke told Carly.

Sirens were loud in the night, and they were fast. There was no help for Milly Blair; she had aimed true at herself.

Carly wasn't sure what would happen, if the woman's organs could be donated. At the end, her last words had been to give her organs.

But could that change anything? No one, no matter what their knowledge or degree, had a right to play God, to decide who lived and who died.

They had taken lives they thought were…

Not worthy.

They had stolen those lives. And no one had that right; no one had the right to judge the heart and soul of another human being when it came to the precious things that could be given...

They did not have the right to decide life or death.

Campbell arrived with the first of the cars.

"Didn't we just do this last night?" he asked dryly.

Luke was glad to see Carly manage a smile.

"Well, you know. Can't let the grass grow under your feet."

"No. We can't do that," Campbell agreed. "Do your reports at the house. Call it a night—we now have all the players. Good work, good work! And...thank you!"

After the night in hell, there was something wonderful when they reached the house.

Jordan had already been released; he was waiting for them at the table. He'd brewed coffee and tea and set out shortbread for them to enjoy while each wrote up their report for the night.

They couldn't have been happier to see him well, out of the hospital—and not in a jail cell. He was ridiculously grateful to all of them.

Mason and Della joined them, and they learned they had finally managed to discover and arrest the last of the would-be Holmes Society killers who had been operating in France.

"And we came right here!" Della said. "We're still trying to piece it all together."

"There wasn't a Burke or a Hare," Luke explained. "There were several pathetic pawns, down-and-outers or those who were terrified for loved ones—to do their bidding. But there were a few major players. Rusty Teller, or Vince, and Milly Blair at the hospital. Milly was a shock. She hadn't been on our radar at all. The best we've figured is Lily had a transplant years ago. An illegal transplant. She paid a fortune and lied to her husband. She learned then, however, that there was a way to recoup her fortune by becoming a broker in organ transplants herself. Somewhere along the line, she and the man Angela just informed us is really Stanley Morton, a surgeon who lost his job for losing patients—came in contact. Stanley left the States, took on the esteemed identity of a man who had died far from home with no relatives, and came to Scotland to start over. But his attitude kept him out of the hospitals, and he met Lily and…Burke and Hare began with a little help from Milly, Vince and the man Cullen, the first *friend* Stanley found in Scotland. There is going to be so much for the National Crime Agency to sort out. So many charges that must be decided. But that's not for us."

"No," Mason said, "that's not for us."

"Well…" Jordan said, wincing. "I am Police Scotland."

"And," Daniel added, "I'm National Crime Agency."

Luke grimaced. "Sorry, guys! All those charges will fall on you two to file."

"Not to worry. That's really all up to the legal world here," Jordan assured him.

"Oh!" Della said. "The couple discovered in the house were Celia and Ted Smith, from the Shetlands. That's why they weren't on our radar. They had been planning a move to the mainland so when they disappeared, their neighbors thought they had completed the move. They have been reunited with their children and will be able to head back soon."

"They didn't do any of the killing, did they?" Carly asked.

Mason shook his head and quickly told her, "She is a pediatrician. Different from a surgeon, but that wasn't what they wanted from her. She and her husband were to watch over the patients—the ones that organs were transferred into—and keep them alive. That's something else up to the legal community, and I don't know how they'll handle it. You can't return a liver to a dead man or woman, or a heart, or lungs, or kidneys."

"Who did do the…physical killing?" Carly asked.

"Well, your two men. Stan and Cullen," Luke said. "Even Jared Stone was just a pawn, just the man who was to get a woman to the van. And while we don't know and may never know, it's my belief that Milly was the one to lure the men to their deaths."

"And Dorothy Norman?" Jordan asked.

"I think that might have been Milly—with a little help from her friends," Luke said. "But…all this will take time to completely unravel."

"Truth and court dates…we're talking lots of time," Mason said. "But I have good news for our little Blackbird division."

"Oh?" Carly asked.

"A few tie-up reports, and we're off!" Della said.

"Off…of?" Luke asked her.

"Ordered to take some vacation time," Mason said. "Wherever we want to go."

Carly smiled, glancing at Jordan and Daniel. "I love Scotland. I will always love Scotland with all my heart. Right now…"

"Beach?" Luke asked.

"Not just a beach!" Carly said. "A charming seaside village. I was thinking Italy. They have some great places on the coast. Days of just lying in the sun, jumping in the water—"

"I want a Jacuzzi!" Della said.

They all laughed and then Luke sobered, looking at Jordan and Daniel. "I…"

Daniel laughed. "We have both been given vacation time, too, but closer to home. We may be needed—and, of course, when we get to the trials, you will be called back. But I… I may be going with you."

"What?" Carly asked.

Daniel laughed. "Well, not on vacation with you, Carly, or a Jacuzzi with you, Della. But the powers that be are working together. I am a Scot, but they feel they can have a representative of the National Crime Agency be part of Blackbird—an international law enforcement entity, though its base and origins are America." He looked from Luke to Carly and they both understood why immediately.

Daniel had loved working with Keith. He had learned to use the strange ability he had; he didn't want to go back.

He felt the need to be with those who shared it.

"All right, then! Come the morning, plan the vacation. But now let's clean up."

Jordan and Mason carried the cups to the kitchen.

"And something else that's incredibly important," Carly said.

"What's that?"

"Find Keith MacDonald and thank him. And then we must also find the lovely woman who helped us at the very beginning, Kaitlin Bell. We need to make sure she knows how grateful we are for her help, just as we must let Keith know how grateful we are to him."

Daniel smiled. "And they will be pleased. They witnessed this horror before and could do nothing. Now, they have helped in a different time and place, but I think it will help them both!"

"All right," Carly said, rising. "I'm for bed! Oh, how rude! Mason, Della—"

Jordan, coming back from the kitchen, glanced in Carly's direction. "I do have a home here and I can go to it. Oh, I will be buying an alarm as soon as possible. I just wanted to thank you all tonight—"

"Jordan, we're fine. We're in the last room of the house. No one goes anywhere, not tonight!" Mason told him, coming up behind Jordan.

Good-nights went around. And they began to peel off, heading to their separate rooms.

And when they were in theirs, Carly turned into Luke's arms. "We… I can't believe it's really over, and we have all the puzzle pieces falling in."

"We do. And we get to go on vacation!"

"Vacation. Hey, do you think that…"

"We'll be able to just enjoy the sights and sounds, the art of Italy! Italian food, a beach… Yeah, well, you know, not forever. But do I think we will really, truly, get a few days? Yes! When the paperwork is tied up here. And we will need to come back when our players go to trial. Because they can never, never be let out!"

"Of course. Luke, we also need to go by and thank Kevin and Catherine. They were the real deal. Oh! And Dr. Forbes. We might never have discovered the truth without him."

"Right. One might first suspect a doctor there—but it

makes far more sense that such a killer might be someone who would never be hired at a place where the mission was to save lives—all lives—and not just the lives of those who had money or prestige."

"We will get it all in," Carly said.

"Shower?"

"Shower!"

She headed in. He followed. And it was amazing. Soap, suds, the feel of someone you loved, and loved you in return, against you.

Later, as they lay curled together, Luke said, "It's amazing."

"What's that?"

"Being with you."

"May I return the compliment?"

He grinned, turning to her. "But I was thinking…on bad days, being together seems to alleviate the worst. And on good days…the celebration of touching you is purely amazing."

"And I am grateful beyond measure that we have what we have."

He curled an arm around her. Smiled.

And slept.

Thanking everyone and making plans wasn't going to be quite as easy as Carly might have hoped. Despite all the help that MacDuff and Campbell intended they have, there was paperwork, mounds of it, and that took the morning.

When they left, Jordan stayed behind. He still had work to do regarding what had been done to him, papers to fill out so that his name was fully cleared.

They were sorry to leave without him, but when they

did, Daniel said, "I'm sorry Jordan isn't with us today, but…you do realize that it's going to be easier to say thank you to spirits when all of us can see the spirits."

"He has a point!" Carly told Luke.

"That he does," Luke agreed. "But we do have a few of those still living that we need to thank, too."

It was just after noon when they were able to get to the hospital and see Dr. Forbes—and Dr. Douglas as well.

They learned that life was going to be painful for Ewan Connoly, but he had truly been oblivious to what his wife had been doing. The future would be hard for him and his son; however, Westin Douglas informed them his father was going to do all that he could to help his old friend.

But they were grateful, and the doctors were grateful. It was still good to see them.

They decided to have lunch at Filigree and hoped to find Kaitlin Bell.

They did. And since they were a group, it was easy to speak with her and explain all the pieces that had been identified and fit together to make the picture whole.

Carly thanked her especially. She had been a beginning for them in knowing what paths they needed to follow.

They headed to Kevin's, where, again, they were able to thank Kevin and Catherine. And Kevin assured them he and his livelihood—the pub—thanked them in turn.

They hadn't seen Keith yet and Carly knew they must.

They headed for the dark paths and streets that led behind the kirkyard.

And there, they found him. He'd been waiting for them.

"So, my friends, I… I have been blessed to see you, to be a part of this!" he told them. "And I was hoping…"

"What's that, Keith? What can we do?" Carly asked him.

"I've had a strange feeling. Will you come with me to Arthur's Seat at Holyrood? I've a feeling, well… I needed to see you. But I wish we might go there."

And so, they did.

When they arrived, the sweeping green of Arthur's Seat seemed especially beautiful, dotted here and there with wildflowers. Keith thanked them again, and they insisted once more that he had been the help they needed.

And then Carly knew. He stood before them, the soft feel of his hands on her shoulders, and he told her, "It has come full circle. I have done what I was meant to do."

She wasn't sure why but she felt tears sting her eyes.

"Be happy for me!" he said.

And she nodded. "I am!"

He waved to the others and stepped back on the highest point. He gazed at them all, smiled and waved.

The he lifted his arms, and it seemed the sun burst a little brighter, sending a special ray down to kiss the earth.

And then Keith was gone.

And while tears still dampened Carly's eyes, she was glad. So glad.

Luke's hands fell on her shoulders and she knew. He would always be there with her. They would both miss Keith.

And they would also be happy. They had finished a case. Keith had finished his mission, and it had taken decades. He would go on.

And find his own peace and happiness.

Epilogue

"This is lovely. But…" Carly sipped her whiskey sample and gave the young man serving her a brilliant smile. "Do you have anything stronger?" she whispered.

"Um… I don't know. No, no, I don't think so," he told her.

She leaned back. She watched. An older man came out just to look around the room.

They'd had this one piece of unfinished business to tend to—and even facing charges that rather desperately needed mitigation, there was one piece of information that Stanley Morton and Lily Connoly had refused to give them.

The identity of the person supplying their "killer" whiskey.

And so, before taking off for the beaches of Italy, they'd decided to do a few whiskey tastings—something that could take a long, long time in a country renowned for its exports of the liquor, but they had taken the divide-and-conquer approach.

Luke was across the room from her—while "Burke and Hare" and their minions were now safely incarcerated, they were still approaching all aspects of the case with teamwork.

She rose, hurrying after the older man who had looked around the room. He had to be the proprietor. "May I speak with you?" she asked him.

"Of course, lass. I hope you're enjoying the distillery tour!"

"I am," Carly assured him. "But… I'd like to know if you don't have anything stronger?"

He frowned, looking at her, indicating that she take her chair at her table again while he joined her, leaning close to ask suspiciously, "Why are you here, lass, and asking about whiskey?"

She arched a brow at him. He knew, and there was something about his attitude that was both suspicious—and regretful.

"I've heard there's something out there in the Scottish whiskey world that is super-charged," she told him. She quickly pondered a lie. "All right, I'm terrified of flying! I was hoping I could get something incredibly strong that I could slip into a tiny container to have when I made my way through the airport and that would… well, knock me right out for the trip across the pond!"

He sat back, closing his eyes. Then he leaned forward. "All right. We have created such a special batch, but just for the family. And," he added, "just for that reason. Me daughter, Rebecca, she's terrified of getting into an airplane and… But we had a few bottles stolen from the distillery and… I have decided there will be no more."

"Stolen?"

He nodded gravely. "Strange! Just those bottles gone, no sign of a break-in, but—"

Carly saw the young man who had first been helping her watching them—and then he suddenly disappeared into the back.

"I think I know your thief!" she murmured. She stood to follow him; Luke was already doing so.

He had, in fact, caught up with the young man just outside. And there were tears in his eyes.

"They told me it was for private consumption!" he cried. "That they couldn't sleep, that they were desperate, they'd tried pills, they'd tried everything on the market, and they paid me enough for my school bill and... Oh, God! Then I heard that victims of our new Burke and Hare were extremely intoxicated and..."

He broke down in hysterical sobs.

Carly looked at Luke. She was glad she wasn't going to be part of the legal system that moved against the young man.

And she was equally glad that finally the pieces had all fallen into place. The young man had done something very wrong and yet she couldn't help but feel sorry for him.

It was one thing to steal a few bottles of whiskey.

Quite another to realize they had been used in heinous crimes.

But for them...

It was time for MacDuff and Campbell to take over.

And for the two of them and Della and Mason to have a little bit of coveted time off!

Liguria, Italy. Breathtaking mountains, an exquisite beach. The charm of the Italian people who did their best attempt at signing when Carly's not-quite mastery of the language failed her.

They had an amazing time. Of course, as much as
they needed what Della liked to call their "chill" period between cases, and as much as she loved lying on
the beautiful beach, she was fascinated by the area as
well. Balzi Rossi offered them an incredible day wandering through prehistoric sites. Having enjoyed that
trip, they went on to Grotte di Toirano, with its ancient
"footprints" and stunning rock formations. Of course,
Italy was famous for so much more, but then again,
there were those idyllic days on the beach.

They'd all opted for a lazy day after visiting numerous magnificent castles and cathedrals. And lying next
to Luke, Carly let her fingers run through the sand,
marveling that there was so much beauty to be seen
in the world.

"Missing Scotland?" Luke asked her.

She smiled. "I will love Scotland as long as I live,"
Carly told him. "I will never forget trips with my grandparents. I will never forget Keith. But I must admit, I
think the beach is a little better here!"

He laughed. "We'll get back. We have great friends
there now—and one day, it will be nice to go and see
them when we're not looking for a conspiracy of killers."

"Ah, good point! That will be nice!" Carly told him.

"Daniel will be joining us. I don't know all the mach-
inations they're doing to make him part of an American extension of the Krewe, but—" Luke broke off,
grinned at her, and said, "I'm glad. Daniel is great. A
great asset for us. And, I think he'll get to feel sane
working with us."

She grinned in turn, still running her fingers through
the slightly cool and damp sand, loving the feel of it

between her fingers along with the golden touch of the sun on her skin.

"Daniel is great," she agreed. And she couldn't help herself. She tossed a little sand on Luke's bare chest.

"Hey!"

"Look at you, you're all sandy. Ready for a dip to clean up a bit?" she teased.

"You want to see sandy?" he threatened.

She burst into laughter, lay back and closed her eyes, waiting.

But no sand touched her. She opened her eyes to see that Mason had left his blanket on the beach and was standing over them.

"Sorry, guys, we'll be leaving tonight."

Carly jolted up and Luke did the same, helping her rise to her feet as he did so.

"What's happened?" Luke asked.

"Well, I'm glad Della and I had some time to brush up on our French. We'll be heading to Paris tonight."

"Paris, what—" Carly began.

"There you go. That's the thing about a vacation," Mason said. "We don't watch the news—because we don't want to. Except, I don't think there's much on the news about this yet."

"About what?" Luke persisted, frowning.

"Jackson got a call from an old friend of his, a French detective, Gervais LeBlanc. There's a vampire or some such creature loose in Paris, so it seems."

"What?" Carly and Luke looked at one another. "But you put Stephan Dante away about a year ago. You mean—"

"I mean that LeBlanc is afraid there will be a *vampire* panic when certain aspects of murder cases become public. Visitors to Paris have now been found in the nearby wine region of Reims—dead, and completely drained of blood. Young women. They know of two victims. Because they've been discovered out in the fields…they don't know how many more there are. No *fang* marks on these victims. But they are…bled dry. Razor slashes on veins and arteries…"

"That's not a vampire," Carly said thoughtfully. "That's someone who wants copious amounts of blood. Ritual? A cult. A single person doing this?"

"Jackson has sent a Krewe member, a young woman named Jeannette LaFarge, out to speak with Gervais LeBlanc—she has just come off an undercover assignment investigating a cult, bringing it all to a conclusion. We're to meet her there and Daniel will join us, too." He offered them a smile. "Hey, we've had almost two weeks of vacation. That's almost—normal."

"True," Carly said. She looked regretfully at the beautiful sandy beach. "And…what's not to like about Paris?"

"Except for a killer needing buckets full of blood," Luke mused. "Not in *vampire* mode, not displaying bodies, just disposing of them as if they were used-up, empty receptacles…"

"Exactly. So, time to head back, pack up and go to Paris," Mason said. He walked back to his blanket where Della was already picking up their beach goods.

"Back at it," Carly said, looking at Luke.

He took a minute to smile. "And that's all right. It's what we do. And do you know what is now best about our work to stop murderers and hopefully save lives?"

"What's that?" she asked.

"We do it together," he said quietly.

And she had to smile in return. Because it was true.

They were the Blackbird division of the Krewe of Hunters, and that was lucky. They could use their most unusual talents for good.

And he was right.

They could do it together, and that was amazing.

"All right—I'll grab the towels. You grab the picnic basket!"

Paris. City of lights, city of love, city of fashion or Capital de la Mode.

And now...

City of blood.

* * * * *